THE
BAD ONES

STYLO FANTÔME

Published by BattleAxe Productions
Copyright © 2016
Stylo Fantôme

ISBN-13: 978-1530113361
ISBN-10: 1530113369

Editing Aides:
Ratula Roy

Cover Design
Najla Qamber Designs
www.najlaqamberdesigns.com/
Copyright © 2016

Formatting
Champagne Formats

DEDICATION

To anyone who has ever been frustrated, or anxious, or scared of being different, or uncomfortable in their own skin, or wondered why they couldn't just be normal.

I know exactly how you feel.

THE
BAD ONES

PART I

ONE

"Ms. Travers, I know we're not even half done with this year, but I think it's crucial we develop a plan for next year. You'll be a senior, and frankly, I'm worried," Ms. Poulter, the guidance counselor at Fuller High School, said with a sigh.

Dulcie Travers nodded, but didn't look at the other woman. She kept looking out the window. There was a huge maple tree just outside and the leaves had all begun to change. It looked like the tree was on fire, with the fronds rustling in the wind likes sparks in the sky.

I wish I could take my camera out.

"Ms. Travers!"

"Yes," Dulcie responded quickly, finally looking across the desk. "Yes, I'm listening."

"Now, I see here that at the conclusion of this year, you'll only have two credits in math. What kind of math will you be taking next year?" the counselor asked.

"No math next year."

"None?"

"I only need two math credits to graduate. So once I'm done with this year, I'm good," Dulcie explained. She felt like this was something the guidance counselor should've known on her own.

"Well, yes, two is all you need to graduate, but many colleges require three credits. Possibly more! Now, I'm going to sign you up to take -" Ms. Poulter began prattling away as she clicked away on her keyboard.

"No," Dulcie interrupted her.

"Pardon me?"

"*No.* I don't want anymore math classes."

"But Ms. Travers! If you want to get into college -"

I'm gonna lose this amazing light if I don't shut her up, and I have to get a picture of that tree.

"This is stupid," Dulcie snorted, and she picked up her bag as she stood up. "Let's be real. I'm not going to college."

"Your grades are perfectly acceptable, you could apply -" Ms. Poulter was practically sputtering.

"My grades are 'perfectly' average – who's gonna pay my tuition, huh? I'm not getting a scholarship, and no school is just gonna let me in based on my GPA. I'm like you, I'm like my family, I'm like everyone else in this town. *Stuck here.* One more math class won't change that; I know it, and you know it. So how about I get out of here, and you can use the rest of our scheduled hour to look up cat videos on the internet," Dulcie suggested.

There was silence for a moment. She began to think the counselor would argue with her. But Dulcie was right, and Ms. Poulter knew it. Unless a student's grades were astronomically good, or he could throw a perfect spiral straight to its target, he was stuck in Fuller, West Virginia. Basically like purgatory, adjacent.

"It's your future. If you can't be bothered to care about it, then I simply don't have time to help you."

It was a dismissal, and Dulcie didn't hesitate. She muttered a hasty "thank you", then bolted out the door.

She threw the strap of her bag over her head before she began digging around inside it. Normally, she was okay with using her phone's camera, but for really spectacular shots, she pulled out her precious.

The ridiculously expensive digital camera she'd bought herself for Christmas.

School wasn't over for another two hours, she should've gone straight back to class. Or hidden in the library. She supposed she could've cut and just left for the rest of the day, but she didn't really have the means – she didn't have a car, and no one was around to give her a ride. Dulcie usually avoided trouble, she liked to fly below the radar as much as possible. But she couldn't resist getting a picture. Just a couple snaps, then she'd go back to class. No one would even know.

A couple snaps turned into about fifty pictures. She got the tree from almost every angle. She even laid down at one point and took a shot straight up. That's when the magic happened. Just before she pressed the shutter, a leaf fell loose from its branch. It spiraled slowly towards her, and she got pictures of it every inch of the way down, all the way up until it landed on her lens.

Dulcie smiled as she slowly sat up, plucking the leaf away from her camera. She twirled it around in her fingers, then on a whim, she took a textbook out from her bag and pressed the dry leaf between the pages. A memento of a stolen moment and a beautiful picture. Then she put it away and climbed to her feet.

She was staring at the screen of her camera, not paying attention to what was going on around her. She was heading back to the front doors of the school and was vaguely aware of someone yelling in the distance, but figured it was some luckier students, escaping in their car for an early day.

When the sound of footsteps broke through her deep thoughts, though, she realized she wasn't alone. She looked up just in time to see a guy barreling towards her. His head was turned around so he could look behind him and as a result, he rammed right into her. She shrieked as they tangled together. Limbs were everywhere and she got a mouthful of his jacket collar. Her camera was momentarily crushed between them and when they ricocheted off each other, it fell to the ground. She, however, didn't fall. The guy grabbed her arms, holding her upright. She lifted her head to see what the hell was going on.

"Jesus, Dulcie, I didn't even see you."

She stared up into a pair of very deep blue eyes and was shocked into silence. Everything seemed to grow quiet for a second, then a gust of wind ripped across the front of the building. It was strong enough to push her forward, into his chest, and a whirlwind of leaves flew through the air, surrounding them for a moment.

His full name was Constantine Masters. It just had an evil ring to it, like a crazy megalomaniac. Or an insane preacher, leading a doomed cult to its judgement day. Maybe even a serial killer, stealing through a window late at night. His friends called him Con for short, and so much is in a name. Con didn't seem quite as scary as *Constantine*. But still, there was something about him that had always given her the shivers.

She wasn't sure how long they would've stood there just staring at each other. It was a surreal moment, with the wind and the leaves and the quiet. But then it was ruined when someone began shouting from around the corner.

"What are you doing?" Dulcie asked, and the spell was broken. The wind died down and Con stepped back from her.

But he kept a hand on her arm.

"I was just -"

"*Masters!*"

They both turned and looked at where the voice was coming from – its owner had appeared. It was the gym teacher. He was jogging towards them, huffing and puffing away. He looked *pissed*.

"Mr. Tully, hey, what's up?" Con replied nonchalantly as the out of breath teacher came to a halt in front of them.

"Don't you give me that shit! I got you now, you little bastard! I don't care who your daddy is, I'm gonna nail your ass to the wall," Mr. Tully swore. Dulcie was shocked. She'd never heard a teacher talk to a student that way, and had never heard anyone say anything but glowing remarks about Constantine Masters. She glanced up at the boy who still held onto her arm, as if he was afraid she'd leave.

4

Or as if he doesn't want me to get away …

"I don't know what you're talking about, sir," Con replied in a calm voice, which to Dulcie just made it seem as if he *definitely* knew what the teacher was talking about.

"Don't give me any of your bullshit. I know it was you who lit that car on fire. I got your ass now, Masters. No more football, no more parties. I got your number, alright. Stupid punk. Thought you got away with it, huh? No alibis this time," Mr. Tully sneered.

Dulcie watched as Con winced at first, but then his eyes grew hard. He was staring very hard at Mr. Tully, and a muscle began to tick in the side of his jaw. But his breathing stayed even and the rest of his body appeared relaxed.

Still, though. That muscle.

"What are you talking about?"

Dulcie was shocked to hear her own voice. She'd just blurted it out, no discussion between mouth and brain. Mr. Tully started at her voice, too. As if he hadn't even realized she was there. Con didn't look stunned at all. He looked as if he'd been waiting for her to say something.

"None of your damn business, missy! What're you doing out here, anyway? You should be in class!" the teacher snapped at her. She took a step closer to Con, surprising herself even more.

"I know. I really wanted to get a picture of the tree, but I wasn't tall enough for the angles I needed – Con offered to take the shots," she lied smoothly.

"Like hell, he did! He was just -" Mr. Tully began to argue.

"Look what you made me do," Con interrupted. "All your shouting, I dropped her frickin' camera. You made me break it."

Dulcie watched as Con squatted down and collected the shattered remnants of her camera – she hadn't even realized it had gotten damaged. Her heart broke a little as Con stood up, the pieces cradled in his hands.

A year's worth of tips, gone. All because some jock wasn't looking where he was going.

"What? You expect me to believe you were out here, taking pictures of a goddamn tree?" Mr. Tully sounded incredulous.

"It was for an art project, for a class," Dulcie's voice was soft as she continued staring at her poor camera.

"Nice going, Mr. Tully. Sorry, Dulcie. Maybe the school can reimburse you," Con suggested.

"This is all horse shit. If you've been out here playing photographer, then explain to me why a car in the back parking lot is *on fire!?* Did it just spontaneously combust?" Mr. Tully demanded. Con shrugged.

"How should I know? I've been out here."

There was another long moment of silence. Dulcie finally glanced between the two men. Con looked completely at ease. Mr. Tully was quickly turning red, but his mouth stayed shut. He had no evidence, Dulcie realized. He'd probably happened upon the scene just as Con had been fleeing it. Mr. Tully had most likely only seen the younger man's back, if even that much. He couldn't actually prove Con had done anything wrong.

Though Dulcie didn't doubt for a minute that Con had done exactly what the teacher was accusing him of.

"Okay, Masters. Okay, you win this time. You think you're so slick, getting your girlfriend out here to cover for you," Mr. Tully hissed.

"Oh, I'm no-" Dulcie began to argue.

"And *you*," the teacher turned his anger on her. "Don't think I don't know who you are, *Travers*. I remember your brother. You a dope head like him? A bunch of good-for-nothings."

Dulcie was used to people talking about her *half*-brother. Comparing her to him, bringing up the family connection. Didn't matter that she wasn't anything like him – his name had haunted her for a long time. Probably would for a lot longer. So she didn't let it bother her. People could assume whatever they wanted.

"Hey, don't fucking talk to her like that," Con swore, taking a challenging step forward. Dulcie was blown away, then she collected herself enough to grab his arm, halting his movements.

"Whatcha gonna do about it, boy?" Mr. Tully asked, puffing out his chest. "That's right, *nothing*. I'll get you yet, Masters. You can bet on it."

"Hmmm, I think I'll keep betting *on me*."

When Con finished talking, Mr. Tully's head looked like it was gonna pop off. He got right up in their space and while Con didn't back down an inch, Dulcie shrunk back, even moving behind the star quarterback a little.

"Just a punk, Masters. It may not be me. May not be anyone in this school. But someone, some day, will see you for what you really are, and they'll put you in your place."

The two men were almost nose to nose. Dulcie held her breath. She'd always thought there was something a little … *off*, with Constantine Masters, but she'd always assumed it was just her. She had an eye for certain things, she was more observant than most people. *Stranger* than most people. But apparently, she wasn't the only one who sensed the darkness in him.

"I'm excited for that day, sir."

"Front office! Both of you! *NOW!*"

A car really was on fire in the back parking lot, but of course, it was easy to prove Dulcie couldn't possibly have been there. She'd been in Ms. Poulter's office at the time. And Dulcie had provided Con with a solid alibi, so now it looked as if he couldn't have possibly been there, either. So in the end, the only thing they could pin on them was cutting class.

Detention. After school. Two hours.

Fuck my life. I hope I don't get fired over this bullshit. Why did I help him? Why did I say anything? And how does Constantine Masters even know my name!?

"Were those pictures really for an art project?" Con asked when they were well away from the office. She turned to take the pieces of her broken camera back from him.

"Yeah," she replied, shoving the bits into her bag.

"Are they gone forever?"

"No, the memory card should be fine."

"Got any other cameras like that one?"

"Nope, that was it."

There was an awkward silence. Well, Dulcie felt awkward. Con looked completely at ease. She was beginning to wonder if anything made him uncomfortable.

"Thanks for the help," he finally said. She shrugged.

"Your welcome. Can I ask a question?"

"Go for it."

"Why did you set someone's car on fire?"

She thought maybe it would rattle him – her thinking he'd actually done it. But of course it didn't. He chuckled, and she was treated to a patented Masters grin. It started at one corner of his mouth and eventually moved to the opposite corner, slowly revealing perfect white teeth and a razor sharp smile. He leaned close to her, and as his lips pressed against her ear, she could've sworn the temperature dropped.

"Because I thought it would be fun."

TWO

DULCIE TRAVERS. WHAT THE FUCK KIND OF NAME IS DULCIE? CON had looked it up one time. It was a British name, and came from the Latin word for "sweet".

It was very fitting for her. She had sandy brown hair, almost a super dark blonde, which she usually wore in a messy braid over one shoulder. She was on the shorter side, with a slender frame and no figure to really speak of. Her large, expressive eyes were an amazing whiskey color – almost amber, and topping it all off was a wide mouth and almost heart shaped lips that were made to smile, but rarely ever did.

She was soft spoken. Soft mannered. Soft in generally everything she did. Unobtrusive to the maximum. She slipped around unnoticed. Had become so good at it that by the time they were all upper classmen, people hadn't realized what a beauty they had in their midst. What an interesting soul.

He was obsessed with her.

Of course, her living in a trailer park on the outskirts of town worked against her, not to mention the fact her mother used to be a pro over in Charleston and her step-daddy supplied the outlying communities with most of their meth. Her older brother, Matthew Reid, was a known meth head and had already been arrested for armed robbery.

Several times.

Constantine was the star quarterback. All-American, three years in a row. He had a full scholarship to Ohio State, he was homecoming king, and his father was the mayor. Maybe of a tiny little middle-of-nowhere town, but that was almost worse. In a small town, everyone knew everyone, so being mayor was a big deal. Being the son of the mayor, almost just as big a deal. Con didn't hang out with the kids from the trailer parks. He didn't hang out with chicks like Dulcie. No, Con did what Con was expected to do – he dated cheerleaders, he hung out with jocks, and he went to awesome keggers. He had lots of sex and played a lot of beer pong.

Even as he did those things and played his little part in the universe, he watched Dulcie. As she walked down the hall. As she tried to hide in the library. She called to him, and she didn't even know it. Didn't know that he understood why she worked so hard to remain obscure – because she didn't want people to see the real her. A feeling he was very familiar with, since he always kept a large part 7of himself hidden.

Maybe, just maybe, their hidden pieces matched.

Con very much wanted to see the real her.

Detention wasn't so bad. It meant missing practice, but Con owned the football field. Had practically built it. He could say he needed the afternoon off to go fuck the coach's daughter, and the man would probably just tell him to go easy on his arm.

Detention was held in the library, and he strolled in after the last period and immediately sat down with some friends, slapping high five, laughing and being loud. When Dulcie entered the room a couple minutes later, he didn't acknowledge her, just kept talking to his buddies. But he watched out of the corner of his eye as she disappeared down an aisle. There were study carrels in the back of the room, offering more privacy. She was probably heading to one of them.

She'd saved his ass, Con was very aware of that – as well as completely surprised. While he'd been noticing Dulcie, she'd never once seemed to pay any attention to him. But the way she'd stared at him, like she'd known him. Really *seen* him, through and through. A little scary. *A lot* exhilarating. Then she'd opened her mouth and covered for him. No hesitation, no questions asked. Well, at least not until the end.

The car that was now a burned out husk belonged to the junior varsity quarterback. A punk kid who had long been giving Con shit. Beyond a punk, the guy was a bully and also had a reputation for getting aggressive with girls at parties. He cast a bad light on the whole football team, which made coaches and teachers come down harder on them. It was already hard enough for Con to sneak off to indulge in his own wants and needs; he didn't appreciate the extra eyes on him.

If junior varsity boy didn't watch his step, he'd find more than just his car on fire.

"Masters! Got your costume planned out?"

Con snapped back to attention, dragging his eyes away from the aisle Dulcie had gone down.

"What? Oh. Yeah, I got something," he answered his friend.

"What is it?"

"You know I can't tell you."

"Just a hint, man."

Halloween was only a couple weeks away. The holiday was a big deal in Fuller. The high school went all out, putting on a carnival and then having a large masquerade ball. People went nuts for it, traveling into Huntington and Charleston to get costumes, or having them hand-made sometimes. Con always kept his outfit a secret.

"Okay, a hint," he started, and slid out of his seat. "It's something historical. In fact, I gotta look something up for it."

The teacher who was presiding over detention was sitting behind the check out counter, reading a book. He glanced at Con once, then nodded and went back to his novel.

She was hunched over in front of her carrel, a pair of large headphones covering her ears. Con stood behind her, his hands in his pockets, and he just watched her. Her right hand was moving rapidly, brushing back and forth, and it took him a second to realize she must have been sketching something. She was known for being quite the artist; Con was very familiar with the sketchbook she carried everywhere.

He moved up behind her, close enough so he could hear the music trickling out from her headphones. She had a smell like clean linen and it suited her. He would've bet money that she was a virgin. Wondered if she'd ever even kissed a boy.

Wondered if she'd been waiting for him.

He couldn't get a good view over her shoulder, so he began moving around the carrels. When he got to hers, she still hadn't noticed his presence, so he tilted his head to the side, trying to get a good angle on her drawing.

He couldn't quite tell what it was, at first. She was drawing with a pencil and dark shading covered the top of the sketchbook paper. In fact, it covered most of it, though it lightened at the center of the page. There, she'd sketched out a figure. An exaggerated image of a man with impossibly long legs, giving him an eerie, skeletal look. His shoulders were broad, coming to razor sharp points. He was extending an arm down, and like the legs, the appendage was ridiculously elongated, ending in sharp, pointy fingers. They were all hooked, like he was about to snatch something.

Just under the hand was what appeared to be a little girl. She was small and wearing a dress with a hooded cloak, and immediately Little Red Riding Hood came to mind, though there were no colors. The picture was haunting in its nature. A shadowy figure with a claw for a hand, reaching out of the blackness to snatch away an innocent little girl. Very dark.

But as Con looked closer, he noticed other small details about the picture. The hood of the cloak hung down in front of the girl's face, hiding her eyes and nose in shadows. Her mouth was visible, though, and upon closer inspection, it almost looked like she had fangs. Tiny little fangs, biting over her bottom lip.

And the shadow man. There was more to him, too. He was completely shaded in, there was barely any detail to his form. But his thin waist and broad shoulders seemed familiar. Then Con saw it. It was barely noticeable, but on the chest of the figure, there were two letters. They were barely bolder than the shading surrounding them, but they were there. A jagged F, and a jagged H.

F.H.

Fuller High.

He glanced down at himself. He was wearing his letterman jacket, and on the left side of the coat was a patch – a football, with a very clear "F.H." on it in big, bold letters. They rested in the exact same spot on his chest as they did on the man in Dulcie's sketch.

Very intuitive. And if that's me, are you the little girl?

"Nice," he said in a loud voice.

Dulcie shrieked and jumped in her seat, the pencil flinging out of her hand. She glanced up at him before slamming her sketchbook shut.

"Jesus, you gave me a heart attack!" she hissed, pulling her headphones away and letting them rest around her neck.

"I've been here for a while," he commented, leaning his forearms over the back of the carrel. He watched as her face lost some of its color. She cleared her throat.

"You have? I didn't even notice you," she replied.

"Music must be too loud."

He stared at her. He could tell it made her uncomfortable. Those amber eyes stayed locked on his for a moment, then she licked her lips and looked away. Shifted in her seat. Licked her lips again. He watched as her fingers clenched and unclenched around the edges of her notebook, and he smiled.

"Did you need something?" she finally asked.

"Is that me?" he returned her question with one of his own.

"What?"

She licked her lips again. He wondered if she had any idea how sexy her mouth was, or how much time boys probably spent thinking about it.

"Your drawing. It's me, right?" he asked again, and leaned forward enough so he could tap a finger on top of her sketchbook.

The color that had drained away came rushing back to her face, and the tops of her cheekbones turned a pale shade of pink. She slid her book further away from him, almost into her lap.

"Why would you think that?"

"Because it looks like me," he pointed out. She frowned.

"It looks nothing like you."

"Give it to me."

Con held out his hand, and was honestly a little shocked when she immediately complied. She looked surprised at herself, too, but couldn't do anything when he took the book from her. She stared, wide eyed, as he walked back around the carrels while flipping through pages till he found the one she'd been working on.

"Shouldn't you be studying, or something?" she suggested when he came to a stop next to her. He snorted and leaned back against a chair.

"Shouldn't *you?*"

"*I am* – I wasn't lying, I have an art project due at the end of the semester," she was quick to respond, her voice snide. He smiled. She had a backbone, it just seemed to be buried. It only came out when provoked.

"Gotcha. So tell me something," he sighed, turning the book around so the picture faced her. "Why am I in your art project?"

"It's not you," she denied it, but she wouldn't look at the picture.

"It's definitely me."

"Why would you think that? It's a shadow, there's no face. No features," she argued. Con turned it again so he could look at it.

"No. But still. Those shoulders, that hand," he mumbled, smoothing his fingertips over her pencil strokes. It almost felt like he was touching *her,* and he took a deep breath through his nose.

"You think you look like that?" she asked, her voice soft. He glanced at her, then back at the picture. At the little girl. Then back at Dulcie. She was wearing a red plaid shirt.

"Sometimes. Yeah, sometimes I think I do. And this," he traced a finger over the little girl. "This is you, isn't it?"

There was a long silence and he finally looked at her again. She was hunched over in her seat, her hands together and pressed between her legs. She looked small, almost vulnerable. But her eyes were wide and her mouth was set in a firm line. She wasn't intimidated by him. Nervous, maybe. But not scared. No, she was something else, entirely.

"Sometimes, I think it is," she whispered, mimicking his own response.

Con did not want to be in school at that moment. He wanted to grab her by the arm and drag her out of the building. Take her into the woods and tear her apart. Become one with her, consume her. Find out what was wrong with him, and see if maybe she could cure him. Or even better – *maybe find out she was the same.*

"Yo, Masters, you slummin' it back here?"

Again, the spell was broken. Con glanced up to see his friends come around the end of an aisle. He smiled and stood upright. Dulcie hunched over even further and looked like she was thinking of making a run for it.

"Jesus, is that Matt Reid's sister? You scoring some drugs, Masters?" another friend joked.

"Nah, I told you. I was doing research for my Halloween costume. What do you guys think?" he asked, flipping her sketchbook around so they could all take in the picture.

Dulcie's gasp was audible and she instantly reached for the book, but Con lurched forward, moving away from the carrels. The other guys crowded around, looking over the drawing.

"This is what you draw? You're a twisted chick," one guy commented.

"I don't get it. Why doesn't he have a face?"

"Who's got time for picture books? Let's get the fuck out of here."

Everyone leapt on the last comment and in the moment of distraction, Dulcie yanked the book out of Con's hands. The she stood up abruptly, her chair coming out so fast, he needed to jump out of its way. She began shoving things into her messenger bag while his friends filed out a back door.

"You know," she began, her voice low. "Just because everyone around you acts like an asshole, doesn't mean you have to, too."

She could've stomped off. She was pissed, Con realized. But he didn't want her to have the wrong impression of him. He roughly grabbed her arm, halting her movements.

"See, that's the problem. With me, it's not an act," he warned her. She stared at him for a second, then stepped closer.

"There's a difference between being an asshole, and being a *monster*. One is much better at hiding his character."

He was so shocked that when she pulled away, he let her go.

Dulcie stood out in front of the second hand store for a moment, her hand on the doorknob. She stared into the distance, up at a house that sat on a hill. At Constantine's house.

His father was the mayor, so *of course* they lived in the biggest house in town, the one with white pillars and green shutters. His mother was an interior designer, she traveled into Charleston and Huntington to work with clients. Rumor had it she'd been a big time designer in New York, but financial trouble had convinced her to marry Mr. Jebediah Masters, who really only wanted her for breeding purposes. Mrs. Masters had given her husband a son, and from that point on, was rarely home.

Constantine was clearly beyond anything his father could've hoped for, and then some. He was tall and strong, with brown hair and smiling blue eyes. He could throw a football like he was born to do it. Like wherever he wanted the ball to go, that was the only choice it had – Con Masters did not miss. He had strong legs, could run fast. Broad shoulders, could knock anyone down.

He was beautiful.

Con was a year older than Dulcie, which was part of the reason they'd never shared a lot of classes. He was also exceptionally smart and took a lot of AP classes. Dulcie took the bare minimum of requirements, then filled up the rest of her schedule with as many art credits as were allowed. He spent all his extra time on the field or with friends. She spent all her extra time either at work or at home. They had no reason to interact. Had gone to school together their entire lives, and had barely ever spoken.

So why do I think about him all the time?

"Did you need help?"

Dulcie was startled into the present when a store clerk pushed open the door. She managed a smile and shook her head no, then walked into the building. She began pawing through aisles, looking for anything that would work for what she had in mind.

She didn't usually wear a costume to the Halloween dance – she'd always taken pictures for the yearbook. It's what she'd planned on doing that year, as well. But ever since their little tête-à-tête in detention, she'd known she would be dressing up.

The clerk wandered over and smiled at her, then poked at the clothing Dulcie had in her basket.

"Shopping for Halloween, huh? How fun. Do you know what you're going to be?"

Dulcie smiled and grabbed a thick, felt, burgundy coat from off a shelf.

"I'm going to go as Little Red Riding Hood."

THREE

I T WAS DARK, AS DANCES TENDED TO BE, AND SHE COULDN'T TELL who anyone was, obviously. No one really noticed Dulcie, but she was pretty sure that was also because no one recognized her. Her dress was indecently short, matching a lot of the other girls' costumes, and she wore a demi-mask over her eyes, along with the hood of her red cape pulled low over her forehead.

After laughing and chatting with a few friends for a while, Dulcie broke away and slowly walked around the room. The organizers had really outdone themselves, going all out with the decorations. A mummy hung from the basketball hoop and every now and then, it twitched and writhed around. Other displays had been set up in the corners, and where the bleachers were stretched out, fake spider webs had been thickly stretched across either side.

A DJ spun remixes of old Halloween classics, and some upperclassmen spiked the punch. A fight broke out at one point between a Legolas and a Frankenstein. It was actually pretty funny, watching while a sexy cat screamed at both of them.

She wasn't sure how long she'd been walking around when she realized someone was watching her. She hadn't noticed at first because his mask made it hard to tell. And on top of that, she stupidly realized she'd been looking for him in normal clothes. How ridiculous. Con Masters was like the first son of Fuller, so of course he *always* dressed up for Halloween.

Dulcie wasn't sure what made her recognize him. She'd been in the act of turning around and had stopped mid-spin when she noticed the figure standing against a wall. He was dressed as a plague doctor, and absurdly, her first thought was to wonder who'd made his mask. It was gorgeous, crafted out of dark lacquer wood, with what looked like onyx for the eyes. A wide brimmed hat and black material clung to his head, completely hiding any trace of his identity.

But she knew it was Con. He wore a long black duster to go with the theme of the mask, and the belt was cinched tight around his waist, accenting his narrow hips. The material fell away from his shoulders in a cape, highlighting how broad across he was, and all the black made him look even taller; he was every inch the shadowy figure from her drawing.

It seemed inevitable that she should walk over to him. They had dressed to match each other, after all. When she went to step forward, though, someone blocked her path.

"Dulcie! Lookin' *hot*."

Chuck Beaty stood in front of her. He was in her class, a junior, and talk around the school was saying he would be the new quarterback after Con graduated. That was still almost a year away, but he'd already started acting like cock of the walk – emphasis on *cock*. Like he expected the entire student body and staff of Fuller High School to fall at his feet.

"Um, thanks?" she managed a reply, then she glanced over his shoulder. The plague doctor was gone, replaced by a werewolf.

"How come you don't dress like this more often?" Chuck asked, his eyes traveling over her form.

"What? I should wear a babydoll dress and mask to school every day?" she snorted, looking down at herself. The thick petticoat made the skirt of the dress stand out from her body, barely clearing the tops of her thighs. Her cloak fell just past the hem in the back, leaving most of her legs on display.

"I wouldn't complain," Chuck leered. She rolled her eyes and went to step past him, but he moved with her. When she tried to go the other way, he took a step forward.

"This is fun and all, but I'd like to get back to the dance now," she said, moving back with every step he took forward.

"Sounds good. I'd love to dance," he laughed. When he reached out to grab at her ruffly petticoat, she jerked backwards and bumped up against a wall. He'd trapping her between a corner of the gym and the bleachers.

"I don't dance," she told him.

"C'mon, babe, what's the deal? I'm the quarterback, you're hot. Let's see what we can work out," he suggested, crowding in so close she was able to smell the tainted punch on his breath. She pressed herself flat against the wall.

"If you don't get away from me, I'm gonna work out how to plant my knee in your nuts."

"You're a fucking snob, Dulcie. Always walking around acting like you're better than the rest of us," he suddenly snapped at her.

"What are you talking about? You're drunk, Chuck. Get out of my face," she ordered, and she placed her hands against his chest, trying to push him away. He didn't budge.

"Shit, this is the first time you've ever even dressed up. You too cool for Halloween, Dulcie?" he snarled, then he surprised her by reaching out and ripping off her mask.

She should've been scared – she was in a dark corner with Chuck Beaty. There were all sorts of rumors about him, about how he treated girls, about how he liked to get drunk all the time.

But Dulcie wasn't scared. She was angry, and she was annoyed. As was apparently becoming her new habit, she didn't even think about what she was doing – she just launched her hand at his face, raking her nails down the side of his cheek.

I want to see his blood.

Chuck was shocked for a moment, then he looked really pissed. He grabbed the front of her dress and twisted the fabric in his fist before jerking her forward, then he slammed her against the wall. She immediately started slapping at his arms and yanking at his wrist.

It never occurred to her to scream. Not once. She wanted to rip him in half, she was so angry, but she never got the chance. A dark figure stepped out from underneath the bleachers and grabbed Chuck by the back of the neck, pulling him away from her. Constantine Masters had lost his mask, but he still looked haunting and formidable in his all black costume, and it seemed easy for him to hold the smaller guy in place.

"You wanna know why I lit your car on fire?" Con growled, and Dulcie watched as Chuck's eyes opened wide in shock.

"You fucking did that!?" he shouted.

"Because," Con ignored him. "*I thought you were in it.*"

He moved forward and Dulcie leapt out of the way, tripping under the bleachers as Con slammed Chuck's head against the wall. He did it two more times, until the other guy was unconscious and falling to the ground in a lump.

Dulcie gripped onto the network of rails that surrounded her and tried to catch her breath. She was almost panting, and her heart was racing. She stared at Chuck for a moment, at his figure as it lay prone on the floor. Then she moved her gaze to Con. He was staring down at Chuck as well, and even in the dim lighting, she could see the muscle in the side of his jaw. Watched as it ticked away.

When he moved, Dulcie stayed still. He slid between the rails, moving undern the bleachers till he was standing in front of her. He looked a little crazy. His face was flushed and his eyes were wild. He moved so they were touching, so she could feel his chest as it rose and fell with his heavy breathing. He was so much taller than her, she'd never really realized. She had to tilt her head back to look up at him and her hood fell away from her hair.

"Are you scared of me?" he demanded, his voice hoarse sounding.

"No," she answered straight away.

"I think you should be," he warned her. She took a deep breath.

"I think *you* should be scared of *me*."

When his mouth fell on hers, it felt natural. He needed to devour something, it was clear, and she was fresh meat. She wanted to split open for him and lay at his feet.

She moaned and grabbed the edges of his jacket, yanking him even closer. They stumbled backwards till they hit the wall, then Con's hands were moving over her body. Scratching across her chest, pulling at her skirt. When they slid around to her back, he grabbed onto the material of her cloak and yanked hard, causing the knot at her throat to pull tight. She gasped as her head was pulled away from him, but she still wasn't scared. As his teeth left bite marks down the side of her neck, she thought maybe she didn't need oxygen anymore. He could just breathe for her.

Dulcie had been kissed before, but not in the way he was kissing her – she was pretty sure no one had *ever* been kissed like that. She was still a virgin, but at that moment in time, she didn't care. She didn't care that she was young and stupid, or that they were in a gym full of people, or that she barely knew the boy who was touching her. She wanted his darkness to swallow her whole. She wanted to be a part of it. She wanted to give her own darkness back to him.

He let go of her cloak, allowing her to breathe again, but his hands didn't remain idle. They immediately moved under her skirt, pawing through all the ruffles, finally finding skin. Nails dug into the soft flesh on her thighs and she groaned into his mouth.

"Please. Please, I want this," she assured him, though he hadn't voiced any questions or concerns.

"I know," he growled back.

She would never know how far they really would have gone. Con was so much more experienced than her, maybe he would've had more self restraint. She certainly didn't have any – she'd been ready to start ripping off clothing. But then a series of flashing flights played across her closed eyelids and she blinked back to reality, holding up her hand as another bright flash went off.

"Whoa ho ho there! Dulcie! Now I see why you didn't wanna take the photos tonight!"

It took a second for her brain to stop spinning and recognize the voice. Gary was a sophomore who was on the yearbook committee with her. And the little asshole had just taken their picture. One of Con's hands was up her skirt, and both her arms were wrapped tightly around his neck.

"You little shit, I should make you eat that fucking camera," Con started to threaten, and he moved towards the younger kid. A frightening gesture to be sure, and Gary quickly backed away. Then he stumbled over something and when they all looked down, they realized he was tripping over Chuck's unconscious body.

"What's going on here? What did you guys do!?" Gary yelled.

"Nothing, Gary. Just wait -" Dulcie tried to calm the situation down.

"Nothing he didn't fucking deserve, and you're gonna be next," Con interrupted.

There was silence for about a second, then Gary took off running, yelling for the principal.

Well, shit. There goes the night.

"This is gonna be worse than detention, isn't it?" Dulcie groaned.

"It'll be fine, c'mon."

Con didn't explain, he just grabbed her arm and began pulling. She stumbled as he dragged her down the length of the bleachers. When they got to the other end, he still didn't say anything, he just pushed his way through the fake spider webs before yanking her to a set of double doors. They led to the back parking lot, and Con pushed one of them open.

"What are you doing?" she asked, a little confused as he shoved her outside.

"I'll take care of all this," was all he said, then he went to shut the door between them. She reached out and grabbed it, stopping his momentum.

"What is going on here?"

It was the million dollar question – and she wasn't talking about the dance. She wasn't even talking about the kiss. She was talking about the *feeling* she was having whenever he was near. She knew he felt it, too. She was pretty sure if they'd been out in the open, the entire student body would've felt it. That's why he'd pulled her into the dark to kiss her. If they'd been standing in front of other people, they might have seen their true forms.

Whatever those are.

"Nothing, Dulcie. Go home."

And with that, Con yanked the door out of her hand and slammed it shut in her face.

FOUR

BY THE TIME CON GOT BACK TO CHUCK BEATY, THE KID HAD BEEN coming to, thank god. Con was able to get him onto his feet before the principal showed up. At least it didn't look quite as bad as it had before, and despite the little shit Gary whining about being threatened, Con was able to convince the principal it had just been a scrap. Just boys being boys, some healthy rivalry.

If there hadn't been a game the following weekend, Con was sure he would've been in big trouble. But the match was an important one against a long standing rival, and without Con, their team would lose. He watched as the principal struggled with what to do about the situation.

"I can't keep letting these things go, Masters," he grumbled. Chuck was leaning up against a wall, his head in his hands, not quite "there" enough to offer his two cents. "I *have* to do something."

"Understandable," was all Con said in response

"Alright. Three days suspension. Banned from any future dances. And I have to call your parents. Okay?" the principal asked. Gary made a noise like he wanted to argue, but Con just nodded.

"Fine."

"No more fighting, Masters."

"No more."

"And no more funny business. I heard something about a fire a couple weeks ago, your name was -"

"*Got it*. Let's go."

Con didn't bother waiting, he turned and led the way out of the gym.

Being a teenager was a strange process, Con had always felt. He didn't feel young. He didn't feel any particular age. He felt like he was always going through the motions, always pretending to be something he wasn't; something he didn't want to be, anymore.

The only time he felt real was when he was doing something *wrong*. And not like cutting class or cheating on a test. Like setting Chuck's car on fire. Or the time he'd beaten the shit out of some guy, after a game in a neighboring town. Or when he'd kissed Dulcie. Only when he was completely letting go did he truly feel free.

So sitting in the office, listening to his dad yell at both the principal and himself, Con didn't feel real. He felt like a paper doll, just sitting in a chair, waiting for his dad to pick him up and move him. Tell him how to be, tell him what to do, until the moment came when he could be himself again.

After the principal had been reminded of exactly *WHO* Con's father was, and exactly *HOW* valuable Con's arm was to the town, they left. The elder Masters went home in his own car, and Con followed close behind in his truck. He didn't want to go home. He wanted to find Dulcie and finish what they'd started. Whatever the hell it had been.

It was a human sacrifice, and she was offering herself to your altar.

"What the fuck is wrong with you, Constantine!?"

Con sighed as they walked through their front door and his father instantly began yelling. It wasn't a surprise. Once upon a time, Jebediah Masters had used his fists to keep his son in line. But then Con had gotten bigger than his dad, and he'd never been afraid to hit back. So the striking had taken a back burner to preaching. His father could talk and talk and talk – before becoming mayor, he'd been a very successful lawyer.

"Don't you talk to my son that way!"

Ah, Mrs. Masters joined the fray, complete with martini in hand. She, unfortunately, was not bigger than her husband, and her face sported fresh bruises to attest to that fact. It didn't bother Con – his mother had been an absent figure in his life, spending most of her time in bigger cities. When she had been home, she'd always turned a blind eye to the hitting and shouting. Defending Con now, it was just ammunition against her husband. Another reason to yell at each other.

While the two "adult" Masters screamed and shrieked at each other, Con sat down at the head of their twelve seat dining room table. It had been set for the holiday season, complete with garland laced with purple tinsel and orange candles burning down the length of it.

He stared into a flame while he listened to his parents argue. *Parents.* More like animals. It would explain a lot, really. A harpy and a snake, snarling and hissing at each other. Trying to draw blood, but neither brave enough to actually do it.

Con was brave enough, though. He was a different kind of beast.

Just burn it all.

He reached out and tipped over the candle that was directly in front of him. The flame flickered as it hit the table top, but didn't go out. The pillar of wax rolled into the garland, which quickly caught on fire. The plastic tinsel acted like a fuse and it was only a matter of seconds before the entire runner was up in flames.

Con wasn't a pyromaniac, not at all. Fire was just quickest and easiest. He'd set Chuck's car on fire simply because he'd had a lighter on him. If he'd only had a bat, he would've beaten the shit out of the car. If he'd had a gun, he would've shot his parents. But all he had was a flame and a thought, and without bothering to dwell much on either, he set their dining room table on fire. While he watched the flames grow and spread and drip down onto an expensive Persian rug, his mind was miles away.

I wonder what Dulcie tastes like. I wonder if she'd let me bite hard enough to find out.

FIVE

NO ONE KNEW GARY ECKLAND EXISTED, LET ALONE LISTENED TO him, so word never got around about Dulcie and Con's private little moment. No one would have believed it, anyway. Half the time, even she didn't believe it had really happened.

News about the "fight" between Con and Chuck did spread around, though. Some stories claimed Con had beaten him to within an inch of his life. Other tales claimed Chuck had almost won, and Con had just gotten in a sucker punch. No one knew the truth, except for Dulcie and Con. She wasn't talking and Con was suspended, so the stories went unchecked.

She didn't speak to him for almost the entire month of November. More rumors swirled, talk of the fire department being called to the Masters household. He came back to school for one day, then the team left for an away game, which they of course won. Two weeks later, Thanksgiving break happened. Two weeks after, Christmas break. The Masters took their annual trip to Vail to go skiing.

Dulcie worked through the holidays and avoided home as much as possible. Matt, her crazy half-brother, had been getting even crazier. She'd come out of the bathroom fresh from a shower more than once to find him lurking near the door. Her mother was also spending more time at home, but that wasn't any help – she turned tricks to her husband's friends in exchange for drugs, which her husband then sold for money that he kept for himself.

Weeks turned into months. Winter into spring. Dulcie had dreams about a shadowy man, stealing her away and carrying her into the night. Kissing her in the dark and touching her in ways that had her waking up in a hot sweat, panting for more.

But Con wasn't saying anything. It was like nothing had ever happened. The most profound moment in her short life, and he acted as if it hadn't even mattered. Of course, maybe it hadn't. Con kissed lots of girls. Had slept with lots of girls, had lots of girlfriends. Kissing Dulcie was just more of the same for him, probably.

No. He felt it. We were in that space together.

It didn't matter. They bumped into each other a couple times. One time, they'd even somehow wound up in the main hallway together, after the last bell for class had rung. She'd been fighting to get her portfolio into her bag and had dropped it. Before she could pick it up, someone was standing in front of her and grabbing it off the floor.

He'd asked her how her art project had turned out, if she'd been able to make it work without her camera. She'd been shocked he'd even remembered breaking her camera. Before she could answer, though, half the football team had flooded into the hallway. Con made a joke about asking if Dulcie did nude portraits, and everyone laughed. Then he winked at her and walked off with his friends. As if she was just some regular girl he could flirt with and tease.

I am NOT a regular girl, Constantine Masters.

Similar incidents happened. He'd magically appear in a place she'd be – the library, the art room, the back gym – but before anything could be said, someone would interrupt them. And it was like watching a mask fall over someone's face. He would smile and he would be cute, but it wasn't Con. She just *knew* it wasn't him.

Graduation day came and while most kids were excited, Dulcie felt like she was being strangled. It was like Con had brought something to life in her, then taken it away just as abruptly. Most juniors were celebrating become seniors, and all the seniors were celebrating the end of high school. There were parties everywhere, every night. She wanted to go, wanted to corner him somewhere, wanted to kick and scratch and bite until he recognized her for what she really was – *his reflection.*

But she was weak, and she was nervous, and when all was said and done, she was just a seventeen year old girl. A stupid, stupid seventeen year old girl, who had been cliché enough to fall for the good looking jock.

Little red riding hood fell for the wolf.

And so it was that Constantine Masters graduated with valedictorian honors, to high praise and accolades, and gave a grand speech at the commencement ceremony. People cried and people laughed. Oh, that Con, so good at saying all the right things.

Dulcie didn't see any of it. She sat under the bleachers and put her headphones on and drifted away. To a shadowy place, where evil things could fulfill their dark wants and needs, and not be troubled with the bright and shiny world.

Being a teenager is so very black and white. I long for technicolor.

Dulcie held out hope that after graduation, after everything had settled down, Con would seek her out. He knew where she worked, knew she spent a lot of time at the library. But her dream quickly died – she found out Con had left town one week after graduation. He would be spending the summer in California with family, then he'd go directly to school in Ohio. There was a very real possibility Dulcie would never see him again.

Once again, she wasn't sad. She was *angry*. Con had ruined something great. Taken something away from her. She couldn't possibly have imagined it. It had only been a moment in time, but it had been one of the greats. Something she'd remember for a long time. One kiss, and no other guy would compare. It wasn't fair.

About a month after graduation, she came home in the afternoon from working a breakfast shift at the diner. She grimaced at the sight in the living room. Her step-father in his boxer shorts, sitting on the couch spread-eagle while he snored away. Her mother was in a slip and she sat up as Dulcie entered the trailer.

"Hey, baby! Glad yer home, I feel like I haven't seen you in ages," her mother cooed as she climbed to her feet.

Mrs. Bottle – formerly Mrs. Travers, formerly Mrs. Reid, formerly Tessa Banks – had the soft accent that was common in the area, yet had somehow missed her daughter. Not quite southern, but almost. Country, that's what Dulcie called it in her mind. A distinct twang. Not everyone had it, and she wasn't quite sure why that was, but her mother's family had lived in West Virginia for years. All the Banks' had it – Dulcie's grandpa's was so thick, sometimes he was hard to understand, but she loved it. Sometimes wished she had it. Wondered if it would soften her.

"You saw me last night, Momma," she sighed, keeping her head down as she headed towards the hallway.

She hated looking at her mother because they looked very much alike. Her eyes, her lips, her hair color – her most distinct features, she'd gotten them all from her mother. Looking at Tessa Bottle, Dulcie felt like she was looking at her potential future, and it wasn't pretty.

"I did?" Tessa sounded unsure. Dulcie wasn't surprised, the woman had been high out of her mind.

"Yes. Look, I'm really tired. We can talk later, yeah?" Dulcie suggested, knowing full well that wouldn't happen. Later, Tessa would either be high, or busy "earning her keep".

"Sure, baby. Oh! You got a package. I left it on your bed," her mother informed her.

Dulcie froze for a second, then rushed down the hallway. Nothing was safe in the house, she never left anything private or worth money in her room. She wasn't expecting any packages, had no clue what it was, but knew it would draw unwanted attention.

She wasn't wrong.

"What are you doing!?" she shouted, bursting into her room just in time to see her half-brother Matt standing by her bed, shaking a brown box between his hands.

"Wha'd you get?" he asked, holding the package up to his ear and shaking it harder.

"How would I know? I haven't opened it. Get out of my room," she demanded, hurrying around her bed and reaching for the box. Matt backed up and held it out of her reach.

"Aw, c'mon, we're family. You have to share," he teased, stepping backwards.

"Give me the box, Matt," she growled, reaching for it again.

"Work for it, Dulcie."

She jumped up, trying to snatch the box, and he snaked an arm around her waist, yanking her close. She almost gagged as she fell against his bare chest. He was only wearing a pair of baggy jeans, showing off a sickly thin torso that was covered in misspelled tattoos. She forgot the package and tried to pull free from him, causing them to stumble across the room.

"If you don't get your goddamn hands off me, I swear to god, I will _"

"Mmm, Dulcie, you smell you good."

She felt his nose against her hair. Matt had always been ... *strange* towards her. They'd never been close. He was eight years older than her, and when he'd been thirteen, he'd run away to live with his father. She'd only been five at the time. Then he'd shown back up when he was twenty-one, and she'd been thirteen. She'd never felt like he was her brother, and obviously, he felt the same way.

I wish he would just overdose already and put himself out of my misery.

They were near her door and Dulcie managed to wiggle an arm free of his grasp. She reached out and grabbed a piggy bank off her dresser, swinging it around and slamming it against the side of his head. The thick porcelain shattered, showering them both in loose change and sending Matt to his knees with a groan. She yanked the package out of his hands and tossed it onto the bed.

"Don't ever fucking touch me again!" she hissed, moving around and planting her foot squarely in the middle of his back. He fell forward, through the open doorway and into the hall. Then she slammed her door shut behind him.

She immediately went around to the other side of her dresser and shoved as hard as she could. The piece of furniture was old and made of a heavy wood, not to mention the fact it was full of her clothing. But she'd had a lot of practice moving it, and after she gritted her teeth and put some extra elbow grease into it, it slid across the floor. She kept pushing till it blocked the entrance to her room. Matt had apparently gotten to his feet, because he started banging on the door. Dulcie ignored him and picked up a thick piece of two-by-four that was just inside her closet. She dropped to her knees, wedging the wood between the dresser and her bed frame. Her door was now impossible to open.

"You stupid bitch! You better stay in there, cause if you come out here, I'll make you sorry you ever fucked with me!" Matt was practically screaming.

The door was shut, so he was no longer an issue. He could scream all night and it wouldn't bother Dulcie. She knew he'd eventually lose interest, or get into a fight with Tessa's husband, or get high and forget he was mad. Whatever.

She dropped her messenger bag to the floor and crawled to the center of her bed, picking up the package. It was wrapped in brown paper and had her name on it, along with her address, written in big block letters. No return address. No other information, period. She frowned and began ripping the packaging paper away.

There was gift wrap underneath, with a large, square envelope taped to the top of the box. Again, her name was on it, but just in plain capital letters. Nothing distinct about it. She pulled it away and sat it next to her on the bed, then continued unwrapping her mystery mail.

When about half the paper was ripped off, she was shocked to the see the product on the box's label. She didn't want to get her hopes up, though – people packed socks in blender boxes, so who knew what was really inside it. She quickly ripped through some tape and yanked the box apart.

Nope. The label hadn't been a lie. Someone had sent her a brand new digital camera. *Better* than the one that had gotten destroyed last fall. She turned the machine over in her hands. It was nice, and probably very expensive.

Who the hell would send me a camera!?

Dulcie scrambled to open the envelope that had been taped to the camera box. There was a card inside, but it was blank on the cover. She opened it and there was no printed message inside, either. Just a personal, handwritten note to her.

Dulcie –

I couldn't say goodbye. I won't say I'm sorry, because I'm not, and I think you know why.

I should've gotten this for you sooner. You see things other people don't. Take pictures, and then look at them and draw what you really see in the frames.

Don't be afraid.

And don't disappoint me.

Constantine

Dulcie was breathing hard by the time she got to the end of the note. She'd known it. She'd been right. It wasn't just her, it wasn't just some random moment in time. It had been realer than anything she'd ever experienced. This life, her home, her job, all of it was dishwater bland. Out of focus and blurry. Constantine Masters, now there was some high-definition for her life.

I'll take those pictures, and I'll draw what I see, and when you come back for me, you'll see that we're the same.

PART II

SIX

"**N**O NO NO, THIS SIDE! GET MY *GOOD SIDE!*"

Dulcie sighed and pushed a button. The camera flash went off, which seemed to appease the girl who'd been whining. Or at least it distracted her from realizing the shutter wasn't moving.

"Thanks, Dulcie. You rock."

Whiny girl's boyfriend fist bumped Dulcie, then the pair pranced out of the room and headed back into the dance.

The Halloween dance.

Senior year wasn't all it was cracked up to be. Maybe knowing college was on the horizon made it more exciting for some people, but Dulcie knew she wouldn't be going to college. She'd been saving up to move into her own apartment the moment she turned eighteen, but the diner paid barely enough to cover her extracurricular activities and text books, let alone to save up oodles of cash for rent. Her eighteenth birthday came and went, yet Dulcie was still living in the trailer.

Still blocking her bedroom door.

"Dulcie! Over here!"

A blonde girl was waving at her from inside the gym, and Dulcie smiled and put down the camera. No one was in line to get their picture taken, so she figured she could have a couple minutes of freedom and she headed into the dance.

Senior year wasn't all bad, either. When they'd gotten their yearbooks during the summer, she'd discovered the picture of her and Con kissing had gotten published in the "Hall of Shame" section. It was semi-tasteful, she supposed, and only showed them from the shoulders up, their lips barely touching.

At first, she'd been annoyed. She didn't want anyone seeing their kiss, it was a private moment between her and Con. She worried that when he came home, he'd be mad about the picture. Or embarrassed.

But Con never came back. Never called, e-mailed, wrote, *nothing*. Her sketchbook was overflowing with drawings, her walls were lined with them.

And no Constantine to look at them.

She got mad. Over five months had passed, and there had been no communication. She knew it wasn't him not having the time – she'd heard through school he'd been in contact with other friends. With other girls.

Meanwhile, the infamous kiss photo had given her a bit of celebrity. If Con Masters had found her attractive, well then, she *must be* attractive. And witty, and funny, and something worth looking at twice; suddenly, boys who'd never given her the time of day were chatting her up in the halls. Stealing seats next to her. Asking her on dates.

She ignored them, at first. Then, more time passed, and she got angrier at Con. Angry at herself. Angry at the town she lived in, and angry at her life. Why should she live life on the fringe? Just biding her time, trying to slip by unnoticed. Before, she'd begun to think really, she'd been waiting for Con to notice her.

Now, she realized she'd just been scared. Well. Not anymore. She hated the thought of being scared of anything, so one day, when a relatively good looking guy asked her out, she said yes.

Jared was nice enough. He played football – had played with Con, even. He was the same age as her, and was actually in a few of her art classes. He liked to laugh and he was very polite. He was also super understanding of the fact her legs seemed to be welded together at the knees.

It wasn't that Dulcie was scared of sex – she was very familiar with her own body and was perfectly comfortable giving in to her baser desires. She had a very active fantasy life. Unfortunately, though, none of those fantasies featured Jared, so she just couldn't bring herself to sleep with him.

No, all her fantasies featured a man made of shadows. A boy with a golden smile and a dark heart.

"Hey, ditch the photo room for a while – let's make fun of peoples' costumes," her friend Anna laughed when Dulcie finally reached her side.

"Too easy. What's happening after this?" she asked, glancing around the room.

Oh yes, Dulcie even went to parties now. She felt very accomplished.

"Bryce said something is going on at the lake," Anna started, referring to her own boyfriend. "Jared mentioned you guys might go."

"Hey, you guys talking about me?"

Dulcie didn't get a chance to turn around before an arm slid around her waist. She felt Jared's warm lips against the side of her neck and she smiled as she leaned back into him. He was so comfortable, like an old sweater. A comfy blanket. Her grandma's house.

Not sexy at all.

"Yeah, you guys gonna go to the lake later?" Bryce piped up. Jared moved around so he was at Dulcie's side.

"I dunno, it's so far out there, and I have practice in the morning," he replied. Dulcie let out a sigh of relief. She went to parties, but she didn't particularly like them.

"C'mon, you gotta go! Didn't you hear who's gonna be there?" Bryce exclaimed.

"No, who?"

"Constantine fuckin' Masters!"

Gravity quadrupled for a moment and Dulcie felt like she was going to collapse. All other sound receded and all she could hear was the conversation that was happening between the boys.

"Con's in town? I heard he was like moving up the ranks in Ohio – he's gonna be starting line next year, easy. Dude is gonna go to the NFL," Jared commented.

"Yeah, but his mom died. He came back for the funeral, got here a week ago. He called the other day, just to catch up. I mentioned the party, he said he'd try to make it."

A week. He'd been in town a week, and had made no attempt to contact her.

Nothing. It was all in your head. Just a stupid boy, kissing an even stupider girl.

"What do you say? You wanna head up to the lake?" Jared asked, shaking her shoulders gently. She shook her head.

"No. No, I don't want to go to the lake."

They left the dance and drove towards her home. He parked the car on the other side of a covered bridge and pulled her across the seat, pressing his lips to hers. She sighed and leaned into him. Maybe she *should* sleep with Jared. Get it over with, relieve some tension.

But as his hand fumbled around ineptly in her underwear, she could feel herself growing cold. It always started at her core and worked its way out to her extremities, till she was numb all over. The idea of having sex, of him being inside her, made her feel physically ill. So she pushed him back into his seat and surprised him with a blowjob instead.

At least someone gets a happy ending.

SEVEN

THE TOWN LIBRARY HAD A COURTYARD BEHIND IT WITH SEVERAL large benches, and Dulcie sat outside on one. The days were still a little warm and she wanted to soak it up while she still could, keep some of the cold in her at bay. A young woman was sitting on another bench and her three year old daughter was toddling around the area. Dulcie made faces at the little girl, making her laugh and smile. She tried to capture it all with her pencil, sketching out the child's giggling face.

"It's a good picture, but if you wanted it to be great, you'd make her cry."

She froze up, but only for a second. Then she took a deep breath and continued sketching.

"Maybe that's not what I'm going for," she replied. She was sitting lotus style on top of the bench, and she listened as Con Masters sat in front of her.

"I find that hard to believe."

She glanced up at him, but he was looking at her paper, watching her pencil strokes.

"What're you doing here?" she asked, looking back down at her work.

"I was dropping off some of my mom's book collection, as a donation. Saw you sitting out here," he explained. She nodded.

"Oh."

Suddenly, he grabbed her sketchbook and pulled it out of her lap. At the same moment, a strong gust of wind blew through the courtyard. The little girl began to cry and her mother picked her up, cooing sweet nothings as she carried the child back inside.

"These are good," he commented, flipping through the pages.

"Hey, you don't have any right to look at those," Dulcie snapped, reaching for the book.

"Don't I? I told you to draw them."

He could've slapped her and she would've been less surprised. He seemed completely at ease, leisurely turning each page, as if her reason for being outside had been to wait for him. Like an appointment. She couldn't stand the tension and she jumped up.

"It's been a long time, Con. Thank you for the camera, but that's my book, and I would like it back," she said in the voice she usually reserved for talking to rude customers or belligerent parents.

"Oh, really?"

He closed her sketchbook and slowly stood up. She'd forgotten how tall he was, how imposing. He looked so different. He was only a year older since she'd last really looked at him. Just a nineteen year old boy, that's all. Nothing to make her nervous.

Except, he didn't seem like some nineteen year old boy. He looked like something else. Like a man. Like something *starved*. Like something she had been missing for far longer than he'd been gone.

She wasn't cold anymore. Oh no. Now she was hot all over, every inch of her. She licked her lips and watched as his eyes followed the movement.

"I'm sorry about your mother," she suddenly blurted out. He raised an eyebrow.

"Why?"

"Because she died. I'm sorry."

"I'm not. We weren't close."

"How did she die?"

"Fell down some stairs."

"That's too bad."

"Or was pushed."

That made her pause for a moment. She may have been over-heating, but Con had reached new levels of cold. He was approaching sub-zero temperatures.

"You think she was pushed?" Dulcie clarified. He shrugged.

"I don't really care, either way. She hated her life, she's probably glad she's dead. My father hated her, so he's probably even happier about it."

"If you don't care, then why did you come back?" Dulcie was confused.

He smiled, then. She'd forgotten his smile, forgotten the effect it had on her. That slow grin, leisurely traveling the length of his lips. Suddenly, she was starving, too.

"I came back for this," he said, waving her sketchbook in front of her face.

Then he turned around and walked away, taking her book with him.

When Constantine had come home for the funeral, he hadn't bothered with his old room. He wanted as much distance between him and his father as was possible. He stayed in an apartment over their detached garage.

After he'd left the library, he'd gone back to the apartment and stripped down before getting into bed. There was no air conditioning and the garage was heated. Combined with the warm spell that was gripping the county, it all made the small living quarters sweltering hot.

He laid naked while flipping through Dulcie's sketchbook. He'd been lying to her – the funeral really was his reason for coming home. Of course he'd thought about her, though. Not a day went by where he didn't think of Dulcie. But she made him nervous. He couldn't tell where he was when he was with her. Was he bad for her? Or was *she* bad for *him?*

When he was surrounded by plastic shiny people, he had an easier time pretending he was normal, and an easier time pretending his dark thoughts didn't exist. When he thought of Dulcie, though, all the pretending stopped. He hated that, it was like a bump in the road. It caused him to stumble.

He'd had no intention of seeking her out while he was in town. School was going well for him. He wasn't going to go into the NFL, like everyone expected and wanted. No, he had other plans. He was going to get his MBA, then move far away, from everything and everyone. Dulcie could ruin his plans, could destroy his carefully built facade.

But as Con examined each page, as his eyes wandered over all the black paint and the dark lines, he knew it wouldn't be so easy anymore. He got to the picture she'd drawn the year before, in that long ago detention, and he traced his fingers over the shadowy figure.

So much darkness. Falling in love with this chick would be easy, but surviving each other … that's an entirely different story.

EIGHT

"**C**'MON, IT COULD BE A LOT OF FUN!"

"Yeah, Dulcie, c'mon! Have you ever been up there?"

"You could probably get some great pictures, more stuff for your creepy book."

Dulcie rolled her eyes at the last pitch. Besides, she couldn't add anything to her "creepy book" – Con still had it. It had been a week. She was beginning to wonder if she'd ever get it back.

Do I really care?

"I don't know, you guys. I get off work at eleven, will it even be worth it?" she asked, then she bent over and wiped down the table they were all sitting around.

She was at work and the gang had come in to beg her to go to a party that night. Apparently, the football team had decided to throw some huge kegger up in the woods, near an abandoned mine shaft. A hot spot for parties because the cops could rarely be bothered to trek into the woods to shut them down. Dulcie had never been, had no interest in going, but she'd heard some pretty wild stories.

"It'll just be getting started," Jared assured her. She grimaced. That wasn't a selling point, in my mind. That just meant everyone would be wasted by the time she got there.

"Why is this party such a big deal?" she was curious. Jared grabbed her hand.

"Cause it's in the woods, and all secluded and private. It'll be fun," he assured her, then winked.

Her grimace got worse.

Luckily, at that moment a customer called for her. The diner was railcar style, so she moved down the narrow walkway between the counter and the tables. She took an order, cleared another table, then made her way back behind the bar. As she dumped dirty dishes in the sink, she heard the bell above the door go off. A gust of wind rolled through the restaurant, then the door closed.

"Be with you in a minute!" she called out. She dried off her hands, stuck the new ticket on the order wheel, then turned around.

She moved around the counter with her order pad in hand, but when she looked up, she didn't seen any new patrons at any of the tables. She scanned the small space once, then began looking over the people at the counter, wondering if maybe the new arrival had simply stepped in and then stepped back outside.

No such luck. She spotted him on her second glance around. He'd slid into the booth next to Jared, his arm stretched out along the back of the seat. He looked so at ease, laughing at whatever silly story Anna was telling. So normal, sitting amongst normal people.

There is nothing normal about Constantine.

"What are you doing here?" she blurted out as soon as she walked up to the table. Con turned his smile on her, but she was better prepared for it this time around and it didn't quite knock the breath out of her.

"Came in for a cup of coffee, saw these guys. I forgot you worked here, Dulcie," he lied. She could tell. She could just *feel* the lie, like a cold snake wrapped around his words. He'd known exactly where she'd be, exactly where she worked.

"Well, I do. Did you want something?" she asked. Her voice was loud and flat, and she watched as Jared winced.

"Jeez, babe, what's got you all riled up?"

Con's smile got bigger.

"That's right, I heard you two were going out. How long has it been now?"

Now it was Dulcie's turn to wince.

"Eh, like two months?" Jared estimated. Dulcie nodded.

"Yeah, almost," she agreed. The way Con was sitting, Jared couldn't see his face, but Dulcie was only about a foot away from him. She could see the knowing gleam in his eye. The malice.

Could see he knew Jared was nothing more than a placeholder.

"How *cute*."

"So!" Anna's high voice cut through the growing tension. "We've been trying to convince Dulcie to go to the mine party tonight."

"Yeah, tell her how fun they are," Bryce added. Con's eyebrows went up.

"Never been to a party at the mines?" he asked, though she was sure he already knew the answer.

"Never sounded like very much fun," she replied.

"Remember the one last year, Con? After homecoming? Man, it was epic," Jared chuckled.

"They are pretty '*epic*'," Con agreed with a sigh. "Sounds like a good time. Maybe I'll check it out."

"See, Dulcie? If Masters is gonna be there, it's gonna be epic," Bryce assured her.

If another person says epic, I'm going to scream.

"I don't know, it's gonna be so late, and I -" she began to make excuses.

"Of course, if you're *scared*, don't go. It's dark up there. Dangerous. Wouldn't want you running off, getting lost."

He'd said it to ruffle her feathers, and it worked. She stared down the length of her nose at him, like he was a bug she wanted to squash. She wasn't scared of anything, least of all some stupid party in the woods. And definitely not Con Masters.

*No, I'm not scared of him. I'm **terrified**.*

48

"I'll go. But it better be pretty fucking epic."

He smiled again.

"Oh, it will be."

His smile unnerved her more than just about anything. Con had picked up on that a long time ago, and he almost laughed when she turned and hurried away the moment he showed some teeth. She went back behind the counter and pretended to be busy with washing cups.

"You really gonna go tonight?"

Con turned back to the table. He'd almost forgotten he and Dulcie weren't alone. Bryce, a third string player he'd barely spent any time with, was smiling eagerly at him. A blonde thing sat at his side, a girl Con didn't recognize at all.

It was Jared who'd spoken to him. Jared had played on the team with him, was varsity, but they'd never been close. Hadn't really been in the same circles. They'd been to a couple parties together, and of course a lot of stays at away games, but that was the extent of their friendship.

"Yeah, why not. For old times' sake," Con replied. The couple laughed and turned to chatter excitably about the upcoming night. Jared smiled and clapped him on the back.

"That's awesome. I gotta ask, though ... this isn't weird, is it?"

"What?" Con was confused.

"This ... y'know. Dulcie and me. Dulcie and you. You two had a thing, right?" Jared asked.

Con had to stop himself from replying with *"there is no 'Dulcie and you', so why would it be weird?"*

"No," he cleared his throat, stopping the other words from coming out. "Not weird. It was just one kiss, one night. Dulcie and I were never 'a thing.'"

No, we were almost **everything**.

NINE

DULCIE FELT UNEASY FROM THE MOMENT SHE GOT OUT OF THE CAR. Not because of the dark, or the woods in front of them, or the thought of being in the middle of nowhere with a bunch of drunk teenagers. No, it was something else.

Something bad was going to happen that night.

"Do we have to do this?" she asked as they trekked up a hillside. Jared laughed and grabbed her hand, linking their fingers together.

"It'll be fun, I promise," he said, then leaned down and kissed the side of her head.

She frowned.

It was actually a decent hike, taking them almost twenty minutes. Dulcie wondered how anyone made it back out after they were drunk or high. She was sober and she was pretty sure she couldn't find her way back to the car if she needed to get to it.

There was a huge bonfire raging in front of the mine shaft, with a couple kegs just inside the entrance. People were scattered about and someone had set up a bunch of wireless speakers. The woods were filled with the sounds of the top hits.

Dulcie wasn't a big drinker, she'd seen what substance abuse did to the people in her family. She'd never met her real dad, but she'd heard some pretty awful stories about him, and of course her mother and Matt were daily reminders of why she shouldn't drink. So when Jared got her a beer, she took it and smiled, but she barely sipped at it.

"Could you imagine being here this time last year?" Anna squealed. Dulcie glanced at her.

"No, I honestly can't," she agreed. November of last year, she would've been sitting at home, pining away for Constantine.

Now she was in the middle of a party, and she was still pining.

"Can I ask you something?" Anna asked in a soft voice the moment the boys wandered off.

"Sure."

"So that picture ..."

Good god, the picture of her and Con kissing was going to haunt Dulcie for the rest of her life.

"What about it?"

"Well, you never told me the story behind it, and now he's back, and you just seem ..." Anna stopped speaking as she searched for the right word. Dulcie felt her pulse quicken.

"I seem like what?" she demanded. She thought she'd been doing a damn fine job of seeming like nothing was different.

"I don't know, distracted. I haven't seen you sketching anything, you haven't taken any pictures. I just thought maybe ... maybe there was more than just that kiss. Thought maybe you'd like to talk about it," Anna offered.

Dulcie knew she took the other girl for granted. Anna had been there before Dulcie's "stock had risen", as it were. She deserved a better friend, really, someone who could handle sleepovers and giggle about boys. Someone with some warmth.

"No," Dulcie said, then she looked around to make sure they were alone before stepping closer to her friend. "We only ever kissed. But it was ... intense. Remember how my camera got broken? Cause he bumped into me? When we were in detention, he looked through my sketchbook, and it was like ... he just understood, you know? He didn't think it was weird, he didn't question anything. He saw everything exactly how I saw it. That's why I dressed up for the dance, because of a picture I'd drawn of the two of us. He did the same thing. That's why we wound up under those bleachers."

"Oh my god," Anna gasped. It wasn't the whole story, but it was juicy enough for the other girl. "Oh my god! So like, it *was* a thing! Oh my god, he got in trouble that night, didn't he? Oh my god, what if he hadn't? What if you two had gone out? What if you were like meant to be together and have a hundred babies and that night ruined it? *Oh my god does Jared know!?*"

"No! No, he does not, and I don't want him to," Dulcie replied quickly.

"Do you still like him?" Anna asked. Dulcie glanced around again.

"I'm not sure I ever liked him. We were just … something weird. We barely ever talked, before that and after that, even now. He graduated and left without even saying goodbye," she explained. Anna winced.

"Harsh."

"But then two weeks later, he sent me a new camera and told me to make sketches of the pictures I took."

"*Oh my god he's totally in love with you you should go have all the babies with him.*"

When Anna got excited, her speech would approach light speed. Spaces between words and breathing became optional.

"He is *not* in love with me. I never heard from him again after that, not once, not till he came back to town. Like I said, it was just a weird thing, and it happened a long time ago. It's done, it's over with, and now you know, so now we don't ever have to talk about it again," Dulcie said, her voice growing hard.

"But what if -"

"I'm serious, Anna."

Anna tried to glare, but being upset wasn't in her nature. She pouted her lips and sighed dramatically, then finally laughed.

"Okay, fine. So he doesn't like you."

"Yes."

"And you don't like him."

"Correct."

"So you won't care that he's hitting on Frannie McKey right now."

Dulcie froze for a second. Of course when they'd first gotten to the party, she'd scanned the area, looking for him. She hadn't seen him in the crowd, though she supposed he could've been in the mine, or off in the woods. She'd halfway hoped he hadn't come.

But mostly really hoped he'd be there.

She glanced over her shoulder, trying to be nonchalant. Probably failing. He was standing maybe fifteen feet directly behind her. A girl was next to him, her back against a tree, and he was leaning over her. Smiling his evil little smile, his arm braced against the trunk over her head. Frannie beamed back at him, laughing and flirting. Dulcie remembered they'd dated briefly, when Con had been a junior. There'd been wild stories about the two of them getting caught in some interesting "situations" in the boys' locker room.

He's only ever kissed me, and he's seen what she looks like naked. Why did I come here?

"No. No, I don't care. I have a boyfriend, remember? Why should I care who or what Constantine Masters is hitting on?" Dulcie responded, but her voice was so quiet she wondered if anyone heard it.

Then she chugged down her entire beer before walking off to grab another.

She was in the middle of guzzling her third straight cup when Jared found her again. He laughed and pulled the red plastic away from her lips, causing foam to dribble down her chin.

"I've never seen you drink like this before, someone's in a crazy mood," he teased, reaching out to wipe off the foam. She slapped his hand away and took care of it herself.

"I'm crazy, alright," she agreed, then followed him as he led her away from the kegs.

"So I was thinking," he started, and she groaned inwardly. "Thanksgiving break is coming up. Wouldn't it be cool to take off? My parents have a cabin out on the lake. We could head there on Friday, stay till Sunday. Snuggle in front of the fire, take walks around the lake."

Hmmm, a whole weekend alone in a cabin with him. She tried to picture what it would be like, did her best to conjure images of burning fireplaces and romantic evenings and sexier night times.

But all that came to mind was the unbearable desire to shove him away. To hold him down and scream at him and make him understand that she didn't want to "snuggle". She wanted someone to take a bite out of her. She wanted someone to bleed for her. She wanted to make him understand that she would rather stab him in the eye with a hot poker than get naked with him.

Jesus, just break up with his poor kid before he realizes you're fucking psychotic.

"I don't know," she sighed, then stumbled over a root. She wasn't a complete novice to alcohol, she wasn't drunk, but her head was spinning a little. He'd led her into the treeline, where it was dark and the bonfire's light didn't quite reach all the way. She couldn't see her feet in the blackness.

"C'mon, babe. We've been going out for a while now," he reminded her as he pushed her up against a tree.

"Two months isn't so long," she argued, then hiccuped. He laughed at her.

"You're cute when your drunk."

"I am *not* drunk."

His tongue was in her mouth and she almost gagged on it. She put her hands against his chest, intending to push him away, but he took it as an invitation and leaned all his weight on her. She could feel his erection against her hip and the urge to vomit intensified.

"God, you have no idea how much I want you," he groaned, his hands sliding underneath her shirt.

"I have a very good idea of it right now. Get off me," she instructed, grabbing at his wrists.

"C'mon, Dulcie. No one can see us," he assured her while trailing sucking kisses down her neck. She shuddered and pulled hard at his arms.

"I don't care."

"Please. It'll be so hot, I promise."

"Not gonna happen, Jared."

"How about like in the car? Just real fast, and I won't come in your mouth."

Dulcie briefly wondered if boys actually thought that was a selling point. Was this something they regularly used as a bargaining chip? Did it work?

"I'm not blowing you in the woods while a group of people stand twenty feet away from us. Now get off me!" she snapped, and shoved at his shoulders. He stepped away and stumbled, almost falling over.

"What's your fucking problem?" he demanded, and she was a little shocked. Jared was always so calm and collected.

"A lot of things," she sighed, rubbing her hand across her forehead. She'd known they wouldn't last. Con coming back to town had really driven it home. She knew she had to break up with Jared, but she hadn't wanted to do it at a party. Now it looked like it was going to happen anyway.

"No shit. I've tried with you, Dulcie, I really have," he pointed out. She nodded.

"Yup, you sure have. I'm sorry. I'm just some fucked up chick. You picked the wrong girl to like, Jared. I'm really sorry," she told him.

He looked sad for a brief second, as the fact that they were really breaking up sank in. Then anger washed back over his features.

"So this is all my fault, huh?" he asked. She shook her head.

"No. No, it's all me. I shouldn't have gone out with you," she told him.

"Why not?"

"Because … it wasn't fair. I'm not normal."

"No shit," he growled. "Always in your stupid book, drawing. Won't let me touch you, won't touch me. What the fuck!?"

"Okay, just because we're breaking up and I won't blow you doesn't mean you get to be nasty. Just go back to the party," she instructed.

"Screw you, Dulcie. Oh wait, *you don't do that.*"

What he was saying didn't hurt, because Dulcie was beyond hurting most of the time. But it did surprise her, and it did make her mad. Sure, she'd been dating Jared for the wrong reasons, and yes, that made her a bad person. But it didn't mean she was required to take his shit.

She went to open her mouth to make some sort of comeback, but there was a loud snapping noise. They both jerked their heads to her right and watched as Constantine came out of the shadows. Dulcie groaned and fell back against the tree.

This night just gets better and better. Why did I come here again? Oh yeah, cause Constantine fucking Masters dared me to.

"Sorry, guys, we got a little lost out here," he chuckled. There was a giggling sound, and Dulcie watched with wide eyes as Frannie came out of the dark, as well. She was buttoning up her shirt and kept on giggling.

Oh. Of course. Yes. I see now. I'm fun enough as an appetizer, but not good enough to be the full meal.

"Lost, yeah, right. Thanks for interrupting. Sorry your girlfriend's a frigid bitch," Frannie snickered and giggled, glaring at Dulcie. Frannie was the quintessential high school cheerleader who just loved to pick on the weird artsy chick. Jared swallowed thickly and glanced around the group. Con just smiled.

"Hey, don't talk about her -" Jared began putting up a token resistance.

But Dulcie was so very tired of pretending. Tired of being too young, and too confused, and too cold. Tired of *everything.*

"Don't be sorry, Frannie. I'm not. And I'm not his girlfriend anymore. He just dumped me," she interrupted. Frannie laughed harder. Con kept staring, his stupid smile still in place.

"I didn't dump you, Dulcie," Jared said in a low voice.

"You should. If you don't, I'll just do it to you. Either way, I'm walking out of here single," she told him, then pushed away from the tree to emphasize her point.

"And a virgin," Frannie called out. Dulcie stopped moving. Sighed and looked straight up.

"I love it. Because I didn't want to fuck some guy up against a tree in the woods, *I'm* the weirdo. *I'm* the loser. Good luck with your hopes and dreams, Frannie. I hope they're easy to accomplish while you're laying on your back."

Jared's jaw dropped open. Frannie started hissing and yelling.

And Constantine, well. He just kept on smiling. Just kept pouring salt in the wound.

Dulcie strode off, not bothering to look back when Jared called out her name. She skirted the edge of the party, then took off into the woods where there was a sort-of-trail. A foot path, really, which she prayed would lead her back to where they'd parked the cars. She didn't want to spend the night in the woods.

What the fuck. *What in the actual fuck.* She was gasping for air and realized she was almost jogging through the forest. The moonlight was barely filtering through the canopy and she was amazed she hadn't smacked into a tree or fallen down. She leaned against a stump for a moment and tried to catch her breath.

She wasn't upset about Jared – she'd been telling the truth. If their fight hadn't happened, she would've broken up with him, anyway. And she wasn't even mad at Frannie – everything the girl said had technically been the truth. Dulcie *was* frigid and she *was* a virgin. Getting upset over facts would be ridiculous.

She was angry at Con, but most of all, she was furious with herself. For not understanding what was going on in her head and in her heart. For not being able to read such a strange boy. For having the ultimate stupidity to believe he felt something for her. And for feeling like her heart broke a little when he came out of the darkness with another girl.

I want to be in the dark with him.

She finally got control of herself and she continued blundering through the woods. Her mind raced as she stalked along. She would drop out of school. Not like it mattered anyway, right? She would drop out and she would move away. She would steal Matt's drug stash, sell it as she went, and go anywhere else. Somewhere she could hide in a dark corner and paint out her dark thoughts. She would go anywhere Con Masters wasn't, that's where she wanted to go.

I can't even get out of these fucking woods, how am I going to run away?

Dulcie was pretty sure she was lost. If there was a path, she'd long since left it. She was regularly kicking her way through bushes and shoving her way through branches. The party was long gone behind her, she couldn't even tell which direction she'd come from anymore. She was on a slight incline, so her only choice, really, was to keep walking down and just hope for the best.

It was so dark in the woods that when she finally broke free of the tree line, she was shocked at how bright the moon was, so big and full in the sky. It shined down and illuminated a set of rusty railroad tracks, making them almost glow. They looked very old, like a train hadn't gone over them in a long time, and she realized they were the abandoned lines just outside of town. She'd been walking away from home. All she had to do was follow the rails and eventually she'd wind up right near where they'd parked the cars.

She began walking down the center of the tracks. She really wished she'd brought her camera. Everything looked dark and eerie, she felt like she was walking through the underworld. Like maybe something magical would happen.

Wishing for a boy to like you. Wishing to run away. Wishing for magic. You are so tragically young, it's not even funny.

Dulcie was practically in the hobo camp before she was even aware there was one. The tracks went around a sharp bend and *bam*, there it was; an abandoned train station loomed in front of her. There were candles burning in a couple windows and tents had been set up along the platform, as well as on the actual tracks.

While she wasn't afraid, she also didn't particularly feel like getting raped, so she left the lines and scrambled up an embankment that ran alongside them. A couple voices called out of the darkness below, a couple hisses and rude comments, but Dulcie ignored them. Just wrapped her arms around herself and walked against a stiff breeze.

The tents eventually thinned out, and when she finally saw one without another right after it, she moved back down to the tracks. The ground was more even and there was some shelter from the wind that was picking up. She came across a large piece of quartz and kicked it along as she went, bouncing it off the rails. She stared at the large white stone and thought about a very dark boy.

What's wrong with me? What do I want? Why can't I push past this … this curtain in my head. Like a black curtain, just blocking everything until I pick up a pencil. I need my sketchbook to see anything. I need something, I need -

"I got watcha need, lady."

The voice was so low, so resembled a hiss, that for a moment she genuinely thought it was a snake. No, not that a snake was literally talking to her. She thought she'd finally gone insane and was imagining things.

But then a form crawled out from under some cardboard boxes and slithered towards her, and she saw it was a man.

Eh. Close enough.

"I don't even know what I need," she replied, pausing to look down at him. "How could you possibly know?"

"Because," he croaked out, shifting form and climbing to his feet. "I'mma man. Yer a woman. I got whatchu *need.*"

He fondled his crotch as he shambled forward and Dulcie rolled her eyes.

"Nobody needs that, I promise you. Good night," she said, and began marching away.

Fingers, suddenly, tearing at the back of her shirt. Taking hold and yanking her backward, pulling her off balance. She squawked and flailed her arms before falling into him. They both went down, one on top of the other, and ended up in a heap on top of the tracks.

"Oh, *yesssss*, jus' like that, baby," he grunted in her ear as she wiggled around, trying to get free from him.

"Oh, for fuck's sake, get the fuck off me!" she yelled, finally crawling out from under him. She managed to get to her feet and she took a step back, wiping the grime and dirt and feel of him off her body.

The homeless guy had gotten to his knees and he lunged forward, wrapping his arms around her legs. She shrieked and pounded on his shoulders, trying to break free from him. Still, she wasn't really afraid. Mad again, yes, and very frustrated. That black curtain in her mind began to ruffle and move, as if a strong breeze was threatening to rip it open.

"Ain't no one gon' help you, baby. Jus' you and me out here. Ain't no one gon' hear you, lady," he hissed up at her, and then bent his head forward, directly into her crotch.

His teeth. She could feel his teeth against the seam in her pants, directly under her zipper. His hands were raking up the backs of her thighs and clawing at her ass, pulling at her jeans.

This man, this filthy excuse for a human being, had the *audacity* to touch her. To think he was *allowed* to touch her. That she would let him get away with it.

With a primal scream that most definitely came from behind the curtain, Dulcie yanked her knee up as hard and as fast as she could. It connected with the underside of his jaw and she heard his teeth clack together, felt him spit blood out as he fell backwards.

"Who the fuck do you think you are!?" she screamed at him, walking up to his side. He went to sit up and she stomped on his chest. When he fell back again, she moved to kneel over him, digging one knee into his breast bone. He groaned in protest.

"Please, baby ..."

"I am *not* your baby," she growled through clenched teeth, then she reached out, digging her fingers into his hair and pulling. "I should fucking kill you. Fucking touching me. For even *thinking* you could touch me. *Disgusting*. Don't even look at me when I walk away."

She slammed his head back onto the ground, eliciting another groan from him. When she stood up, she kicked him once more in the ribs, then spit in his face. He was a baser life form in comparison to her, and she wanted to make sure he knew it; make sure he *felt* it.

Her warning hadn't been strong enough, though, because when she went to walk away, he grabbed her ankle. Her leg was pulled out from underneath her and she went down fast, striking the side of her head against the rail. Her brain stepped in and out of reality.

Is this the curtain? Or is this behind the curtain? Am I real?

There were hands on her body and weight on her legs. Dulcie was aware that she was screaming, but not out of fear. It was more primal instinct. Something within her, tearing free from years of oppression. She screamed and screamed while the wind howled, and she beat her fists against the man who was crawling around on top of her.

Then a shadow moved in the darkness that surrounded them, and the hobo was ripped off her. She gasped for air and just stared as Constantine all but threw the other man across the tracks.

He didn't look at her, not even once, as he stormed after his prey. Dulcie sat up, watching while Con drove his fist into the man's face. Again and again. But it wasn't enough. While she climbed to her feet, Con grabbed the man by the hair and repeatedly slammed the back of his head into the rail line.

There was a loud growling noise and she looked around, halfway expecting to see a bear or a coyote. But it wasn't coming from the woods above her. It was coming directly across from her. It was Con, growling as he beat the absolute shit out of the hobo.

Dulcie stumbled over so she was right behind him. His growling grew to an open mouthed yell. His hands were coated in blood and he struggled to keep his grip on the hobo's hair.

Well now, let's just rip this ol' black curtain away and see what's been hiding behind it!

"He fucking touched you," Con was gasping for air as he finally stepped back from the damage. "No one is allowed to touch you. I can't believe he fucking touched you."

He was right. She'd thought it before – what had made the man think he could possibly be allowed to touch her, to sully her with his presence, and not pay the consequences? Didn't he know he was trespassing on private property? The sole property of one very dark boy?

Dulcie looked around her, almost manic in her movements. A couple feet away, there was a metal rod laying in a ditch, and she hurried to pick it up. It was a post for a stop sign, though the sign itself was long gone. The edges were rusty and a couple of mean looking bolts jutted out of the top.

This'll do.

She calmly walked back to the *thing* that was laying on the tracks. Con hadn't moved at all, though he still had a wild look in his eyes, and he kept staring at the man. Dulcie moved so she was next to him and looked down as well. The hobo was gurgling, spitting up blood, but still managing to laugh.

"Baby … this what … whatchu *need* …"

With a shout, Dulcie swung the post in a wide arc. It landed smack across the man's face, driving his head harder into the rail underneath him. She could hear bone break, hear teeth crack, and it was like music to her. She swung the post again, and the man's face was unrecognizable as human. Another swing, and an arterial spray of blood shot through the moonlight. Finally, one last swing, one last primal scream, and there was a crunch. Something hard crumbling against something soft. Mr. Hobo would never be touching anything, ever again.

She realized she was panting again, and she dropped the rod. It hit the rail and sent a gonging noise echoing off into the night. Somewhere in the distance, she heard an owl scream.

"*Move him.*"

Con's voice was deep, like normal, but also slightly breathless. She didn't even ask what he meant, she just walked around and grabbed the hobo under his shoulders. Con grabbed his legs and they lifted together.

Half of the man's head stayed on the track.

While they carried the body to the ditch, she could feel his blood running over her hands. She glanced at Con and realized his hands and forearms were coated in the red substance, as well. It was dark out, and there was only a full moon for light, but for some reason, the blood was scarlet in color. Shiny and bright.

They didn't say a word. They dropped the body and Con rolled it onto its stomach. Then he grabbed her hand and began pulling her along behind him. She still didn't say anything, just jogged to keep up with his pace.

They were around the corner from where a bunch of cars were parked at the base of a hill. He didn't lead her to them, though; he pulled her in the opposite direction, through an old railroad crossing. There was rusty fencing that ran along the side of the tracks and they followed it almost all the way back to the station. His truck stood there, easily within five hundred feet of the old building. Why had he parked so far away from the trail?

Because he knew he'd be bringing me here. Because he knew we'd need privacy.

While he dug around for his keys, she stared at her reflection in the passenger window. There was a bright slash of red going across her neck, and there was blood all over her arms. She looked like the walking dead. She began wiping her hands against her clothing, getting rid of as much of the mess as she could.

"*Here.*"

There was a case of water in the bed of his truck, and he tossed her a bottle. She dumped the water over her hands, rinsing as best she could, scrubbing with the hem of her shirt. She glanced across the truck and watched as he did the same thing.

Con finally unlocked the doors and she hefted herself into the massive vehicle. They sat in silence for a while, their breath fogging up the glass. Then he opened his mouth.

"Did he touch you?"

Dulcie knew he wasn't asking about the homeless man.

"Not in any way that counts," she replied, turning to look at him. His hands had moved to grip the steering wheel.

"So he *has* touched you."

"Jared was just an experiment, I wanted to see if -"

"You let him fucking touch you."

"*You fucking left me!*" she was suddenly screaming. He didn't even flinch, just gripped the steering wheel harder. "You fucking left me in this fucking town, without a goddamn goodbye! Without a goddamn word! God, you have *no idea* what it's been like. That fucking camera, all those drawings. And there's all these people, and talking, and feeling this way, and all the blackness, and I don't even know what's wrong with me, and *nothing*. You come back, and it's like *nothing to you*. Oh hey, Dulcie. Where's your sketchbook, Dulcie. Come to a party, Dulcie. Let me just fuck this chick in the woods, Dulcie. So you know what? Yeah, he fucking touched me. I let him fucking touch me. And I hated every minute of it, and I would pretend it was you, and I would hate you, and I would hate myself, and I just *let it happen*."

Con lunged across the seat, and absurdly, her first thought was "*wow, he's really fast*" before his fingers wrapped around her throat. She wasn't fazed, though, and she pushed right back, slapping him across the face. This only caused him to clench both hands around her neck and he yanked her forward, dragging her to him so their faces were only inches apart.

"Stupid little Dulcie," he whispered, his breath hot against her lips. She held onto his wrists and glared at him, but didn't try to pull away. His fingers got tighter. "So scared of the big bad wolf."

"I'm not ... scared of you," she managed to gasp out, but then his grip grew so tight he completely cut off her oxygen.

"Of course you aren't scared of *me*. *I'm* not the wolf. *You are*."

So that's what was hiding behind the curtain. I wish you'd told me sooner, Con. We could've reveled in our darkness together.

It felt like a weight was lifted off her back. She'd been pretending for so long, and she hadn't even realized it. Had conditioned herself to do it. It was easier to believe Con was the darkness, and she was simply drawn to it. Basking in his wake. But that was a lie – she was every bit as dark as him. They were the same animal. She'd just been better at deceiving herself. And now they'd evolved into something else, into a new, higher being.

Her lungs were throbbing, screaming for oxygen. She could feel her pulse pounding behind her face. Her mouth was open, but she couldn't make a sound. Black spots danced in front of her eyes, yet still they stared at each other. Recognizing each other, maybe for the first time ever.

Maybe for the last time.

What a way to die, looking into the face of this beautiful boy. What a gift.

He let her go and when she went to gasp in air, he leaned in and kissed her, instead.

Just like she remembered. He was a tidal wave crashing over her, destroying her, and she welcomed the destruction. She pushed her tongue against his, dragged her teeth along his lip, clawed her fingers through his hair.

Con moved towards her and she shifted around him, crawling onto his lap. He ripped her shirt open, sending buttons ricocheting all around the cab of the truck, and then his face was between her breasts while she shimmied out of her top.

"It's not nothing," he breathed, his tongue tracing along the lace of her bra. "You weren't nothing."

"You didn't sleep with Frannie up there," she stated, then pulled at the back of his sweater. It and his t-shirt came loose, and he let her slide them over his head. She tossed his clothing onto the floor and then stared at his chest, smoothing her hands over it. He was incredible.

Carved out of marble, etched out of stone. She wanted to paint him. Wanted to immortalize him.

"No. She followed me. I was watching you," he replied, reaching around to unhook her bra. It joined his shirts.

"You should do less watching, more talking."

Suddenly, he swung her around and slammed her down onto the bench seat. He promptly began pulling at her pants and she scrambled to unbutton his, as well. She'd barely gotten his jeans past his hips when he was moving away, yanking her jeans down as he went. They slid down her legs and were gone with a whisper, then his body was hovering over her.

"Did you let him do this to you?" Con asked, his rough hand moving over her breasts. Her eyes rolled back in her head and she nodded.

"Yes."

"Ah. And what about this?"

His voice was a purr in the darkness, and she felt his hand cupping her crotch, warm through her panties. She groaned low in her throat as he applied pressure.

"Yes, that too," she sighed.

"*Dulcie.*"

The purr had turned into a hiss, and it set her blood on fire. Made her feel at home. She lifted her hips as he peeled her underwear away from her body. Once the material was pulled over her feet, she felt him moving over her and she opened her eyes.

It was the first time she'd ever been completely naked with a boy, but she didn't care. What was the point in being shy? Her body belonged to him as much as it belonged to her. Moonlight was filling the cab of the truck, and she watched him as he stared at her.

"God, you are so beautiful," she whispered.

"What about this?" he continued with his questions, shifting around so he was between her legs. "Was he ever here?"

"No," she answered, propping herself and wrapping an arm around his shoulders. She dragged her tongue along his clavicle, wanting to taste him. He moved even closer.

"Was he ever *inside you?* Did you let him *fuck you?*"

"*No.*"

It hurt, but she didn't care. She cried out, but he didn't care. She bit down on his shoulder so hard, she tasted his blood in her mouth, but neither of them cared. She wanted his pain to mix with her pain. Wanted them to be seamless.

She was a virgin, no amount of soul connection between them could change that fact, so of course it was unpleasant. He was large, and rough. She was tiny, and inexperienced. But she loved it. Loved being full in a way that made it hard to breathe, loved that she was feeling a pain only he could give to her.

"I thought about this," he was breathing in her ear as his hips picked up speed. "In high school. While I was away. When I was looking at your pictures."

A tear streamed down her cheek, but before it could tip over the side of her jaw, his tongue was sweeping it up.

"All the time. I think about this *all the time,*" she whispered back.

He moved them again, gentler than he had earlier, and they were back in the same position as before, with her straddling his lap. If she had thought she was full before, she'd been mistaken. Her whole body shook as she slid down the full length of him.

"Look at me," he growled, and his hand painfully gripped her jaw, forcing her head up to face him. "God, you look amazing when you cry."

She kissed him, pouring everything she had into it, and she wrapped an arm around his neck before moving her body up and down. The pain was still there, sharp and insistent, but something else was beginning to blanket it. Con's hands moved to her ass, urging her faster, and she complied.

As if she had a choice in the matter.

She gripped onto the back of the seat, used it for leverage to push harder. To grind down against him. She shouted as a tremor ripped through her body, surprising both of them. His mouth went to her breasts, his lips locking around a nipple and sucking hard enough that she knew there'd be a bruise. She returned the favor by pinching his ear lobe between her teeth and biting down. She didn't stop till he yanked her away by her hair.

"Oh my god, *Constantine*," she whispered. More like prayed. All the coldness was gone from her body, *finally*, and she knew it wouldn't be long before he ripped her apart. Just like she'd always wanted.

His hand was still tight in her hair, forcing her head back and her spine to arch. The position caused her to thrust her chest out and one of his hands moved to her breast, pinching at the bruised nipple. It was like lighting a fuse – one that led directly to where he was thrusting back against her. Her movements became erratic and she dug her nails into his shoulders. Dragged them down his chest.

"Such a good girl, Dulcie. You would do anything for me, wouldn't you?" he sighed, leaning close to kiss along the side of her neck. She was whimpering and moaning, and when another tremor shook her, she heard him groan, as well.

"Yes."

"Any time I asked, too."

"*Yes.*"

"I like that. Right now, though," his voice was getting breathless. The hand in her hair pulled tighter and his hips thrust harder. The pain was dull now, but the pleasure, good god. That was sure to kill her.

"Anything," she cried out. "Anything you want."

"*I think it's time for you to come.*"

Jared had tried, and failed, multiple times to give her an orgasm. She wasn't shy about playing with herself, but they were almost as elusive for her as they had been for Jared. She hadn't expected to orgasm her first time having sex. Hardly anybody ever did, from what she'd been told.

But stupid girl. When Constantine Masters said something, well, *so shall it fucking be.*

She screamed, beating her hand against the window behind his head. Her orgasm was electric, boiling her blood and frying her brain. While she sobbed and whimpered and writhed against him, he just gripped stronger, dug in deeper, and pounded harder. He was fucking the last pieces of the old Dulcie right out of her, and by the time he came, that girl was long gone.

*What took her so long to leave? I feel like I've been waiting for this night **forever**.*

TEN

"I CAN'T BELIEVE WE JUST DID THAT."

"What, killed a man?"

"No. I can't believe we just fucked in your truck."

Con laughed.

"Eloquent. Keep digging."

After he came with a shout loud enough that she was sure they'd heard it back at the party, Con had collapsed onto the seat. He took her with him and she spread out on his chest, listening to his racing heartbeat.

It was freezing outside, but all their activity had warmed up the car, and they laid naked for a while. Catching their breath. Coming back to reality. When the cold air finally started to creep inside, Dulcie slowly sat up. Everything from her hips down was sore, and when she pulled herself clear of him, there was a sharper stab of pain making her wince. Con had certainly left his mark, alright. She'd wondered if she'd be able to walk right.

She wiggled back into her pants and he gave her his sweater. He was a lot bigger than her and it almost fell to her knees, making them chuckle. After they were both decent, they hopped out of the truck. He locked the doors and they didn't say anything, just both started walking back to the railroad crossing. When they got to the tracks, they immediately began to walk up them. After a couple steps he grabbed her hand, twining their fingers together. She smiled and balanced on one of the rails as they walked. Just a couple of teenagers, holding hands while taking a romantic stroll.

Of course they couldn't just leave the body there. Dulcie didn't particularly feel like going to prison. While Con dragged the corpse back to the haphazard cardboard shack, Dulcie searched the area, using her phone as a flashlight. She made sure there was nothing left behind, not an earring or a button or a piece of trash that could be linked back to either of them. Then using a bottle of water she'd brought with them, she washed away the blood from the rails as best she could, tossing bits of skull into a plastic bag as she cleaned.

Am I really supposed to go back to school on Monday?

When it was as good as it was gonna get, she went to help Con. He'd moved the cardboard and was working on scooping out a shallow grave. Dulcie dropped to her knees and gave him a hand with the digging. When the space was big enough, they dragged the body into it. She tossed the plastic bag into the hole, as well as the rusty sign post she'd used to finish the hobo, then they covered it all back up. When the ground was flat and even again, Con moved the cardboard back into place. There. Like nothing had ever happened.

"What time is it?" she asked. They were standing in the middle of the tracks, both looking over their handiwork. He glanced at his watch.

"A little after one," he answered. She groaned.

"Shit, I'm supposed to be at work at eight."

He grabbed her arm and turned her towards him. She almost laughed. They were absolutely filthy, both their hands almost black from all the dirt, their clothing covered in soil.

"We really did this. This actually happened," he informed her. She stopped smiling.

"I know, Con. I know it did."

"And I don't care. I don't care that we killed him. Not even a little bit."

"I know."

"That doesn't bother you? That I'm fucking crazy?" he checked. She shook her head.

"No."

"Why? Why has that never bothered you? You've always known it, right?" he kept going.

Dulcie stared up at him. This boy, *this man*, that she barely knew, but somehow knew all too well.

"It doesn't bother me," she said in a soft voice, "because I'm pretty sure I'm just as crazy. Maybe crazier. At least you knew what was going on inside your head. I didn't … I didn't know I could do something like this."

He frowned at her, and it didn't seem natural on his face. Real emotion in general looked strange on him. She wanted to see that smile, that Cheshire grin.

"I knew I was fucked up, and I knew … I knew something was going on with you. With us. And I thought I'd just fuck you up, too. I didn't want that, so I went away. I come back, and look what happens. I don't want to be responsible for you, Dulcie. I don't want to be the thing that wrecks you," he tried to explain. She finally laughed again.

"Stupid boy, I was wrecked long before you showed up."

His hands were on either side of her face and he was kissing her. Trying to swallow her whole. She gripped onto his t-shirt and braced herself, trying her best to not get eaten.

Too late.

"You're goddamn amazing, you know that, right?" he breathed.

"Tell me why."

"Because you helped me kill a man."

"That's it?"

"And you're the more beautiful thing I have ever witnessed in my entire life."

"Hmmm, good, but still not amazing."

"Because you were made for me," he whispered, his forehead against hers. "And you didn't even know it. I had to show it to you. That's the most amazing part, right there."

"Now you're catching on."

They went back to his place. She'd never been to the Masters estate before; it was the biggest house in town, and by no small amount. No other house even measured close to it. It was large and white, with big columns and dark green shutters. She'd always been a little in awe of it, and when they came up the drive, she stared out the window, still impressed.

They didn't go in the house, though. They parked in front of a big garage and Con led her up a set of stairs on the side of the building. There was a large studio apartment at the top, and it appeared to be where he was staying while at home.

"Why not stay in your old room?" she asked.

"Because I'm not that person anymore."

He pulled her into the bathroom and stripped her naked before hauling them both under the shower. It still didn't occur to her to be shy, not even under bright white lights. Her hair was a mess and she was dirty from just about head to toe, but still, she didn't care. Because *he* didn't care.

He helped to scrub away all the dirt and grime and blood and bad memories, then he pushed her up against the wall. Grabbed her legs and forced them around his waist. She was still sore and he was still too big, but she loved the pain. Loved that he was the cause of it. This time when she came, she left welts on his back.

They laid down on his bed, naked and squeaky clean. His apartment was too hot for clothing – they even laid on top of the covers.

They talked for a long time, about wants and needs. Fantasies and nightmares. Almost one and the same.

Con explained how he'd always felt the need to do something like what they'd done; that things just didn't matter to him. He'd rather remove something than deal with it, and people most definitely fell under the category of "things".

Dulcie explained how she'd never much cared for people anyway, and cared even less about how they felt or what they thought. She saw them more like cattle. While she'd never particularly wanted to kill anybody, she also didn't care that she'd done it. That, Con told her, was one of the things he found particularly attractive about her.

They whispered a lot, and even laughed a little, as the hours rolled by. Missing work was a forgone conclusion. They laid on their backs with their heads pressed together, and when Dulcie shifted to be closer to him, she felt something poking her. She pulled out her sketchbook and held it above them.

"You looked through the whole thing?"

"Yeah," he answered, reaching up and grabbing it from her. "You didn't think I would?"

"No, I didn't," she was honest. He rolled his eyes.

"This drawing," he said, flipping to the one she'd done the year before. "This is the drawing that *really* made me fall for you."

"That long ago? So much time," Dulcie whispered, mourning the time they could've spent together.

Though really, the first time we come together, and we kill somebody. God knows what would've happened if we'd had a year to operate together.

"But my favorite is this one. I want to see the picture that inspired this."

He kept turning till he found a drawing closer to the back of the book, then he handed it to her. She squinted and held it close.

"Matthew," she whispered, and saw Con glance at her.

She'd been taking pictures at the football field. Her charming half-brother had been peddling drugs under the bleachers. He'd come up and grabbed her from behind, catching her off guard. A brief tug-o-war had ensued, full of groping hands and rude words. She'd finally set the flash off in his face, and when he'd held up his hands to block the light, she'd kicked him in the balls.

Turned out, she'd also taken his picture. It was a close up, with the flash washing out most of his face. The angle was awkward and upside down, making it impossible to tell who was in it.

She'd stared at the picture for barely a minute before she'd yanked out her sketchbook. Con had told her to draw what she really saw – so she'd done just that, covering the paper with violent pencil strokes and heavy lines. A mouth, spewing poison and venom, because that's all Matt did. Veins, split wide open and gushing blood, because Matt was already dead.

He was just too stupid to know it.

"Is he a problem?" Con asked, still staring at her. She shrugged.

"Sometimes. Like one of those bugs you can't catch to squash," she tried to explain.

"Your brother, right?" he checked. She cleared her throat.

"*Half*-brother."

"He wants you."

"I know."

"Has he ever touched you?"

"No."

"If he ever does, I'll kill him."

Dulcie tossed the book to the foot of the bed, then rolled onto her side so she could face Con. His brows were knitted together in anger as he glared at the ceiling. It was too dark to see the blue in his eyes, but she could imagine them being icy and cold.

She let her eyes wander to his chest. To the body of a lifelong athlete. She trailed her fingers down his sternum, then splayed her hand flat against his stomach. How interesting, to feel so comfortable in another person's skin. To want to rip him open and crawl inside him and never see the light of day again.

"I know," she whispered, then she leaned forward and placed a quick kiss to his lips.

"I'd kill anyone who hurt you."

"And that's one of the things *I* find particularly attractive about *you*," she mocked him. He moved fast and rolled on top of her.

"I have to go back to school tomorrow," he told her, his lips smoothing along the side of her jaw. She stared over his shoulder.

Oh yeah, tomorrow. That's still a thing.

"Oh."

He chuckled and she felt his teeth against her ear.

"Dulcie," he whispered, and for a moment, she wondered who he was talking to.

Dulcie? Dulcie who? No Dulcie here. She's buried in a ditch by an abandoned train station.

"What?" she asked, moving her hands to his back. She found her claw marks from before and slowly ran her fingers down them.

"You can't tell anyone about what happened."

"Of course not. I don't want to go to jail."

"If anyone comes asking about it, you don't know anything."

"I don't even know what you're talking about."

He laughed again, but only for a moment.

"A secret. Between us. Promise me. This is just between us."

He'd braced his forearms on either side of her head and was staring down at her. From that angle, she could finally see his eyes. So blue, looking straight into her soul.

"Only us," she whispered, then dug her nails in and dragged them down his back. He hissed as she reopened the wounds.

"It's only ever us, Dulcie. Now, yesterday, tomorrow. Whenever. You get that, right? You believe that?"

"Of course I do, Constantine. Of course I do."

PART III

ELEVEN

FALL WAS DULCIE'S FAVORITE TIME OF YEAR. SHE WAS A BACKWOODS country gal at heart, she loved when the leaves would change. Loved the crisp air, the first frost. That feeling of waiting for school to start, for new beginnings, even though she was long done with school.

Not to say she didn't enjoy summer, either. That country gal wore shorts more than she wore pants, and warm weather was so much nicer on bare skin. June was turning into a scorcher, so she pulled out some old pants and turned them into cut-offs, preparing for the heat.

I always said I'd be stuck in this town.

She supposed it wasn't all bad. She was twenty-one and she was the evening shift manager at a restaurant in a country club, only half an hour outside of town. Not too bad, and it paid well enough that she was able to buy herself a beater car to get back and forth. Paid enough to get her out of the shitty trailer and away from her mother.

Apartments weren't easy to come by in Fuller, and she didn't want to live in a trailer, either. She'd found an awesome loft space in an old warehouse – it was commercial, but the landlord hadn't been able to rent it out in over two years. Dulcie was able to sweet talk the woman into letting her have it. It was all open floor space, no rooms, and no kitchen to speak of; but there was a bathroom with a shower next to the elevator, and that's really all that mattered.

She bought a mini fridge, a microwave, a hot plate, and a queen sized mattress, and she moved in the moment she made the first payment. She put the mattress on top of pallets, right underneath big windows that still had their original glass. They faced the sun first thing in the morning – the whole room was actually lined with huge windows, though, so she got light from every angle. Even at night, the street lamps would flood the space with an orange glow. She was always illuminated.

Constantine would hate this place.

But his opinion didn't matter. Because she hadn't seen or spoken to him in almost three years.

They had killed a man. Then he'd taken her virginity in the front seat of his truck. Afterwards, they'd buried the body, then they'd gone back to his place and talked all night.

Silly girl, it didn't mean anything. Just because you shared a moment of darkness didn't mean it was forever.

Except, she thought it had. After Con left, Dulcie stayed behind. It was for the best. They had real lives, and really, if someone found the hobo's body, it wouldn't look good if the two of them had disappeared together. So Con went back to college and she finished high school.

He didn't contact her, but she'd been expecting that – she dealt with bullying from Frannie and looks of hurt from Jared. The two of them had apparently hooked up at the party after she'd left, and they started dating soon after, but it was clear Frannie was holding a grudge against her. Constantine had left the party right after Dulcie had left, after all. The two of them hadn't come back. The next day, Dulcie had been sporting some interesting bruises and hickeys. One and one aren't terribly hard to add up, even for a cheerleader.

Dulcie could endure all of it, though, because in her mind, Con would come back to save her. Maybe right after graduation. Maybe before the fall. Sometime. Two people didn't share what they'd shared and simply walk away. They'd made promises to each other. Bared their souls.

But he didn't come back. Fall came and went. By the time Christmas showed up, Dulcie was losing her mind. She dreamed about blood, all the time. Blood and darkness.

She tried to call him, but the cellphone number his friends had no longer worked. She hunted him down on social media, but he wasn't posting anything. Wasn't looking at messages, wasn't opening e-mails. She wrote letters, but they were all returned. It was like he'd disappeared.

Except she knew he hadn't – his father was still in town, after all. And Mr. Masters loved to brag about what a success his son was, about how Con had graduated from Ohio State with top honors and was looking into other options for grad school.

None of those "options" were even remotely close to West Virginia.

Fuck him.

Dulcie wouldn't be depressed, she'd decided. She'd killed a man and she'd fucked the high school heartthrob. She was a badass. She was goddamn invincible. She wouldn't cry over Constantine Masters. She would forge her own path. Her curtain had been ripped away – it was time to find out who she *really* was, with or without him.

So she got a job and she got an apartment and she painted her pictures and drew her drawings.

And sometime, late at night, when there was a full moon, she would walk along the train tracks and pray for something to come out of the shadows.

"I'm not putting up with this shit anymore, Dulcie. He keeps stepping on my toes, I'm gonna pop him."

Dulcie rolled her eyes and looked up from her tablet. Her bartender was glaring at her, his arms folded across his chest.

"So do it," she told him. He looked surprised for a second.

"I'm serious. Frank barrels around back here, fucking with my bar, talking shit to me and the waitresses. I'm gonna hit him one of these days," he assured her. She nodded.

"You keep saying that. I've yet to see it happen. *Do it.*"

They had a bit of a stare down. David was twenty-six and when he'd been hired on as bartender at the Blue Rock, he'd had trouble adjusting to having a twenty-one year old as his supervisor. Eventually, though, he'd recognized Dulcie for what she was – a ball buster who didn't take shit from anyone and would do absolutely whatever it took to see a job done well. Being a like minded individual, he respected her. So he just laughed at her dare.

"You'd like that, wouldn't you. Just waiting for an excuse to fire my ass," he teased her. She shook her head and went back to the tablet.

"No, I keep waiting for an excuse to fire both of you. If you start a fight, it'll solve my problem. If you're going to do it tonight, please wait till after nine. Usually most of the members are gone by then."

He threw a dish rag at her face and they both laughed.

"When you gonna go out on a date with me, Dulcie?" he asked, for the hundredth time. She threw the rag back at him.

"I told you, when you leave this job and make a million dollars. Then I'm all yours."

They laughed again, but she wasn't joking. Dulcie didn't date anyone. Boys were irrelevant to her. Just a means to an end. Young men were the worst, thinking they had something to offer her. Ridiculous.

The only people Dulcie looked twice at were the visitors of the club. Part of the reason she'd taken the job there was because she knew the wealthy elite of the area flocked to the pristine golf course. Belonging to the club wasn't easy, membership was not cheap.

Neither was Dulcie.

She had rules to her little scam. No one young – only men over forty. They were easier to wear out, easier to manipulate. A young, hot woman paying them attention. Flirting with them. Flashing a bit of skin as she delivered their cocktails and meals.

No one staying at the club – she didn't want to lose her job if she could avoid it. She preyed upon guests of the members. Convinced them to take her to seedy motels off the highways surrounding the golf course.

No one single – she had to have ammunition, in case they got frisky and hunted her down, whether to look for more of what she had to offer, or to get her in trouble. She had to protect herself.

And most important – never more than once a month. Getting greedy is what got people in trouble. Slow and steady won the race. Opportunities like the one she had didn't come around often in her small town, and she was sure she couldn't compete in a bigger city.

So she stayed in Fuller. She worked at the country club. She lured men away, she fucked their brains out, and then she robbed them blind. Any cash, anything of value, it all went home with her. Most men didn't know anything had happened till it was too late. Pride and their positions kept most from saying anything, and the few who did dare to confront her, she would threaten them right back. She had no problem with telling their wives or girlfriends or partners exactly what they'd been doing with her.

So far, it had worked out great for her. She had a small nest egg built up, hidden inside her mattress. She was trying to save enough to move to Europe. Sure, life wouldn't be any different in the south of France. But the scenery would be a lot brighter. Maybe it would help keep the darkness at bay, because lately, it had been getting harder and harder.

"Did you hear me?"

Dulcie snapped back to attention and glanced at David. He was staring at her while he wiped down glasses.

"No, I'm sorry. What?" she asked. He narrowed his eyes for a second.

"Where do you go?"

It shouldn't have made sense, but she knew what he was asking.

"Somewhere you don't ever want to go," she whispered. He looked a little surprised, and she cleared her throat. Shut the curtain in her brain, keeping the darkness in check. "I've just got a lot on my mind. We open in five, make sure those glasses are put away."

Dulcie didn't particularly like her job, but it wasn't hard, she was good at it, and she'd found her second source of income there, so it wasn't all bad. When the doors opened, golfers began wandering in, looking to quench their thirst after eighteen holes in the hot summer sun. The tables began to fill up and food was carted out to hungry patrons. During the summer, it got so busy the restaurant essentially ran itself. There was no time for anyone to screw off, so she usually didn't have to even think much about being the boss once the placed opened.

That night, the hostess got sick. Not just a little, either – like *running-through-the-kitchen-and-barely-making-it-to-a-mop-bucket-to-puke* sick. She'd been battling the flu and had apparently lost. Dulcie sent her home, then took her position at the hostess station.

Again, not something hard. It had been her first job at the restaurant, back when she'd been nineteen, so she slipped into the role easily. The only problem was she now had to directly interact with every single person who came through the doors.

Whether she wanted to or not.

"*Dulcie?*"

She'd been looking down at the reservation sheet, trying to rearrange tables and times, and hadn't been paying attention to who'd approached her. When she lifted her head, she almost groaned out loud. Jared Foster was standing in front of her. The boy she'd left in the woods, right before she'd killed someone. The boyfriend she'd refused to sleep with, right before she'd had sex with someone else.

Not that she was necessarily shocked or surprised to see him. Fuller was a tiny town, they'd run into each other a lot over the years. He was always nice and polite, just like he'd been in high school. No, Jared wasn't the problem. The problem was his wife. Frannie Foster – formerly McKey.

The girl who'd been left behind in the woods, as well.

Frannie had *never* liked Dulcie. The universe had scripted their lives to be that way; Frannie had been the popular cheerleader, had dated the quarterback of the football team. Dulcie was the weird art kid who'd somehow captured the quarterback's attention. Frannie had made it a point to be a nasty bitch in school, and it had only intensified since graduation.

She and Jared had dated throughout their senior year. Dulcie could tell it wasn't really love, though; Frannie was just doing it to piss Dulcie off. Stupid girl – Dulcie would have to care before she could get mad about something.

Then just before the senior prom, a social-bomb hit the school. Frannie was pregnant. *Shocking.* Or least it was to a tiny town in rural West Virginia. Two weeks after graduation, Jared and Frannie got married in a small courthouse ceremony. Clearly, the right thing to do.

Dulcie couldn't honestly say she felt bad for Jared, because she rarely felt bad for anyone. But she could recognize that life had dealt him a shitty hand. There went his hopes for college. Instead, he got locked into a relationship with a girl who thought being a bitch looked good in any season.

Beats burying your heart in a shallow grave by some abandoned train tracks.

"Hey, how are you?" Dulcie said, plastering a smile across her face. Jared began moving around the station and she struggled to keep her smile in place. Then she remembered she was supposed to be normal, so she moved towards him and leaned into the hug he wrapped around her.

"Alright, I guess. Anniversary dinner," he sighed after he finally let her go.

"Oh yeah? Where is the little woman?" she joked, then scanned the grand hall that sat outside the restaurant.

"Helping her parents, they're eating with us."

Frannie's father was the second wealthiest person in Fuller, so it wasn't too surprising that he was a member of the club. Mr. McKey ruled over his daughter with an iron fist, and thus, he controlled her husband. Jared worked for Mr. McKey, lived in a house Mr. McKey had bought for them.

Yeah, actually, that grave does sound like a better option.

"And how's the rugrat?" Dulcie kept on with the questions. Years of pretending to be normal had conditioned her to say the right things.

"Good, good. Starting to talk," he sighed. "We're, uh, we're expecting another one."

"Are you serious?"

Apparently, all that pretending hadn't conditioned her well enough. Dulcie heard how flat and loud her voice sounded, watched as Jared winced.

"Yeah. But it's good, y'know? I love little Amy, and we're hoping for a boy this time. Someone to throw the ball with," he chuckled. Over his shoulder, Dulcie watched as Frannie hurried towards them, leaving her parents to play catch up. She was wearing a skin tight green dress and didn't look pregnant at all. When she reached them, she shook her head, causing her light blonde locks to cascade over her shoulders.

"Ew, you still work here, Dulcie?" she sneered.

"Watch it, Fran," Jared's voice held warning in it, but it had no effect.

"Still here. Would you like me to take you to your table?" she offered, and grabbed some menus.

"I can't believe they let trailer trash work here. Standards have *really* gone down."

"Frannie, cool it!"

Dulcie ignored both of them, just turned and smiled when they got to their designated table. She even waited till the elder McKeys had arrived and pulled out their chairs for them. Frannie made snide comments the whole time, but Dulcie was used to it. Any time she ran into Frannie, whether it be at work, at the store, or on a sidewalk, the other girl took the opportunity to insult her. To "put her in her place", as it were. Unfortunately for the former cheerleader, she had no idea that Dulcie was so far out of place, being put back wasn't even an option.

She took their drink orders, then waited at the bar while David made them.

"Friends of yours?" he asked, gesturing with his head. She laughed.

"No. The bitch hates me. I used to date her husband, for like half a minute, back in high school," Dulcie explained.

"The Ice Queen dated someone, oh my god!" he joked, pressing a hand over his heart.

"I did. Worst five minutes of my life. Now hurry up with those, don't give her anymore ammunition."

He loaded up a tray with glasses and she hauled them back to their table. She delivered Frannie's glass of mineral water first, getting it out of the way, then went to the parents next. Jared was last, and as she was leaning over to place his glass in the right spot, Frannie's arm jerked across the table. Red wine flew through the air, with the bulk of it landing on Dulcie's freshly washed and pressed white dress shirt.

"Jesus, Frannie, why can't you just -" Jared started to bark out, and while Dulcie was impressed with how angry he sounded, she held up her hand to stop him. Making a scene was not her thing.

"Please. No worries at all, I'll have someone come and move you to a clean table. No, no, don't touch it, Mrs. McKey! That's why we have cleaners and bussers. I want you to enjoy your evening out. Please, don't worry about it at all. *Greg!*"

Dulcie called over the nearest waiter, gave him instructions to move the family and have the soiled table stripped down. Then she headed back towards the kitchen. As she passed the bar, David paced the length of it with her.

"'Bitch' is right. Want me to dump some soap in her next drink?" he offered. She snorted.

"Soap might improve her. Got any bleach back there? Maybe mix that in."

David laughed, but Dulcie didn't.

She wasn't joking.

Being a good employee who anticipated everything, of course Dulcie had a spare work uniform. She grabbed it out of her cubby and hurried into the employee bathroom, locking the door behind her.

She didn't undress immediately. She turned on the sink, as hot as she could, then she gripped the edge of the porcelain. She tried taking deep, therapeutic breaths. Tried to calm down. She clenched her teeth together and resisted the urge to scream.

Deep breathing wasn't working, so she lifted her head, exhaling loudly. The mirror was beginning to fog up, but she could still see her reflection. See the heavy red wine splattered down the left side of her shirt. It was all over her hands, some of it even on her neck. Dripping past her collar bone. So much red. All over her.

The last time she'd looked at herself, *really* looked, she'd been staring at a hazy reflection. Looking at a girl covered in red. Standing in one spot and wishing for so many bad things to happen. Only back then, she hadn't been alone. Back then, she'd known there was someone else who wanted all those bad things, too. It was so lonely now, being the only one who thought that way. Being the only one with blood on her hands.

I just wanted to feel normal in my darkness. Why did he take that away?

Of course, there was no one to answer her. So while most girls would've cleaned themselves up or broken down in tears or plotted their revenge, Dulcie stared at her reflection. Then she planted her fist in the middle of the mirror, shattering the image.

TWELVE

DULCIE SAT ON A BENCH, STARING ACROSS THE PARK. THERE WERE some little kids playing on a stone walrus, but she wasn't paying attention to them. She had her dark sunglasses on and she waited for inspiration, her sketchpad sitting in her lap.

She didn't have as many opportunities to draw as she'd had in high school, but on Sundays, her one day off a week, she always made it a point to draw *something*. Life had taken a lot of things away from her, but she wouldn't let it take her art; *that*, she could control.

"Trying to imagine what it would be like to have someone touch you long enough to give you children!?"

Frannie's shrill voice carried across the park. Dulcie hadn't realized the blonde had joined the fray with her little spawn.

"Your ex-boyfriend did!" she called back, smiling brightly. Frannie's jaw dropped open.

"You're disgusting!"

Dulcie held up her middle finger.

It gave her a tickle to see Frannie all riled up. It was the little things in life, after all, which made it worth living. But of course, just as she was starting to feel almost good, something had to ruin it.

And not in a good way.

"*Hey, baby,*" a voice hissed near her ear.

For one irrational moment, one horrifying, vomit inducing, moment, Dulcie thought it was the man. The hobo who was buried by the train station. The man she'd killed. The same hissing voice, the same sound of depravity. The same feeling welling up inside of her, the one that told her to take control of the here and now, to do whatever the fuck it was she felt like doing in order to control a situation. The feeling that told her to rip something apart.

But Dulcie also knew she wasn't completely crazy, so when she lurched off the bench and whipped around, she wasn't too shocked to see it was her half-brother, Matt. Basically a being who was only two-steps above an animated corpse, anyway.

"What are you doing here?" she demanded, shoving her glasses onto the top of her head.

Before she'd moved out of the trailer, he'd reached all time highs of creepiness. It was like he could just smell that she'd started having sex, and he wanted in on the action. Any time she was in her room, she'd block her door. The moment she'd had enough money set aside for her own place, she'd bolted, and she hadn't left a forwarding address.

Of course, Fuller wasn't big. Keeping her location a secret wasn't possible – even a psychopath like her had friends. All Matt had to do was ask a couple questions and before she knew it, he was lurking around her building. Waiting outside the front door, asking her for money. Asking her for a place to crash. Asking her to blow him in exchange for meth.

As tempting as his offer was, Dulcie had punched him in the throat, then threatened to tell his parole officer what a creepy little shit Matt was being and have him thrown in jail. It worked for a little while, but after a couple weeks, he started popping up again. She'd be in a bar, having a drink with co-workers, and suddenly he'd be on the stool next to her. In line behind her at the grocery store. Grabbing her ass as she walked down the street.

Many nights were spent thinking of different ways to kill him. But what would she do with the body? She couldn't exactly carry him any-where, and she didn't want to cut him up. The only thing she could think of would be to lure him to the train tracks some night. There was a lovely spot where the ground was soft, she knew. She could probably dig the hole by herself just fine.

It would be wrong, though. That place was special. Sacred. She couldn't do that on her own, regardless of whether or not she was ca-pable. That place belonged to *him* just as much as it belonged to her. To do such a momentous act, to take a life and to bury a secret … no, it wouldn't be right to do it without her partner in crime.

Still, there were days when her reasoning wore thin.

"It's a free park, I saw you sitting here, thought I'd say hi to my fave *sis*," Matt started to laugh, but it turned into a coughing fit. She made a gagging sound and grabbed her bag from off the bench.

"Don't fucking follow me, or I swear to god, I'll mace you again," she threatened as she shoved her sketchbook into the bag.

"C'mon, don't be like that. We haven't seen each other in a while, I'm just being friendly," he pointed out. Dulcie didn't say anything else, she just turned and started walking away. She groaned when she heard his footsteps pounding after her.

"I'm not joking, Matt. How the fuck did you get out of prison, any-way!?"

For a while, it seemed her prayers had been answered. Matt had gotten arrested on a grand theft auto charge and was sent to jail. She'd figured she'd be long gone before he'd have a chance to get free.

"Fuckin' pigs in this town can't do their job right. Illegal search and seizure, they had to throw the whole thing out. You got twenty bucks?" he asked. She left the park and jogged across the street. He matched her step for step.

"When have I ever given you money? As far as you're concerned, I've never even heard of money, okay? So don't ask me again," she snarled, hurrying to the front of her building.

"Why you gotta be so cold, Dulcie? You don't know what it's like, living in that fucking trailer. You got it so good and won't even fuckin' share," he complained.

"Share!? Why the fuck should I share *anything* with you? A fucking drug addicted loser who wants to fuck his own sister. You're lucky I haven't run you over yet. *Don't bother me anymore,*" she warned him, then yanked open her door.

Matt was grabby, but he rarely worked up the energy to be violent, so she was shocked when he shoved her from behind. She stumbled across the entry way, almost ramming head first into a fire extinguisher. Before she could catch her balance, he was grabbing her by her shirt and slamming her against the wall next to the elevator. She let out a grunt as the air was forced from her lungs. Then he was pressed up against her and she resisted the urge to vomit.

"So I'm just some drug addict, huh? Some fucking loser?" he hissed, using his weight to pin her in place."

"Get off me!" she demanded.

"At least you got one thing right. Someone's about to get fucked," he threatened, and she felt his hand at the top of her jeans.

There it was again, that same feeling of cold rage. Of someone trespassing on private property. Property that didn't even belong to her. She let out a scream and she slammed her elbow into the side of his head. He cried out and stumbled back, pressing his hand to his ear.

She turned and practically dove into the lift. It was a large, old freight elevator with a wooden gate that needed to be pulled shut in order for the contraption to work. She jumped up and grabbed the strap just as Matt lurched forward. The gate came from the bottom and top, closing in the middle, and the two pieces slammed together just as he reached in to grab her. His wrist was pinned in the middle, and while he shrieked in pain, she swung the latch to lock the gate into place.

"I'm sorry," she was gasping for air. "Did that hurt?"

"My hand! My fucking hand! You fucking broke it!" he was yelling, yanking and pulling on his arm, desperately trying to get free. She leaned down close and examined his wiggling fingers.

"No, doesn't look broken. I think it's moving too much for that," she informed him.

"*Open the gate you crazy bitch!*"

"Don't worry, though, we can solve that problem."

With a shout, she swung her heavy messenger bag straight down on his hand. Matt screamed as she broke his wrist. She collapsed against the back wall of the elevator and watched as he fell to his knees. His hand hung limply on her side of the gate. It looked completely unnatural, and it made her smile. A *real* smile, the first one she'd had in years.

He was sobbing too much to be a threat, so Dulcie finally unlatched the gate and set him loose. He cried and cradled his hand to his chest, but she didn't care. She kicked him in the stomach, sending him crashing down onto his back, then she slammed the gate shut again.

"I told you – don't ever bother me again, and don't ever come back here, or I swear to god, I will fucking kill you."

And with that, she slammed her hand on the button for her floor and stared at him till the elevator cut off her view.

THIRTEEN

"**P**LACES! WE DO THIS EVERY NIGHT, WHY ARE YOU ACTING LIKE it's your first time!?" Dulcie yelled out as she strode across the dining room floor of her restaurant.

The Blue Rock Bar and Grill was one of three restaurants at the Blue Rock Country Club. One was much fancier, Dulcie hadn't even bothered applying for a job there. The other was a breakfast and lunch buffet. Not high class enough, she needed bigger fish for her scam.

The bar was the busiest, offered some of the best tips, and was more laid back. In the summer seasons, the staff swelled to accommodate all the guests, and the seasonal job attracted a lot of young workers. She was surrounded by people varying in age from sixteen to thirty. She wasn't involved in the hiring process, the general manager handled all of that, but Dulcie made damn sure anyone who was hired on to her shift was more than capable of pulling their weight.

So why half her staff was stumbling around and giggling nervously, she had no idea. They were easily two months into the really busy season, everyone knew how to do their jobs. The governor had come to play in May and had stopped in for a nightcap, and they'd all handled it fine. So what was going on? She stopped moving and put her hands on her hips, her eyes scanning the restaurant.

David was behind the bar, cleaning glasses, and he winked at her. The action reminded her of Matt, though, and she quickly looked way. After she'd broken her half-brother's wrist, she'd watched out her windows as he'd stumbled away from her building. That had been a week before, and she hadn't seen or heard from him since then. But she was still looking over her shoulder, still careful when she went out at night. She had a very strong feeling the battle had not been won. That in fact, she'd just upped the ante and made a declaration of war. It was only a matter of time before he'd fire back.

Thinking about something didn't change it, though. There was nothing she could do till it happened, or till she had enough money to get away, so she pushed it to the back of her mind and tried to focus on work.

She went back to looking over the restaurant, trying to figure out what the fuss was about. A couple bus boys were putting the finishing touches on the tables, straightening out silverware and placing glasses. A couple male waiters were standing at a wait station, making sure the specials were set up right for the evening. She narrowed her eyes and it dawned on her.

It was all the girls. There were a couple clusters of waitresses, giggling and chatting in hushed tones. The male waiters were going about their business, making sure their sections were clean and tidy. Dulcie sighed and marched up to the closest gaggle of women.

"Okay, what's going on? We open in ten minutes, and I haven't seen you guys check your areas once," she stated.

There was a chorus of sorry's and most of the girls broke away. One stayed behind, though – her friend, Anna. The bubbly blonde had actually made it out of Fuller. Turned out all her giggling hid a pretty smart brain and she'd gone to college on a full scholarship. Now she only came back to Fuller for the summers. Dulcie didn't like many people but for some reason, she'd always taken a shine to Anna, so she'd gotten the other girl a job at the bar.

"It looks good in here and you know it," Anna teased her. Dulcie shrugged.

"I don't care, they still need to do it. Let them slip once, and they'll take advantage of me for the rest of the season. What's going on, anyway?" she asked.

"Haven't you heard?"

"Obviously not."

"The Honorable *former* Mayor Masters is going to grace us with his presence."

Dulcie groaned. Jebediah Masters was of course a member of the club – he was one of maybe three people in Fuller who were rich enough to actually afford it. He rarely visited, but he'd been there before, so it still didn't explain everything.

"Big deal. Warn the girls – after three drinks, he gets grabby," Dulcie said, remembering a time when he'd gotten a hand up her skirt. She'd almost stabbed him with a fork. Briefly considered pulling her scam on him and then killing him in his sleep. Had ultimately laughed it off and flirted her way to a bigger tip.

"Yeah, we *all* know about his grabby hands, but that's not what they're dying over," Anna continued, a grin taking over her face.

"Then what? He's a shitty tipper, they'll have to show a lot of ass if they want more than ten percent."

"He's not coming alone."

Dulcie was surprised.

"Who's he bringing? God, please say he's on a date. I can't wait to see this bitch," she cackled.

"I heard he's bringing his son."

"He doesn't have a so-"

Dulcie's mouth stopped working. Or more like, her entire brain shut down. She'd completely separated Jebediah Masters from Constantine in her mind. She'd had to, after she'd started working at the club. She wouldn't allow herself to think about Con, not at all. It helped that the elder Masters didn't look much like his son.

"Uh, I'm pretty sure you've met him," Anna teased. Frannie had spread it around that Dulcie had stolen Con from her the night of the party, that she was some big boyfriend stealing whore. Never mind the little fact that Frannie and Con hadn't been dating. Never mind that Dulcie didn't care one iota what she, or anyone else, thought of her. Being a whore was not the worst thing a person could be.

A murderer, though … that's pretty high up there.

"Shit. Are you sure?" Dulcie asked, glancing out the windows. The entrance was technically behind her, through the club, but the entire back wall of the bar was glass, stretching all the way up to the vaulted ceilings. There were stunning views of the course, and a walkway wrapped around the building. Guests could be seen coming and going from the green.

"I dunno, just what everyone is saying. Mr. Masters was bragging about it at the store, said Con was coming to town, how he was taking him to dinner, only the best, blah blah blah," Anna explained. "And he has a reservation for tonight, so we all figured it was going down. *Constantine Masters.* God, we haven't seen him in forever! Do you think he's still hot?"

"Yes," Dulcie answered without hesitation. "He played ball all through college, I heard."

"You still got a thing for him?"

Not really. Just a secret buried near the train tracks, that's all.

"No. But I do wonder about something," Dulcie lifted her hand, tapping her fingernails against her bottom lip.

"What?" Anna asked. Dulcie narrowed her eyes.

"If he still has a thing *for me.*"

Mr. Masters' reservation wasn't until eight at night. Dulcie wished Anna had mentioned that; the restaurant opened at five. It would be hours before everyone's curiosity was sated.

"*Stop hanging out up here!*" Dulcie had to hiss more than a few times when the girls would gather around the hostess' podium.

"Who is this guy?"

Dulcie was behind the bar, making a martini for one of the trustees. He claimed she was the only one who made it the way he liked.

"Who's who?" she asked, digging around for a shaker.

"This guy everyone is talking about. Connie?" David asked, leaning over her to grab a glass. The restaurant was packed. It was a Friday night, and the way things were going, they'd be closing down late.

"*Con,*" Dulcie burst out laughing. "His name is Con."

"What the hell kind of name is that?" David snorted. He wasn't from Fuller. Wasn't even from West Virginia. She wasn't sure how he'd ended up at the club, and she'd never asked. She didn't really care.

"It's short for Constantine."

"That's even weirder. What's the big deal with him?"

"Constantine is ..." Dulcie searched for the right words. Well, not really. She searched for words that would be appropriate to use. "He was a big deal in high school. It's hard to get out of Fuller, most people go to work in the glass factories. But he was like a god on the football field, and he got the best grades, and his dad was the mayor back then. I think everyone was a little in love with him. Then he went off to college and never looked back."

"And what about you, boss lady?" David pressed, moving behind her. The bar was narrow and she could feel his warmth against her back.

"What about me?"

"Were you in love with this brainy football god?"

She actually managed to laugh and looked at him over her shoulder.

"Would you be jealous if I said yes?" she teased.

"Devastated. I never played football," he flirted right back.

She chuckled and split the shaker, dumping the martini into its glass.

"Good. I fucking *hate* football."

"You know, I hate to spoil the moment, but I think you like me, boss lady," David warned her.

"Ah, but you're wrong," she sighed, then shivered as a chill ran down her spine.

"How so?"

"I don't like *anybody*."

She looked up then. Stared across the restaurant. Constantine was standing on the other side of the room, staring back at her. That smile she'd worked so hard to banish from her memory, it was back in all its technicolor glory. He nodded his head at her, acknowledging her existence. She returned his stare for a second longer, then went back to garnishing the martini.

"Hmmm. Methinks the lady protests too much."

Dulcie elbowed David before he could make any other smart comments, then she picked up the cocktail and delivered it to its owner. After she chatted with the gentleman for a while, she made her way back into the kitchen. Made sure everything was running smoothly. When she went back out to the floor, Anna was looking for her.

"Oh my god, oh my god, he's asking for you! *He's asking for you!*" she squealed. Some things never changed, and the other girl's excitement for … *anything*, was the same as ever. Dulcie didn't ask her to clarify.

"Of course he is."

"This is it! You can still have all his babies!"

Dulcie resisted the urge to gag and she pushed the other girl out of the way. She made a beeline to his table, then stood next to him, her hands clasped behind her back.

"Mr. Masters, we're so glad you could join us. I hope the table is to your liking," she prattled off in her sweetest voice. Con smiled up at her.

"It is. I got quite a welcome when I arrived," he told her. She nodded.

"Of course, your father is a valued member. May I get anything for you? Anna is one of our very best servers, she should be taking excellent care of you."

"She is – I barely recognized her. Is she the blonde chick from high school you used to be friends with?"

"Yes, she's the blonde chick from high school that I'm *still* friends with."

He laughed loudly at her and added, "I find it hard to believe you *have* friends."

"Thank you," she sighed. "Now if you'll excuse me, it looks like Mr. Jeffries would like to have a word with you." She nodded her head in the direction of a very eager looking older gentleman who'd been staring at them.

"Who the fuck is Mr. Jeffries and why do I care?" Con asked, glancing over his shoulder.

"Mr. Jeffries is the head of the trustees committee here. I'm sure the trustees are hoping you'll join their hallowed ranks and become a member, like your father," Dulcie explained. Her smile was pasted on so stiffly, it was beginning to hurt. He finally looked back at her.

"Are they? And how do *you* feel about that?" he asked, his voice low and his eyes bright.

"I feel like they're making a mistake. Have a good evening, Mr. Masters."

And with that, she turned and walked away.

Later that night, Dulcie laid in her bed. She had all the windows tilted open, letting a cross breeze through the apartment, trying to stifle some of the summer heat. Her large headphones were securely in place over her ears, drowning out all the sounds from the street below. She smiled to herself and hummed along to the tune, letting her eyes fall shut.

She obviously hadn't remained celibate since Con's departure, but she didn't really consider what she did having sex. It was more like doing a job. A particularly unpleasant one. The only time it was good was when it was with herself. And with a new memory of that evil smile still fresh in her brain, her fingers ran a race against her pulse, seeing which would happen first – heart failure, or orgasm.

Jesus, Con, took you long enough to come back, you idiot. Now hurry up and find me again.

FOURTEEN

WATCHING DULCIE TRAVERS CRY HAD BEEN A BEAUTIFUL MOMENT, but getting to see her mad, well. She'd been stunning.

Three years. I suppose I could've dropped her a line.

It wasn't in Constantine's nature, though, to cater to other peoples' feelings. He'd told her it was only them, regardless of the time and distance apart, and he'd meant it. So if it took him three years to find his way back to her, then that's simply how long it took.

Now the real test was to see if she'd meant it when she'd agreed with him.

Finding out where she lived had been easy enough. The town was tiny, everyone knew each other, and on top of that, she was eccentric, she was young, and she was sexy. Everyone knew her, or knew *of* her, in some capacity.

Con also knew that on Saturday nights, the country club closed down at eleven o'clock. He watched from across the street as she parked her car and headed into the old brick warehouse where her apartment was located. She was still in her work uniform, black tights, black skirt, and a white button down shirt. Her hair was in a tight braid that wrapped around the base of her head, and she looked so much like the girl from high school, it made him wonder if any time had actually passed.

When she came back out half an hour later, though, it was very apparent she most definitely wasn't that girl anymore. Con was a little surprised when he saw she'd changed into a short pair of cut offs. She'd always been a very slender girl with a small frame, but she'd filled out a little since he'd last seen her. She certainly filled out her shorts, showing off a pair of very tan legs. She wore a long sleeve shirt on top, and she'd gotten rid of the braid. Her hair was longer, as well, and it fell in waves over one shoulder. She looked every inch the good ol' country girl she really was.

*That she's really, **really**, not.*

She froze for a second when she saw him. They stared at each other for a long moment. She had her phone and her car keys in her hand, was obviously going somewhere. But she didn't move. He slowly smiled and watched as she shivered.

Then she abruptly turned and strode off down the sidewalk, heading in the opposite direction from her vehicle. Con glanced both ways, then jogged across the street and quickly caught up with her. He was so much taller than her, his long strides were able to eat up the distance she covered, even though she was almost jogging.

"You sure three years was long enough?" she called over her shoulder.

"Eh. Want me to check back in three more?" he asked. She threw back her head and laughed.

"Sure! But first, c'mon, let's have some fun."

She actually did break into a jog then, and she'd disappeared through a doorway before he even saw where she was going. He glanced up at a sign as he followed her. *Beavers.* A bar that was quite possibly older than god; Con had never been in it because he'd moved away before he'd turned twenty-one, but he'd heard stories. Lots of crazy rednecks, drinking beer and doing drugs, dancing to honky tonk and blue grass music.

It was so dark inside he couldn't see anything at first, it took his eyes a moment to adjust. He walked down a short, narrow hall that eventually opened into a large area. It was closing in on midnight, so the evening was just picking up speed. There was a band on a stage to his right, and a bar directly across from him at the back of the room. There were a lot of people dancing and laughing, but he was able to make out Dulcie's form as it slipped through the crowd. He took a deep breath and barreled on ahead.

"You a big drinker now?" he asked, getting to the bar just in time to see her neck an entire Corona. She shrugged and dropped the empty bottle onto the bar top before ordering another.

"Only when the situation calls for it."

"What have you been up to?"

"Do you care?"

"Not really, I'm just saying anything to drown out this noise," Con explained. She laughed loudly again and reached out to take a fresh beer.

"Put it on his tab," she said, whacking him in the arm. He rolled his eyes and pulled out his wallet, handing the bartender a twenty.

"So you come here often?" he tried again. She choked on the sip of beer she was taking, then finally turned to face him. He almost fell into her wide amber eyes.

"That sounds like a pick up line, Con. Are you hitting on me?" she asked, making her voice breathy and sexy. He chuckled and leaned down, grabbing her by the back of her neck and yanking her close.

"I don't need a pick up line, Dulcie. *I've already got you.*"

She pulled away from him and took another long drink of her beer, emptying it to the halfway point, then she put it down. She began swishing her hips back and forth, moving to the beat of the music, and she stepped away from the bar.

"I come here," she began answering his question, "when I want to have some fun. Don't you like having fun, Con?"

He narrowed his eyes.

"What kind of fun do you have while you're here?"

"Mmm, I like to make new friends. Meet new people."

She'd been dancing away from him, moving her body in a way that made even his pulse leap. He wasn't the only one to notice, either, and he watched as a large, potbellied man stepped up close to her, moving in time to her rhythm. Dulcie turned her amber eyes on the stranger, giving him her amazing smile. Slicking her tongue over her incredible lips.

"*Enough.*"

Con stepped forward and grabbed her arm, jerking her back to him. She was still laughing, and her new friend shouted at both of them.

"Why are you here, *Constantine?*" she drew out his name.

"You know why I'm here. Is this what you've been doing while I've been gone? Acting like a fucking idiot? Is that why you came here?" he demanded, ignoring the large man who was still cursing in their general direction. Dulcie's laughter fell away.

"No. No, that's not why I came here," she said in a soft voice.

"Then *why?*"

"I came here because I like to fight."

"Have you ever even been in a fight?"

"No, but I'm about to."

Without another word, she picked up her half drunken beer and slammed the bottle against the side of his head. Liquid and glass showered down all around him, and he could feel where the glass had sliced him at the edge of his hairline. A couple of girls standing near them shrieked, but Con didn't move a muscle. Just stared down at her.

"*What the fuck is goin' on here!?*"

The fat man who'd tried to dance with Dulcie steamed up to them. She smiled, but didn't look away from Con's glare.

"My friend was being rude," she explained in a breathy voice. "I think he needs a lesson."

"Look here, fella, I don't know who you think you are, but here, we treat our ladies with respect, so apologize for whatever -"

Con's fist broke the man's nose before he could finish the sentence. Pandemonium erupted in the bar. Girls started screaming. A woman began pounding on his back, but when he looked behind him, Dulcie was yanking the girl away by her hair. The big man tried to take a swing, but he missed entirely when Con stepped to the side and the blow landed on the back of some other guy's head.

And that's all it took. Fights broke out all around them and the bar turned into a mosh pit. Con was tackled from the side and he rolled around before pinning his attacker to the ground. He laid into the man, punching him repeatedly in the face. He didn't stop till he'd knocked the guy out, then he slowly climbed to his feet.

He'd somehow wound up in the middle of the dance floor. People were fighting all around him, he couldn't see anything, so he moved to where a table had been left standing and crawled on top of it. When he stood up, he could see the whole bar.

Dulcie was standing in almost the same spot as before, though she'd moved to kneel on a bar stool, keeping herself relatively out of harm. Her eyes were scanning the room, clearly looking for him, so he jumped down from his table and stormed towards her. She saw him before he reached her and she hopped off her stool, meeting him halfway.

There was turmoil all around them. A pair of screaming girls, their hands locked in each others hair, crashed between them before falling to the ground. One of the bartenders was banging a bat on the bar top, screaming for order, while the other was on the phone, calling the police. Con was bleeding from a cut on his lip, he realized, and he spit blood and saliva onto the floor. But he didn't say anything, just stared down at Dulcie, into her large amber eyes, and finally he smiled.

"I missed you," he blurted out, and she smiled back.

"*Good.*"

She grabbed his hand and pulled him out of the bar. Once outside, she broke into a run, and he jogged to keep up with her. She'd lost her phone in the scuffle, but had somehow held onto her keys, and she let them into her car.

Con didn't ask where they were going, just leaned back in his seat and held a hand over the wound on his head. After about five minutes, she reached over his lap and opened her glove box. She dug around inside for a second, then pulled out a bandana and handed it to him. He took it and pressed it against his cut.

"So that's what you do on Saturday nights? Start bar fights?" he asked after about fifteen minutes. She burst out laughing, but it wasn't the hollow sound from earlier. The cackle she'd been giving him in the bar. This was warm and real and it thawed some of the ice in his heart.

"No, not usually," she finally answered.

"Then what the fuck was that about?"

She stayed silent, and he noticed their speed increasing. They were racing down the highway, zipping around other cars.

"I wanted to see you bleed," she finally answered, then yanked on the wheel, narrowly making it onto an exit ramp.

"You could've just asked. I have a pocket knife," he informed her. She snorted and continued taking turns, navigating down a long and winding road.

"Oh, yes. And I'm sure you would've whipped it out and sliced open your palm at the first mention of blood," she chuckled.

"Yes, I would've."

"Why?"

"Because it would've been you asking me to."

Con had figured out where they were going long before the country club came into view. She bypassed the parking lot and went around the main building, parking in a tiny lot next to a maintenance house. They got out of the car and she headed towards a back door.

"It looks closed up," he commented, looking through a large window into the restaurant she worked at while she fumbled around with her keys.

"It is," she informed him, then yanked open the door. She grabbed him by his jacket and pulled him inside before locking the door behind them. "We actually closed early because tomorrow morning there's going to be a huge wedding, out on the fourth hole. Their reception will be here in the afternoon. They wanted it set up tonight."

When Con had been there the night before, it had been busy, full of loud people with wait staff rushing around. Now it looked so much bigger, devoid of all the hustle and bustle.

Dulcie flicked on the lights by the bar, illuminating a wall of liquor and some paneling. She left everything else off. The entire restaurant was done with dark oak and large rugs, giving the room an eerie, shadowy feel.

"How long have you been working here?" he asked, sliding his jacket off and heading towards her. She shrugged and moved so the bar was between them.

"A little over two years. I moved up pretty quickly, they made me a shift manager."

"Wow, impressive."

"Youngest one ever."

"You like it?" he was curious. She laughed again, and the sound echoed in the vast room.

"Do I *like* it? What kind of question is that? It's a fucking restaurant at a fucking country club, Constantine. What do you think? Of course I don't like it. But I like to eat and I like having my own apartment, and not all of us were born with rich daddies," her voice grew snide by the end of her speech. She grabbed a bottle off the wall and slammed it down on the counter. Johnnie Walker Red stared back at him.

"From what I've heard, you don't even know who your daddy is," he dished her own shit right back to her, then slid onto a bar stool.

"Touché," she twirled the cap off the bottle before pouring a healthy amount into a glass. "I don't. He could be loaded, for all I know. Doesn't really help me."

"And you think my father's money helps me?"

She didn't answer. He watched as she hoisted herself onto the bar top. She moved around till she was sitting next to him, her legs dangling over the side. Then she poured the scotch into a glass for herself and clinked it against the side of his.

"*Cheers,*" she whispered, then took a sip. Con did the same, though he drank everything she'd poured for him. "And yes, I do. Daddy's money helped you run away. Daddy's money helps you forget."

He choked on the fiery liquid for a second.

"Forget what!?" he snapped. She smiled and reached out her hand, wiping some scotch off his chin.

"The person you really are," she called him out.

"Oh, and like you're so good at remembering. Running around this place with your manager title, acting so prim and proper. Acting like you didn't come from a fucking trailer. If I was trying to forget, then what the fuck have you been doing?" he threw back at her.

"Is that a joke? I had to drive past that train station *every day* on the way to school. I live within five miles of it. Sometimes, on a clear night, I can see the chimney from my rooftop. So no, Constantine, I haven't forgotten. It's not possible for me to forget. And you know what? *I don't want to*," she hissed at him.

He got out of his seat then and moved so he was standing in front of her. She didn't move at all, just stared at him with hooded eyes, so he gripped her knees and forced her legs apart. She didn't resist, like he knew she wouldn't, and he moved into the V of her thighs.

"Were you scared?" he asked. She nodded and downed the rest of her drink.

"Yes."

"Aw, poor little Dulcie. Still afraid of herself."

"No," she shook her head, then lobbed the glass over his shoulder. It hit a wall and he could hear it shatter.

"No?"

"I was scared because … because I began to think I'd be the only person who'd know," her voice dropped into a whisper again. "That I'd be the only one who'd know what I was capable of. That it was the last time I'd ever get to feel like myself. That while I was staring it in the face every single day, *you* were running away from it. That you weren't strong enough to handle it, *and I was. That* thought scared me."

"I had to finish what I'd started, I had to … work shit out. I couldn't come back until then. I told you, it's only us, kid. *Only us.* I didn't give it a time frame," he reminded her. She rolled her eyes and shoved at his chest.

"Awfully convenient for you. So what's the plan, Con? Gonna fuck me and then leave for another three years? How about five? I'm not going anywhere. Works out awfully well for you," she pointed out, hopping off the bar and pushing past him.

"I hadn't planned much beyond the sex," he was honest.

"So confident! I admire that," she laughed, then raked her fingers through her hair.

"So who's the bartender? Boyfriend?" he asked.

She turned her head to the side and stared at him, and for just a moment, for the first time ever, Con felt a sliver of fear. He'd watched them the night before, seen how her coworker had been looking at her, how he'd found excuses to touch her. Con had wanted to bury his steak knife in the guy's forehead.

He'd never once lied to her – he'd meant everything he'd said that night. They were special. She was special to him. She was his whole reason for doing the things he did, anymore. He'd stayed away because she brought out the darkness in him. He'd needed to learn some self-control. If he'd stayed home, or if he'd brought Dulcie with him, he would've spun *out* of control. Patience disappeared when she was around, and they couldn't afford that, not with the kind of people they were. He'd just needed some time.

If she had a boyfriend, though, it would create a problem. As Con stared back at her, he wondered if that dead man had decomposed yet, and if there was enough room for another body in the hole.

"No. He's nobody. He thinks I'm cute," she finally answered.

"Ah. You *are* adorable," he teased, and was rewarded with an eye roll. "And what do you think of him?"

"*I don't.*"

"Any other prince charmings come along while I was gone?" he kept questioning.

"Jesus, Con, just ask what you want to ask. Have I dated anyone?

No. Have I fucked anyone? *Yes*," she snapped.

"You used to be so meek and quiet. What happened to that girl?"

"*You*."

He'd been walking forward the whole time, and he stopped when he was looming over her. She didn't back down at all, just glared up at him.

"So you're saying you didn't date them – just a lot of casual sex?" he wanted to make sure what was happening wasn't one-sided. That he hadn't wasted three years.

"I wouldn't even call it that. After I fuck them, I steal their money and threaten to tell their wives," she informed him. He was impressed.

"Clever girl. Do they -"

"Are we going to talk about my sex life all night? You want details? How many times, how many men? How many positions? How about the one time the guy asked me to wear a school girl uniform – which he'd brought with him. I still have the pictures, want to see? Or how about the other time, when the guy asked me to blow him while he was on the phone with his wife. He wanted to see if he could come before she hung up, so I -"

Enough.

Con snapped his arm out and grabbed her face, his fingers digging into her cheeks so hard, he could feel her molars through her skin. She let out a muffled shriek, obviously surprised, then she began hitting him. It was ineffectual; he was so much bigger than her. He could do anything he wanted to her, and there wasn't a damn thing she could do about it.

"I didn't ask for a blow-by-blow of your daily life," he growled, shoving her backwards and forcing her against a table.

"Really? Could've fooled me!" she yelled, her voice muffled behind the palm of his hand.

"I don't care how many people you've slept with, Dulcie," he breathed out her name as he yanked her up onto her toes. "It's still *my property* they're fucking."

"Oh, get fucked, Constantine. I don't belong to you anymore than any of the other guys I've slept with," she hissed.

Now that was simply going too far. He slammed her down onto the table top, sending dishes and cutlery and wedding decorations to the floor. She shrieked and raked her nails down the side of his face, so he pinned her wrist to the table above her head. With his other hand, he let go of her mouth and clamped his fingers around her throat.

"Is that so? Then why are you so worked up," he whispered, rubbing his nose along the side of her jaw, breathing her in. She squirmed underneath him.

"Because you're touching me," she answered honestly.

"I've done more than just touch you, Dulcie."

"Yeah, and then you left. I'm setting a timer for how fast you can run away this time."

"So bitter. It's heartwarming, really, to know you cared so much," he teased her.

She'd pushed his buttons earlier, and apparently he'd just pushed one of hers. She went wild under him, hitting and shoving at his body. Struggling to push him off.

"Is that a fucking joke? Real fucking funny, Con," she was yelling while she slapped at his arms and wrists and shoulders. He ducked his head and rode out the blows while he moved his hands over her body. "After everything we did, after everything we said, and you just did it again! Not a fucking word ..." she was still shouting, still hitting him, but did nothing when he unbuttoned the front of her shorts and began yanking the material down her legs. "... god, I hope someone kills you. I hope someone kills you, and I hope I'm there. I'll bury your fucking body under a cardboard box by the train station, and I won't even fucking care."

Last time we barely got to taste each other. This time, I'm going to swallow her whole.

He gripped the top of her thighs and yanked hard, dragging her across the table and into him. He grabbed a fistful of her shirt and jerked her forward, forcing her back to lift so her face was right in front of his own.

"As long as you promise it's you who does it, I'm fine with that," he growled.

"Such a sick fuck, Con. You're such a sick and twisted *fuck*," she swore, smacking him upside the head. He gritted his teeth and managed to undo his own pants with one hand, shoving them down in a hurry.

"Only for you, babe."

She finally kissed him. Jesus, took her long enough. He'd been dreaming about those lips, those sharp teeth, for so long. While she filled his mouth with her tongue, he ripped her underwear off her body.

"You were gone for so long," she whispered, rubbing her hands down his chest. "Gone for *so long*. I began to think you'd never come back."

"You should've trusted me," he whispered back, then sucked air through his teeth when her hand wrapped around the base of his cock. Yeah, virginal Dulcie was long gone. This creature was not shy or timid at all. She bit down on his earlobe while the palm of her hand rolled over his sensitive head.

"I should've. I missed you. I missed you so much. I would pretend everyone was you," she promised him, her hand picking up speed.

"*Good.*"

"I used to walk down on the tracks, and I'd think about you. Wished you were there with me," she kept going.

"We'll go together."

Maybe it was because she was an artist, he wasn't sure, but she was magically dexterous with her wrist. She could twist and curl her hand at impossible angles. If he didn't stop her, he'd be coming all over her instead of inside her.

Not necessarily a bad thing ... I'll save that for later.

He abruptly shoved her and she fell back onto the table. It broke the hold she had on him and he was able to lay down on top of her.

Their kisses were brutal, full of teeth and biting. Their fingers were mean, scratching over soft flesh and leaving marks. He held her down, wanted to push her through the table. She kept talking, kept reminding him of how awful he was, and he put his hand over her mouth. Not because he didn't want to hear it, but because it was turning him on. At this rate, the moment they'd start having sex, he'd probably explode.

"So bartender boy's never been here?" Con double checked, then roughly shoved three fingers inside her. She cried out, a sharp sound of pain that sent a tremor through his body, then she groaned and writhed against his hand.

"No. Since you left, no one else's fingers have," she was panting for air.

"No one's?"

"Just me. Just you," she assured him.

He was holding both her wrists down with one hand, and with his other hand, he was making her just as desperate as he was; possibly more so, if her movements were anything to judge by. She was making a high pitched whining sound. *Keening*, and it reminded him of the sound an animal made when it was being hunted. When it was close to death.

Sounds good to me.

He dug his fingers into her thighs and wrenched her legs apart. He wanted it to be in slow motion – things had been crazy in his truck, and then hazy in his apartment. He hadn't gotten to witness her in all her perfect glory. He wanted to watch as she took every inch he had to offer.

But he couldn't do it. Something about Dulcie, she'd always brought out the wild animal in him. The one that lived just beneath his skin, hiding just behind his smile. He barely had his tip in and then he slammed forward, giving her no warning. No time to adjust. She screamed and there was a crunching sound. He lifted his head and realized she'd grabbed one of the fallen champagne glasses. She'd crushed it in her fist, and fat drops of scarlet blood were already falling onto the pristine tablecloth.

"*Dulcie, Dulcie, Dulcie,*" he sighed her name, slowly moving back and forth.

"God, yes," she groaned, and her hips worked in a circle against him.

"You can't possibly have any idea what this feels like," he told her. She managed to shake her head.

"No, because it feels *better* to me," she challenged him. He stopped moving his hips and laid down, crushing her with his weight. Impaling her on his length. She let out a lengthy moan.

"I want to fuck you until you have bruises in places you didn't even know were possible," he hissed against her ear.

"I have been *dying* for you to do that to me."

It was as close as either of them were ever going to get to seeking and giving permission, and Con took it. He leaned back from her and while he wrapped one hand around her throat, he began pounding away between her legs. When she was almost gasping for air and yanking at his wrist, he let go, but moved his hand into her hair. He pulled hard, forcing her to look to the side, then he lowered his head so he could bite into the top of her shoulder.

I got blood from her last time. Seems only right I should draw it this time.

"Con … Constantine," her gasps caused her to stumble over his name.

"*Fuck.* What!?" he yelled, hiking his leg up so his knee was on the table. It gave him more leverage to push harder, to go deeper. He wanted to pound her inside out.

"Please, please," she begged, and he felt her arms around him, her hands working their way under his shirt. Felt her nails against his back. Against the scars he still bore, three years after she'd put them there.

"Please *what*, Dulcie?" he demanded, finally letting go of her hair. He was holding onto her thigh with one hand, but with his free hand, he pushed his way under her shirt. Shoved the fabric up her torso so it pooled at the top of her chest. She had small breasts. Petite. They fit perfectly in his cupped hand. Were made to feel his sharp teeth.

"Please make me come," she finally whispered. He bit down on her nipple and she shrieked. "*Please.* Please, only you … only you can …"

She was begging. Actually begging him. Con almost felt bad for her, but served her right. Letting other men touch her. Of course they couldn't give her orgasms; they all belonged to him.

"Poor little Dulcie, can't get what she needs," he chuckled as he slid his hand between their bodies. He briefly spread his fingers around either side of his dick, just for a second, then twined them through her slickness. Tap danced in her heat.

"No, never," she agreed, her hands moving to squeeze her breasts.

"Let's see if I can give it to her," he whispered, then he pinched his fingers together.

Con could feel her orgasm from the inside out. Felt her tremors all along his dick, milking him. Forcing him to pump harder. She shrieked and her hands clawed at the table cloth, shredding it in places. Her entire body seized, coming in fits and starts, causing her spine to arch, her breasts to tremble. It was like she was pulsing in time to his thrusts, and he couldn't stand it. He squeezed her breast as he came, causing her to cry out again, but this time in pain.

She was breathing heavily, he eventually realized. His forehead was pressed against her breast bone. She'd completely drained him, he couldn't remember the last time he'd come so hard. He could feel his legs shaking, so he scooted her up and followed along, stretching them out fully onto the table so he could take his weight off his feet.

When he looked at her face, Con wasn't entirely surprised to see she was crying. She was staring at the ceiling, struggling to catch her breath, and the tears were streaming down her face. He wondered if it was because he'd been so rough. Or because he'd been gone for so long. If she was happy or sad or regretful about what they'd just done.

Instead of asking, though, he just crawled over the length of her body and gave one long, slow lick up the side of her face, capturing as many tears as possible.

"One more question," he was panting, as well.

"Anything," she replied, still staring at the ceiling.

"Did you kill anybody else while I was gone?" he whispered. She shook her head.

"No, Constantine. I was waiting to do that with you."

"Good girl, Dulcie."

FIFTEEN

"**Y**OU CAN'T EVEN TELL," CON MUTTERED. OUT OF THE CORNER OF his eye, he saw Dulcie nod.

"I know. Amazing what time can do."

They were standing on the abandoned train tracks, staring at what was left of the cardboard shack. It was mostly crushed, half of it blown away. The ground all around it was lumpy and uneven, covered in weeds. There was no sign that three years ago, they'd brutally murdered a person and buried his body there.

How tragic.

After Con had gotten off her, Dulcie had assured him she was crying happy tears. She'd been hollow for three years. He'd filled her void. Then he helped her clean up the mess. They had to get a whole new tablecloth – the cut from the broken champagne glass had gone deep and she'd bled all over the place, not to mention all the claw marks that were now in the fabric. He made her sit down and she just instructed him on how everything had to be done.

"Why did you want to do this here? In the restaurant?"

"Because I hate it here, but next time I'm walking across this floor, all I'll see is you fucking me on this table, and it won't seem so bad anymore."

"Well, then. You're welcome."

They drove back to her place and using an old first aid kit she had, he bandaged up her hand. Then they had sex again. Afterwards, they talked for a long time. He told her about school. She told him about her life. They took a shower together.

And then he asked her to show him.

By the time they got to the train station, the sun was just starting to rise. Dulcie led the way, her footsteps sure and quick. It was obvious she went there a lot. She was back in her cut off shorts again, but she'd pulled on a large black sweater that hung so far down, it covered the shorts completely. She almost looked like she was walking around without any bottoms on, and it took him half the walk to realize she was wearing *his* sweater. The one he'd given her on that fateful night.

She's a romantic.

"What does all this mean?" she finally asked. Con turned to face her, but she kept looking at the makeshift grave.

"It means we can do whatever we want," he said, and it was like letting out a breath he'd been holding for too long. Dulcie was wrong – he'd had it much worse. At least at home, in that town, she'd been able to keep to herself. In school, he was always acting a part. Always pretending to be somebody else. He didn't have any drawings he could disappear into, no spare time to visit old ghosts.

"And what do we want?" she pressed. He grabbed her shoulders and forced her to face him.

"I want you," he stated bluntly. She simply nodded. "I want to do whatever the fuck we want. I've got a lot of money, Dulcie. *A lot.* We can go wherever we want, do whatever we want. We can … we can be as strange as we want. As awful. As fucking horrible as we goddamn want."

She let out a deep sigh and closed her eyes for a moment. When she opened them again, she was finally smiling at him.

"That sounds like *heaven.*"

"But we have stuff we have to do," he became serious. He grabbed her hand and began leading her back towards his car.

"Okay," she replied, and now it was his turn to smile. She didn't ask him what, didn't question him. He said it, and that was it, she was going along with it.

"I have to stay in town for a while. Once we leave, I don't want anything left that could bring us back. Agreed?"

"Completely."

"You never told anyone what we did, right?"

Dulcie smacked him across the back of his head. It was comical; she almost had to jump to reach.

"Of course I didn't!"

"Alright! Alright, calm down, tiger. C'mon, let's go back to my place," he said.

"Your shitty apartment was a million degrees. Let's go back to mine," she suggested.

"I'm staying in the big house," he corrected her. She winced.

"I'm sure your dad won't appreciate me just waltzing in, with my trailer trash roots and my lack of a college education," she pointed out. He narrowed his eyes and picked up the pace, forcing her to jog.

"I don't think you'll have to worry about him."

The Masters house was easily the biggest residence Dulcie had ever been in; though really, she'd grown up in a trailer, then moved into an abandoned warehouse. Almost anywhere was bigger than those two things.

"You like living here?" she asked, her eyes wandering over everything as they moved up the stairs and through the house.

"Not really," he replied.

"Then why stay here?"

"Because it's secluded from town."

"You're only like three miles away from downtown," she pointed out, stopping behind him as he opened a set of double doors.

"I like privacy," was all he said, standing to the side so she could move into the room. She stood at the foot of an enormous bed, taking everything in, then turned as he walked up to her.

"Planning something bad? Why do you need so much privacy?" she teased. He smirked, then leaned close to her, clenching his fingers in her hair.

"Because next time I fuck you, I'm going to make you scream, and I don't want anyone to hear it."

She shivered at his words and it made him laugh. Then he kissed her on the temple and walked out of the room.

They'd brought Chinese food with them and they headed into the kitchen. They stood around the large island and ate out of the cartons. She watched him while he picked through his food, setting aside all the onions. She picked out all her peas.

They may have been weird, psychically bonded, sociopathic soulmates, but most hated foods and favorite movies and the items they couldn't live without, those things were still foreign.

"Why do you think we're this way?" she whispered later on in the night. They were laying in the huge bed in the master suite. The room that should have belonged to Mr. Masters.

But Dulcie already knew Mr. Masters wouldn't ever be coming home.

"I don't know. Chemical imbalance," Con offered. His voice was heavy with sleep. They were both on their sides and facing each other, but his eyes were closed. Dulcie was wide awake and she let her eyes wander over his features. Memorizing them, in case he disappeared again.

"Are we crazy?" she pressed.

"*Yes.*"

"I thought crazy people didn't know they were crazy."

"We're evolved," he switched tactics.

"If this is evolution, I fear for the world," she managed a laugh. He sighed.

"You really wanna fry your brain? How about, what are the chances that two people like us were born in the same town, around the same time, and went to the same school? Maybe it was something in the water. Maybe our mothers did the same kinds of drugs. Maybe we're just blessed. Maybe we're cursed," he told her.

She'd never thought of it that way. Jesus, what were the chances? What if he'd been born in Arizona? How would she have gotten through life, never knowing the kind of person she could really be? Con would've been just fine. Maybe lonely, but he'd always accepted what he was; she'd needed him to rip down that black curtain in her brain.

Is this love? What if we're just feeding off each others darkness? What if we're just making each other worse?

"Maybe we're sick," her voice fell back into a whisper. He groaned and wrapped an arm around her waist, pulling her close so she was pressed against his chest.

"If this is a sickness, then I don't want a cure," he whispered back.

"You're very clever for a sociopath."

"Well, cleverness *is* a trademark of being one. Now shut up and go to sleep before I give your mouth something better to do."

SIXTEEN

FALLING FOR CON, WELL. IT WAS ALL DOWNHILL, REALLY. JUST A descent into darkness.

It was like getting to be a teenager all over again, only the way she wished it had gone. They drove to the lake and went swimming. Laid in the grass and looked at clouds. Spent hours talking about absolutely nothing; all those normal things two people did when they were falling in love.

But at night, they would walk down on the train tracks. About six months before Con's reappearance, the hobo camp had gotten cleaned out by the highway patrol. It wouldn't be long before tents popped back up and people were making their homes in the station, but for the time being, the pair had the area to themselves.

They explored the old train station, walked up crumbling stairs and peeked into long abandoned offices. On the top floor, there was a walkway that overlooked the grand entrance to the old station. Con pinned her against the banister, made her sit on top of it while he fucked her slowly. It was a long fall to the marble floor beneath them – death, if he dropped her.

She wasn't scared.

This is so not normal. This is beyond normal. This is perfection.

When will it break down? My life could use a little explosion.

"You should get out of work tomorrow," he was telling her as they walked down an aisle in the local grocery store.

"You realize you say that every day," she pointed out. They were in the candy section and she dug around in one of the bins. When she pulled out a lollipop, she peeled off the wrapper and popped it into her mouth.

"That's because I hate it when you leave every day," he replied.

"If you say anything else sweet, I'm going to kick you in the nuts."

He shoved her hard enough that she slammed into a display of chips.

"Shut up."

Sometimes Dulcie wondered if they would've had as much fun together in high school as they did right then. Con had never seemed like he wasn't having a good time, but still. It just felt so right, standing next to him. How had he denied them this feeling for so long? Sometimes, thinking about it made her angry. Those were the times she left marks on him. Constantine had a set of scars on his back that would most likely never heal.

"How long are we going to do this?" she asked, moving into a new aisle. He shoved his hands into his pants pockets and followed along.

"For as long as I say," he responded. She groaned.

"But why? Why do you want to stay in this small place? In that big house?" she wondered out loud.

"Because. I like watching you be uncomfortable. Have patience, Dulcie," was all he would say. Was all he *ever* said on the subject. She glared at him.

"It's *boring* here," she grumbled. He stepped up close to her.

"So find something fun for us to do."

Dulcie stared up at him for a moment, hypnotized by his blue eyes. Then she handed over her candy and winked at him before skipping out of the aisle.

They didn't need anything from the store – Con had groceries delivered to his house, and Dulcie's little mini-fridge was pretty well stocked. She mostly ate at the restaurant, anyway. They'd been walking across the street when she'd noticed a familiar looking figure heading into the shop. On a whim, she'd altered course and gone into the building, as well.

She found him in the cooler aisle, looking at ice cream. He was wearing a pale orange polo shirt and pressed khakis. He was laughing at something the woman next to him was saying, so he didn't notice as Dulcie walked up and stood next to him. Out of the corner of her eye, she saw Con enter the aisle, but he didn't walk all the way down it. He stayed down by the frozen pizzas, not even looking at her once.

"... babe, there's no such thing as diet ice cream," the guy was assuring the woman.

"But it says right there! *Diet.*"

"*Excuse me.*"

Dulcie leaned in front of the man, inappropriately close as she opened a cooler and reached inside. She pulled out a push-up ice cream pop, then turned to face him. Peeled off the wrapper as she watched the color drain from his face. Watched the recognition flash in his eyes.

"I ... uh ... you ..." he stuttered. Dulcie smiled and turned to the woman next to him.

"How can you possibly diet when something *so good* is staring you in the face?" she asked, then slowly took the ice cream into her mouth, as deep as it would go.

The innuendo was not lost on anyone, and his wife made a choking sound.

Dulcie had slept with the man over a year ago. He was from a neighboring town, but he had a cabin on the lake outside of Fuller and was good friends with some of the locals. One of those kindhearted souls had taken him to Dulcie's restaurant for a fun evening. Then she'd gone back to his cabin with him for even more fun.

He was a total freak in the sack and after their first romp in the sheets, he'd wanted to piss on her. Dulcie was fine with a bit of kink, but she had some hard limits, and urine was one of them. Mr. Kinky didn't understand the word "no", though, and he'd struggled to hold her down and tried to force her to endure it. She'd broken a lamp over his head, knocking him unconscious. She'd stolen his wallet, then left him a lovely note informing him that if he dared to call the cops or call her work, she'd show up at his home and piss on his trophy wife. Fair was fair, after all.

He didn't look like a freak now. He looked like he was going to vomit all over his loafers.

"Excuse me, do we know you?" his wife snapped.

"No, *you* don't," Dulcie replied, her eyes never leaving the man. She tried to recall his name, but couldn't. Once she left them, they all pretty much stopped existing to her.

"Look here, we don't want any trouble," he finally managed to get out, though he stammered a little.

"Mmm, you so sure about that?" she whispered, then gave the side of her ice cream a long lick.

"Look here, you tramp -" his wife began to bristle.

"Shut up, Marcy! She's just some townie, trying to freak us out. Let's get out of here," he urged, turning and trying to bustle the woman out of the aisle. A memory flashed across Dulcie's mind. His hand around her neck, him calling her a whore. Him telling her to beg, telling her to scream his name.

"It was great seeing you again, *Ted!*" she yelled out as loud as she could.

There was silence for a second, then his wife went nuts. The words "not again" were shouted repeatedly while she beat him with a head of lettuce. Green roughage flew all over the place.

Dulcie turned around and walked back up to Con. He didn't say anything, just fell in line beside her as they walked out of the aisle.

"I'm pretty sure you just ended their marriage," he warned her. She shrugged and took a bite of the push-up.

"You said to find something fun to do," she reminded him. He let out a loud laugh.

"How much money did you get off him?"

She'd told Con all about her little scam.

"Pffft, he only had like eighty bucks. A total waste."

"You know what was really impressive, though?" he started, pulling her to a stop. A gaggle of store employees jogged past them, hurrying to the fight that was happening in aisle three.

"What?"

"Your skills with that ice cream," he commented, staring at her mouth. She smirked at him and worked her tongue around the top of the dessert. "You've been holding out on me."

"You never asked," she pointed out.

"That's all it takes?"

"Of course."

"And what if I asked you right now?" he challenged.

"I'd say it's cold here, let's move over by the hot case."

He had that look in his eye, like he wanted to bruise her. It made her pulse leap and she licked her lips, tasting the chemical orange from her treat. She wanted to taste him.

"*Constantine!?*"

Dulcie groaned. *Frannie.* Since Con had come back, she hadn't seen the other woman. She'd begun to think maybe it was a sign, that her luck was changing. Con was her dark little rainbow, spreading peace over her world. But no. Apparently not.

"Hi, Frannie," he said politely, his politician's-smile making an appearance. No hint of the big bad wolf in that grin.

"It's been so long! How are you? *Move,* Dulcie, jesus, I'm trying to talk to my old friend," Frannie demanded, shoving her out of the way. The ice cream fell out of her hand and smacked into the floor.

"It's been a while," Con agreed, ignoring the incident between the girls. "How've you been? You look great."

Dulcie stared at their interaction, dumbfounded.

"Oh, stop. I don't. Do I? Well, not as good as *you*. You look *incredi-*

ble," Frannie gushed. His smile got bigger and Dulcie watched as Frannie fell a little more in love with him.

"Thanks."

"Enough about me. What are you doing here? And god, is Dulcie bothering you? Townies, I swear. C'mon, there's a great coffee shop next door, it just opened. Let me get you a cup," Frannie offered, then linked her arm though his and began dragging him away.

"A coffee shop? Wow, Fuller's almost like a real town," he laughed, and she cackled right along with him as they walked out the door together. He didn't look back, not even once.

What. The fuck.

Dulcie stomped the whole way home. She bypassed her elevator and took the stairs, wanting to burn off some energy. When she got into her apartment, she slammed the door shut behind her and locked it. The knob and the bolt, even put on the chain. Something she rarely ever did; she pitied anyone who would be stupid enough to try and rob her. But that afternoon, she wasn't in the mood for anyone to come inside.

She felt like she was going to explode, she had to do something with all the tension that was threatening to blow her apart, so she tore around the apartment. The bed was a mess, blankets scattered everywhere – they'd stayed the night at her place, but hadn't slept much. So she changed the sheets and made the bed, then tidied up other parts of the room. There was a wash basin set up on a counter top, so she cleaned the meager amount of dishes she had and left them out to dry. She was rinsing off a chef's knife when she heard what she'd been waiting for – scratching, on the other side of her door.

"Fuck off, I'm not in the mood for you right now!" she yelled. Deep laughter rolled straight through the wood and brick, almost filling her apartment.

"That's a lie, and you know it."

She frowned and turned so her back was against the wall between the counter top and the door.

"I don't want you to come in."

"I wasn't asking. Open the door, or I'll open it myself."

She held the knife up, touching the tip of the blade with her index finger.

"*Go ahead.*"

The building was old, she didn't expect the door to put up much of a fight. She turned back to her wash station and went about drying the knife. There was silence for a solid minute after her dare, and she paused in her movements. Then the door almost exploded off its hinges as Con rammed through it, and she went back to drying.

"You can't honestly be mad at me," he said simply, brushing his shoulder off as he moved to stand next to her.

"You didn't think that was possible? I spent three years being mad at you. I'm really good at it," she informed him. He chuckled and put his hands flat on the counter top, leaning down so he was at her level.

"Dulcie, you couldn't be mad at me if you tried. *You're scared.* What are you so scared of, little girl?"

I'll show him scared.

She let out a yell as she stabbed the knife down in front of him. The blade lodged in the wood right between his index and middle fingers, and had gone so deep, it stood upright on its own. Con didn't even flinch.

"*Not her,*" Dulcie hissed. "You can do whatever you want, but don't *ever* play your little pretend act with her. *Got it!?*"

Almost stabbing him was fine, but telling him what do do? That was just going too far. His hand was around her jaw, his fingernails cutting into her skin, and he literally dragged her across the room. She cried out as he slammed her up against a window, the back of her head breaking out a pane of glass.

"If you're actually threatened by a girl like her, then I'm insulted. Then you're fucking stupid, and what's going on here between us isn't what I thought. Don't you ever fucking talk to me like that again," he snapped, baring his teeth against the side of her face. She held onto his wrist, trying to relieve some of the pressure he was putting on her jaw.

"While you were off playing pretend for those three years, I was stuck here listening to her voice. Dealing with her insults, her jabs, her digs. Watching as she sucked the life out of her husband. A guy whose only mistake in life was dating me, yet she won't stop punishing him for it. I've had to listen as she spread rumors about me, about you. Had to deal with not getting hired in places because she had her father forbid it. So you know what? *Fuck you,* Constantine. I'll talk to you any way I fucking want."

He was silent for a moment, his eyes wandering over her face. She knew he was attracted to her, obviously, but she often wondered if he found her half as beautiful as she found him to be. His blue eyes dipped lower, tracing over the outline of her lips, watching as she gasped for air.

"You are the most amazing thing I've ever seen," he said, reading her thoughts. She struggled to take in air and stumbled a little; his hand was still on her jaw, holding her up so she was forced onto her toes. His forearm was resting on her chest, making it hard to breathe. Yet she let go of his wrist. Let him push almost his full weight against her, and against the glass behind them.

"We're going to kill each other, aren't we?" she whispered.

"Baby ..." he sighed, his eyes fluttering shut as he moved to rest his forehead against her. "What a beautiful thing to say."

SEVENTEEN

"EXPLAIN IT TO ME."

"It's stupid. You said it, I'm stupid for letting her bother me."

"Maybe. But make me understand."

Con was leaning over the island in his kitchen. Dulcie was sitting on a stool, her legs pulled up so her feet were resting on the seat top. She put her chin on her knees. They'd gone back to his house to talk. To plan. The dark hardwood floors and closed shutters, it intensified the ominous feeling that always surrounded them.

"She just … I don't get it. If I don't like something, it stops existing to me. It becomes irrelevant. But her, she goes out of her way to make things hard for me. Remember I worked in that diner? Well, it closed down right before the end of school. I tried to get a job at a clothing store downtown – her mom is a 'preferred customer' with a charge account, I found out. She told them not to hire me. Same thing happened when I applied for a data entry job at the glass factory outside of town. Did you know her dad is the CEO, or whatever? Yeah, I didn't either. So basically, I had to go half an hour out of town just to get a job," Dulcie explained.

"Annoying, yes, but that's what's got you all riled up over her?" Con sounded surprised. She shook her head.

"No, that just adds to it. I'm annoyed that she talks shit about you to anyone who will listen, but then kisses your ass the moment you're in front of her. Do you know she tells people you basically date raped her and stole her virginity?" Dulcie asked. He burst out laughing.

"It probably would've been more enjoyable if I had. By the time we started fucking, she hadn't been a virgin in years. We weren't even dating the first time we slept together – she practically attacked me in the locker room after a game, fucked me in the showers while the rest of the dudes were changing. Kind of sad, really," he commented.

"Very sad. And what does that say about you?"

"Hey, you were a sophomore back then, you walked down the halls staring at your feet. I had to wait for you to figure shit out. I had to take care of my basic needs," he defended himself. She laughed and chucked a hot pad at his head.

"You didn't even know I existed back then."

"Dulcie, I have been waiting for you for longer than you can imagine."

Warmth flooded through her veins and she smiled as she stared into his big blue eyes.

"*Anyway,*" she sighed, pulling herself back to the present moment. It was so easy to be consumed by him. "Shit like that. Walking around like she thinks she's better than me, better than *us*, when she's so far beneath us, she shouldn't even be allowed to say our names. And she cheats on Jared. Lives in her fucking perfect house that Daddy bought her, treats Jared like a fucking puppy dog and me like a whore, meanwhile she's fucking the manager of the Piggly Wiggly and is practically a platinum status customer at the pay-per-hour motel off route fifty-two. She's never had to work hard for anything, and she treats everyone like garbage. I want to show her what *real* garbage looks like."

Dulcie was almost breathless by the time she stopped speaking. The warm feeling had turned into a fever and she could feel sweat break out around her hairline. Her hands were cupping her legs and her fingernails were biting into her skin.

Con stared at her, his eyes wide and his pupils *huge*. She was pretty sure if she'd been able to see her reflection, her eyes would look the same. They'd been having fun since Con had come home, getting to know each other. Learning to like each other in the bright light of day. But that wasn't what drew them together, and they both knew it.

It's been so long since I walked in the darkness. Let's see if I still know the terrain.

"Then let's show her. *C'mon.*"

He still had his truck from high school, the one she'd lost her virginity in – her car had blown a tire earlier in the week and he'd been letting her use the large Ford F-150. They didn't take it, though. There was an old restored Cutlass parked on the side of the house, and Con slipped behind the wheel without a word. Dulcie didn't hesitate, she climbed into the passenger side and as she slammed the door shut, he cranked the ignition.

The back tires spit gravel as he gunned the engine, then they whipped out of the parking spot and raced down the driveway. It was late at night – after the incident in her apartment, Con had fixed her door as best as possible while she'd taped up the window. Then they'd gotten dinner before driving to his place. It was after ten o'clock, the sun had fully set a while before, but it was still warm out. Dulcie rolled down her window and let her arm hang outside the car.

"Plan?" she asked. Con chuckled.

"Oh no, little girl, this is your plan. I don't give two fucks about Frannie, but if you want to draw blood, then by all means. I'm at your service."

She thought for a second.

"What did she tell you during your little coffee date?"

"Mostly talked about how good I looked."

"God, the poor girl's gone blind over the years."

"Be quiet now, the adult is speaking."

"You're *one year* older than me."

"Yet so much wiser."

"Stop being cute and just tell me what she said," Dulcie finally cut off the banter.

"That she was unhappy in her marriage and she really wanted to get reacquainted with me. I offered to take her out tonight – I knew you'd be thrilled at the chance for us to get her alone. But she said they were driving over to Charleston, taking their kid for the weekend," he told her everything. She smiled and sunk lower in her seat.

"*Perfect.*"

"I thought you'd say that."

Frannie and Jared's house was nice, albeit simple. It sat at the very end of a cul de sac and its driveway was surrounded by a thick hedge, making it somewhat secluded from the rest of the neighborhood. Con pulled right up to the front of the house and cut the engine. As Dulcie got out, she realized he hadn't come around the car, and when she looked back, he was rooting around in the trunk. By the time she moved to join him, he'd found what he was looking for.

"You just carry this around?" she asked, taking the aluminum baseball bat from him when he held it out to her.

"I used to play ball, remember?"

"I remember you being good at football."

"Baby, I was good at *everything*. Let's go."

The front door was locked, but it wasn't too much of an obstacle. Con led the way to the back of the house. Dulcie was surprised to find a small pool back there – Frannie's dad had been generous. The backdoor had glass panels, and with one thrust of an elbow, Con let them into the dwelling.

It was exactly how Dulcie would have pictured it, if she'd ever bothered. They had beige furniture and cream carpet. An open kitchen overlooked the living room, which had a gas fireplace. The mantelpiece held pictures of the family, as well as some fancy looking candlesticks and other knick-knacks. And above them all, in an absolutely huge frame, was a larger than life portrait of the lady of the house.

"Ug, she's hard enough to look at when she's normal sized," Dulcie grumbled as they both stood in front of the painting.

"I don't know, she's pretty hot," Con was honest. "I was surprised. She still looks so good, especially for someone who had a kid just a year or two ago."

"She's pregnant."

"Even more impressive."

"Want me to leave you two alone?" Dulcie offered, using the bat to gesture between him and the portrait. He laughed.

"No. Now I have a thing for dark blondes with bad attitudes," he replied, winking at her.

"I do not have a bad attitude."

"Pity. Those are the best kind to have."

"Look at all these," she mumbled, stepping closer to the fireplace. One picture was at the town Fourth of July party, just two weeks ago. Jared was holding their kid, and both were smiling at the camera, waving their fingers. Frannie stood off to the side a little, with her hands on her hips and one leg in front of the other, looking for all the world like she was posing for a catalogue photo shoot and had no clue who the happy family next to her was.

"Cute kid," Con commented. Dulcie moved to look at another picture and nodded.

"Yeah. She takes after Jared," she told him.

"Y'know, this could've been you," his voice was soft. She stepped back so she was next to him again.

"Maybe. I don't know if he ever liked me quite that much," she started. "But maybe. He's so easy going, it would've been simple to talk him into it."

"Simple. And then you'd have a three bedroom house and a pool and a white picket fence. One kid already, and a baby on the way. A husband no one would ever be scared of."

Dulcie nodded and kept staring. The lights were on around the pool out back and what little light filtered into the house was all they were using to see. She stared at the perfect family photos and tried to picture herself in them.

"Fuck it. I'd rather scare people."

She swung the bat down hard against the mantel, causing everything on it to jump and scatter. Her next swing, she did it like she was playing baseball, whipping the bat down the top of the fireplace, swiping everything to the floor. A candlestick at the end was launched across the room, where it became embedded in a wall.

"That's what I'm talking about!" Con laughed, clapping his hands together before taking off his jacket. "But you gotta choke up on the bat, babe. You'll never knock it out of the park with that girly hold you've got there."

"Like this?"

She turned around and brought the aluminum rod down on a glass coffee table. It exploded, glass going everywhere. She continued pounding on the metal frame, trying to reduce it to nothing. Then she heard a whistling noise and she looked up. Con had moved so he was behind the couch, and he was tossing something up and down in his hand.

"Question – this is going to upset your little boyfriend as much as it will her. Have you thought about that?" he asked, and Dulcie realized the object he was tossing was a thick metal bookend.

"He should've thought about that before he married her. He's just a casualty in a war for the greater good," she replied, widening her stance and holding up the bat.

"Sweet jesus, I hope you're not implying we're the greater good."

"All depends on which side you're looking at it from. I'm sure the Joker thought he was working for the greater good."

"Well, when you put it like that. *Batter up.*"

Con didn't hold back when he pitched the bookend at her. He cranked his arm back and threw a perfect fastball, with as much speed on it as he could manage. Dulcie completely missed and the chunk of metal flew past her, ripped through the middle of the portrait, and could be heard tearing into the next room over. She stared up at the picture, at the hole where Frannie's face used to be, then she turned to look at Con.

"You have a lot of pent up rage, don't you?"

"Maybe, but still not half as much as you."

They turned the main part of the house into a demolition scene. He was right, Dulcie did have a lot of rage to work out. Like three years' worth. A *lifetime's* worth. She took it all out on Frannie's property, knocking out windows and breaking apart furniture. She turned the bat over to Con and grabbed a poker as her weapon of choice, using it to stab cushions and pillows, to puncture the walls and rip apart the carpet.

When she finally made her way into the kitchen, it was to find that Con had already done a lot of damage. He'd completely gutted the fridge, and all the cupboards were open. In fact, most of the doors had been ripped off their hinges and their contents spilled onto the floor. So she contented herself with pulling down a hanging rack of pans and sent them crashing into the stove. Then she turned on the burners – it was propane, so flames licked over the expensive copper cookware.

She wandered outside and found Con pissing into the pool. He had the bat tucked under one arm, and with his free hand he was sipping at a beer.

"Very mature," she snorted, pulling the beer away from him.

"Are you joking? We're trashing your ex-boyfriend and arch-ene-my-from-high-school's house. Me taking a leak in their pool is possibly the most mature thing we've done all night. Certainly the least destructive."

She sipped at the Bud Light, then tossed the bottle into the air and swung the poker. It connected and sent broken glass flying into the pool. Con zipped up his pants before applauding her hit.

"What happens if the neighbors call the cops? What happens if we get caught?" Dulcie wondered out loud. He turned to face her.

"Then we'd better make going to jail *really* worth it."

They stared at each other for a second, then she took off running into the house. She could hear him right behind her and she started laughing. Loud, unhinged, full on belly laughter. When they got into the hallway, she jammed the poker into the wall and dragged it along-side her, ripping a gash in the sheet rock as she went.

It was such an amazing feeling. *Finally* getting to do what she want-ed, and not caring. Feeling so above everything around her. Her ques-tions hadn't been facetious, the neighbors really could have noticed the noise and the cops could possibly be on their way. But Dulcie didn't care. She wasn't running out of the house – she was running further *into it*.

She finally found the master bedroom and she dashed inside, drop-ping the poker as she rushed to the bed. She yanked back the covers and was pulling all the sheets away from the mattress when Con grabbed her from behind.

"Question," she was panting as he yanked her shirt over her head.

"No talking."

"When we're done, I want -"

"Are you hard of fucking hearing?"

His hand was in her hair, pulling so sharply her eyes instantly wa-tered, and he yanked down, forcing her to drop to her knees.

It was strange, she knew. To be with someone so violent, someone so unafraid of violence, yet to never be scared he would actually hurt her. Maybe it was because she knew the feeling was mutual. Dulcie herself wasn't gentle when it came to him, and she certainly never held back. He had the scars to prove it. Holding back simply wasn't an option for them, not anymore. They'd simmered for too long.

I want a full boil.

She was struggling with his grip on her hair and when he finally let her loose, it was only to find his dick in her face. She remembered their conversation in the store, him accusing her of holding out on him, and she almost laughed.

"You have to do me a favor," she breathed, running her fingers lightly up and down the length of his cock.

"My favor is staring you in the face."

"You can't come in my mouth," she continued, holding him in her palm.

"You think you have a choice?"

"I want all of you, all over this mattress. Got it?"

There was silence for a second, and she took the opportunity to place a wet lick from the base of his dick to the head.

"Fine. *No more talking.*"

She barely had his tip between her lips when his fist was back in her hair and he shoved her head forward. She almost gagged as he hit the back of her throat, but then she managed to exhale as he let her pull back a little. Then he was shoving her again, harder than before. He kept repeating the action, and it was less like a blowjob and more like he was fucking her face. He pulled her hair, forced her head down on him, and thrust his hips forward. He was completely controlling the entire act.

God, is this what it feels like to be out of control? I wish we'd done it years ago.

"This isn't really the same as eating ice cream," she gasped when he finally let her come up for air. His hand stayed in her hair and he pulled her up high enough so he could kiss her, his tongue taking over her whole mouth.

"Next time I'll give you something good to swallow," he assured her, then jerked her to her feet.

She undid her shorts as she stood and she'd barely gotten them loose when he gave her a hard shove. She fell back onto the bed and he yanked the clothing from her body. She tried to sit up, but then his fingers were forcing themselves inside her, preparing her for something even more invasive, and she groaned before falling onto her back again.

"We don't … we don't have time for me," she gasped for air. He lowered himself and bit down on the inside of her thigh.

"I *always* have time to make you feel good," he assured her, his fingers pumping faster. She rubbed her lips together.

"That's nice, but I really want to make sure you have a chance to -"

"Goddamn, Dulcie, has anyone ever told you that you talk too much!?" he snapped, then he yanked his hand away and shoved three very wet fingers into her mouth. They reached into her throat for a moment, and all she could taste was herself as he pumped them in and out. "*There*. See how good you taste? There's *always* time for that."

Well, when he puts it like that, who am I to argue?

He pulled away, but wasn't finished with her. While he stripped down, he ordered her to play with herself. Not a difficult command to heed when she got to stare at his amazing body at the same time. She was close to orgasm when he made her stand up. She pushed herself to her feet, standing so her breasts were brushing against his abdomen. She wasn't quite five-foot-three and always felt so much smaller than him. His presence was larger than life. Bigger than her, in every way. How on earth had they wound up together?

"I'm worried this isn't real," she whispered. He smiled and lifted his hand, gently running a finger down the side of her face. "I'm worried you'll go away. I'm worried that I'll never feel this way, ever again. That there's no one else out there who would do all this with me."

He leaned down so his lips were against her ear and he whispered, "What do I have to do to earn your trust?"

"Never leave me," she replied instantly, and could feel his smile. That evil grin.

"*Deal*," he hissed. A fire alarm in the living room started going off and he pulled back to face her.

"Someone will hear that," she warned him.

"Then we'd better get to work. This is going to hurt," he warned her. She beamed at him.

"That's my favorite."

He slammed her face first onto the bed and didn't even hesitate, just thrust every hard inch he had inside her. Dulcie screamed, then bit down on the mattress as he began pounding away. She was petite in more ways than just her build, but Con never took any notice of it; there was no warm up, no gentle love-making. Just fucking, pure and simple. There were times when she was less of a lover and more of a vessel. Somewhere he could pour all his raw sexual energy into, something he could pound at till he'd fucked some of his darkness away.

I can't think of a more beautiful purpose in life.

It was definitely looking like one of those times. She couldn't even breathe properly, let alone think about what her body was feeling. His fingers were leaving bruises on her hips as he thrust against her and surely at the pace he was setting, he would come soon.

But then he pulled away and he was urging her fully onto the bed, pushing her onto her back. They were both soaked in sweat and he slid against her, his tongue circling her nipple.

"God, I really do, I wish you could experience this from my side," he sighed. Dulcie finally opened her eyes and lifted her head. He wasn't looking at her, though, his head was tilted down. So she followed his gaze and realized he was watching as he dipped the first couple inches of his cock in her. Then he pulled completely out before doing it again. It drove her wild, the anticipation followed by the denial.

"It's pretty good from this end," she assured him, her voice shaky.

"No. No, Dulcie. *This,*" a finger joined his dick at her entrance and he finally pushed until their pelvises met. Her eye rolled back in her head as he wiggled his finger. "Don't get me wrong, pussy in general is pretty fantastic, but this right here? This pussy is the *golden ticket.* I could die right now, and it would be with a smile on my face, because I would die doing something I love."

His hips picked up speed and her breathing quickly got out of control. The fire alarm was screaming, but not as loud as her. She begged him to fuck her harder, to leave bruises, to make her come. Please, dear god, she wanted to come before he did. Wanted to know she'd been in Frannie's bed, having better sex than that woman would ever know, and got to have an orgasm the likes of which Frannie could never experience.

Con had always been good at making her dark dreams come true, so she didn't have to wait too long. He slithered down her body at one point, his tongue taking the place of his dick. She curled her fingers in his hair and pulled, forcing him to press harder.

"Constantine ... oh fuck ... I'm coming ... I'm -"

He moved so fast it kind of shocked her. One moment his head was between her legs, the next he was thrusting his cock inside her. The shift of gears was like a shock to her system and the orgasm just exploded. Her scream came from some faraway pit in hell and when she raked her nails down his chest, she drew blood *again*.

"Yes, *fuck*, good girl, Dulcie. Just like that, *fuck*," he hissed, pressing his hand down flat on her lower stomach. Right over where his dick was making itself a new home.

He's right, one of us is going to die doing this. I hope it's me, I don't know how many more orgasms like this I can survive.

She could feel it when he came, it was so strong. Then he pulled out, his fist working up and down his cock, continuing to milk the orgasm. She groaned as the first ropey strands landed on her stomach, then he stepped to the side and did exactly what she'd asked him to – he came all over Frannie and Jared's mattress.

"How was that?" he asked, completely out of breath. She trailed her index finger through the mess on her stomach, then brought her hand to her mouth and sucked the digit clean.

"That was abso-fucking-lutely perfect."

Con moaned and yanked on her arm. She'd barely sat upright when he was grabbing her by the head and kissing her, his lips crushing her own. She shoved her tongue against his, fighting back, asserting her own dominance.

"*You're* perfect," he breathed when he pulled away. She smiled and slicked her tongue across his bottom lip. "Now let's get the fuck out of here before the house burns down around us."

EIGHTEEN

OF COURSE DULCIE HEARD ABOUT THE *TRAGEDY* THAT HAD BEFALLEN the Foster household. *Did she know* someone had broken into Jared and Frannie's home? *Had she heard* about how the pots had been left to burn on the stove? *Was she aware* that some barbarian had ripped apart all their furniture!? Thank god, though, the fire hadn't spread to the rest of the house! And thank god only the living room and kitchen had been mainly attacked. The bedrooms had been left unscathed.

Hmmm, I guess there wasn't a terribly thorough investigation. Or Frannie isn't letting certain details out.

While Con had made sure the house wasn't actually on fire, Dulcie had cleaned up the bedroom. After everything on the mattress dried, she carefully made up the bed. When she finally stepped away to look at her work, she was pleased – a person would never know anyone had been in the room, let alone that two people had fucked like maniacs on the bed.

"You're fucking crazy," Con had whispered as he'd hugged her from behind. "*I love it.*"

Is that what this is? Love? It's pretty fucking scary.

They drove back exactly the same way they'd come in, and Dulcie had expected to see police. Firemen. At the very least, gawking neighbors. But there had been nothing. A dog a couple doors down had been going nuts behind its fence, but that was it. As they'd driven away, she'd looked out the back window and couldn't even tell anything had gone down at the Foster's home. Their driveway looked the same as ever, there was no hint of the insanity that had taken place within their four walls.

It rattled the community, that something like that could happen. Such a random act of violence. So senseless. The tiny police force didn't know how to deal with it, didn't know what to do. A curfew was instituted for anyone under eighteen, just in case they were dealing with a madman. Dulcie laughed so hard when she read about it in the paper, she started choking and Con had to pound on her back.

A week went by, and then another. There were no hints, no leads, in the case, and time kept ticking along. August rolled into town, even hotter than July. They slept in her apartment with all the windows open, laying naked and praying for a breeze. Making love and not caring about anything at all.

Of course, they could've stayed at Con's house. It had air conditioning and lots of rooms to choose from; Mr. Jebediah Masters wasn't going to complain any time soon. She never asked Con about his dad, but she knew. She just knew Mr. Masters would never be coming home, and that's why they couldn't leave town. It would be too suspicious. They would have to figure out a way to "cover their tracks", as it were. Make it so no one would have a reason to come asking them any questions.

Work was becoming more and more difficult. Con had inherited quite a bit of money when his mother had died, he was wealthy in his own right just from that, but he also had access to his father's fortune, as well. It didn't even need to be discussed – he had money, so he took care of them. If the situations had been reversed, she would've done the same. So really, she didn't need her job. But for the sake of normalcy, she kept it. So even though she hated it, hated getting out of bed when he was so gorgeous and naked and available to her, she got ready and she went to work.

"You seem distracted," David said to her one day. She was behind the bar with him, doing an inventory count on the liquor.

"I do? How so?" she asked, not looking up from her paperwork.

"I don't know. You used to have time to bullshit. Now you're in and out."

"David, I never once stood around and 'bullshitted' with you, or anyone," she pointed out.

"Okay, maybe not. But Anna says you haven't met up with her for drinks in over a month," he added. She finally looked away from her clipboard.

"You've been asking about me?" her voice was hard. He looked embarrassed and he rubbed at the back of his neck.

"No. Kinda. Yeah, okay. I did. I saw you, the other weekend. With that guy," he explained. Dulcie narrowed her eyes.

"What weekend? What guy?"

"I went into Fuller to see a movie," he started. David's job came with room and board at the club, and she knew he usually drove to the bigger town farther south for his fun and games, rather than the thirty minute drive to Fuller. "I saw you in the lobby, afterwards. I was gonna say hi, but you were with that guy. Y'know, the one everyone was geeking out over. Connie."

She almost laughed.

"Yeah, okay, so I was at the movies with *Connie*. That gives you the right to ask about me to our coworkers?" she checked.

"Okay! I'm a dick. I just wanted to know if you guys were dating. You seemed like you didn't care when he was here, but then at the movie theatre, I don't know, you looked … looked like you were together," he tried to explain.

Dulcie and Con went out often, and in very public places, but they were always careful to keep it platonic. They never kissed or touched while they were out and about, by a silent agreement. She wasn't quite sure why that was; it's just how they'd always acted, since he'd gotten back to town. It seemed safer if people didn't know the two wolves in their midst were actually a couple. She felt like it gave them a sort of alibi, if it came down to it. They were just friends in everyone's eyes.

Friends who can't stop sleeping together and don't understand what kind of monster they're becoming and maybe want to burn down the whole town. That kind of friends.

"Look, David. You're awesome. You're ridiculously hot, and you're funny and good at your job," she assured him, and he smiled big. She didn't. "But I never once lied to you about what would happen between us – I will *never* go out with you. My relationship with *Constantine* is none of your business, but since you want to know badly enough to invade my privacy, *no*, we're not dating. We've never dated. But that doesn't mean I'll ever date you. Don't ask about me again."

It wasn't a lie. Con had never once asked her out on a date. She wasn't sure she'd know what to do if he ever did. They were a match and jar of gasoline. Who wanted to waste time with dating when there were explosions to be had?

She didn't wait for him to respond, she just started walking away. The entrance to the restaurant had just been pushed open, and as she headed towards it, she recognized a figure standing out in the hall. She let out a sigh, then continued through the doorway.

"Hey, Dulcie," Jared said, his voice tired and soft. She smiled sweetly at him.

"Hey. How are you? I didn't know you guys were coming tonight, did you have a reservation?" she asked, heading over to the hostess station. He reached out and grabbed her elbow, halting her movements.

"No, no reservations. It's just me," he told her.

"Oh. Well, that's nice, too. We open in about half an hour."

"Yeah, I know. I just … I wanted to talk to you."

She cocked her head to the side and tried to do her best impression of being confused, though really, her mind was racing. The house had been a disaster zone, but she and Con had looked over everything to make sure they hadn't left any clues, that there weren't any hidden nanny-cams or anything. Unless Fuller had an amazing CSI department, which she was confident they didn't, there was no way the vandalism could be linked back to her.

"Talk to me? About what?" she made sure to sound surprised.

"I just really need someone to talk to."

Dulcie lead him to the end of the bar and got him seated before pouring him a stiff drink. She waved David away, then sat down as well.

"What's up?" she asked, crossing her legs and turning to face him.

"You heard, right? What happened to us?" he checked. She managed a frown.

"Yeah, yeah I did. Sounds awful. I heard there was a lot of smoke damage. Are you going to have to move?" she questioned him. He shook his head.

"No, it's mostly in the kitchen. Some dry wall repairs, a lot of clean up. But Frannie's really ... upset. She hasn't been staying at home. It's just me and little Amy," Jared sighed.

Dulcie wasn't surprised at all. Once she'd had time to think about their little house party, she'd figured Frannie would shit a brick. Would pitch a fit. Be so pissed off, so angry, so *secretly thrilled* to have an excuse not to stay at home. More wheels were set into motion and Dulcie made sympathetic noises, nodding while Jared talked.

"That's really sad. I feel terrible for you, and I'm here if you need to talk, but I gotta be honest. We haven't spoken a whole lot since high school, I'm surprised you even thought of me," she chuckled a little. He downed the rest of his drink and Dulcie refilled it.

"I know. I've actually been thinking about you a lot lately," he confessed. Now she was for real surprised. Why was he thinking of her!?

"Me? Why me?"

"I just ... I really liked you in high school. When we dated," he was honest.

"Aw, that's really sweet. But that was years ago now, we were a lot younger. I was never the type of person you should've been dating. You needed to date a cheerleader," she teased.

"I did. Look where it got me."

"Even so, doesn't mean we were meant to be."

"No, I know, but there was just something about you. Right after the house got trashed, we stayed in a bed and breakfast downtown. I went out for a jog one morning, just getting some air, and I saw you in the park. You were drawing something. You're always drawing something," he laughed a little.

"You could've said hi."

"I didn't want to bother you, and what would I say? *Hey, chick I used to date but then treated awful but then still wanted but now hardly talk to, how are you?* Nah, not exactly a good conversation opener. I kept jogging, and I was thinking about you and your sketchbook, and how you always had it with you in high school. How nothing bothered you. All you ever wanted to do was draw. It was like you were on another plane from the rest of us, nothing could touch you. Not Frannie and all the shit she used to give you, not our break up, nothing.

"Then I got to wondering how you would feel if someone had done that to you, trashed your apartment. And I thought, Dulcie wouldn't give a shit. She'd just clean up the mess and keep on drawing. Wouldn't even let it disrupt her day. Who cares about material shit, when you've got a whole other world in your head you can live in?" he chuckled.

Dulcie was a little stunned. She'd had no idea she'd come off like that in high school. She'd placed herself in the "dork" demographic. An art geek. Not anyone worthy of looking up to or admiring. She'd been wallpaper. Or so she'd thought – apparently Jared had seen through all that, perilously close to the real Dulcie. Nothing had ever really bothered her, and nothing anyone said or did ever touched her. She hadn't realized she was so transparent.

I need to be very, very careful how I handle myself in public from now on.

"Well, you're right," she laughed. "I wouldn't care. Not much to bust up in my place, just a bed and a mini-fridge. They're things, Jared. That's how I think of it. Just things. So someone broke your shit, who cares?

Just go out and replace it all."

"Yeah? And what about people? What do you think of them?" his voice was a raspy whisper, and she held herself still.

"I think … I think sometimes they need to be replaced, too," she spoke carefully. He didn't lift his head, just nodded into his drink.

Jared stayed the whole night. He got a little drunk, but not out of control, and after she shoved a plate of fries in front of him, he sobered up. He stuck to the bar for the first couple hours, chit chatting with people, and then their old high school gym coach came in to eat. They wound up sitting and laughing together. She supposed it was nice, in a way. Jared probably didn't have a lot of opportunities to laugh anymore, and she'd definitely given him some more reasons to frown.

But still, those wheels kept turning.

They were the last to leave the restaurant, and it was eleven-thirty by the time she finally walked him to his car. He hadn't had anything to drink for a couple hours and assured her he was good to drive. Then he shocked her by wrapping her in a big hug, squeezing her tight to him. She patted him on the back a couple times, then pushed him into his car.

"Seriously," she said, leaning into his window. "Any time you need to talk. About anything. Just to shoot the shit. I'm here for you."

"I should've been nicer to you, after school," he grumbled, staring up at her. She gave him as big a smile as she could manage, and she watched him light up.

That's right, keep looking at my smile, never mind those pesky fangs. All the better to eat you with.

"Maybe. But I could've been nicer when we broke up, so it's fair. Stop by soon, okay? We'll have dinner," she offered.

"I'd really like that, Dulcie," he said, then he reached out and tucked a loose strand of hair behind her ear. She took a deep breath.

"I don't work Sundays."

"Sunday. Dinner. You and me."

"Meet me here at eight, I can get us in at Tableau," she said quickly, referring to the high end restaurant at the country club. Much nicer than the place she worked, it was easily four-star, and people usually had to book reservations weeks in advance.

"Sunday at eight, I'll be here. Thank you."

She squeezed his hand once, then stepped away from the car. Her heart was beating fast as she watched him drive away.

It was a bold move. Con probably wouldn't like her just brashly making decisions without him. They may have been a demented sort of Bonnie and Clyde, but it wasn't really fair to engage in an act of depravity without asking him whether or not he wanted to be a part of it.

She trekked around the building to the back parking lot and tried to figure out how she was going to explain it to him. He would go for it, of course, but she didn't want him thinking it was to help Jared out. No, this was purely for selfish reasons. This was to stretch the game out a little longer.

Might as well have fun if he's going to keep us cooped up in this town.

Dulcie was so lost in thought she didn't hear the footsteps behind her. She was digging her keys out of her bag when someone grabbed her from behind. She was slammed up against her car door, causing her to drop all her belongings, then she was yanked away and pushed onto her hood. Her head smacked against a windshield wiper and she cried out in pain.

"You thought you'd get away with it, bitch!?"

Goddammit.

Matt, hissing in her face. He was like a cockroach that just would not die. While she felt around the back of her head to see if she was bleeding, he shoved his way between her legs, which were dangling over the side of her car.

"There's security cameras out here," she warned him, struggling against his weight as he leaned over her.

"Then we'd better give them a good show. Remember this?"

He had a plaster cast around his right forearm and hand, and he whipped it across her face. She tried to lean away, but wasn't quite quick enough, and her cheekbone caught the edge of the cast.

"Oh fuck," she groaned, pressing her palm to the side of her face. She could feel where the plaster had scratched away her skin.

"Yeah, think you can pull shit like that and get away with it? You fuckin' bitch, you're gonna pay for it. I should shove this cast up your ass," he threatened. She started laughing.

"Well, it would be the closest you'd ever get to actually having sex."

The cast came down on her chest and she gagged on air. While he pinned her down, he began pulling at her clothing. She started screaming, pure rage boiling in her veins, and she swung her body around, trying to break free from him.

"Give it up, Dulcie! Even if you get away, I know where you work. I know where you fucking live. I'm not going *anywhere* till you've paid for this fucking broken wrist! I won't stop till I get what you owe me!" he yelled at her.

She wrapped both her hands around his neck and squeezed as hard as she could, really digging her fingernails in; she wanted to draw blood. He didn't give her the chance – when he realized she wasn't letting go and that he actually couldn't breathe, he panicked and she got another smack with the cast.

Before he could hit her again, though, the shadows behind him moved. Breathed and came alive. Matt was on the ground before Dulcie even realized it was Con tackling him. She fell off the hood and scrambled onto her knees, watching as the two boys wrestled around. It should've been an easy fight for Con, he was six-foot-two and built out of solid muscle. Matt was maybe five-foot-ten, and would be lucky if he was 130 pounds soaking wet. Meth had not been kind to him.

Still, it was Con who backed down first. He let go of the smaller man and scooted backwards, then climbed to his feet. He moved so he was in front of Dulcie, blocking her view, so she stood up. But when she went to step around him, he put his arm out, blocking her. She peeked around him and saw what the issue was – Matt had a gun. A tiny thing, a snub-nosed pistol, but still deadly. Still lethal. He cocked the hammer back and pointed it straight forward, maybe a foot in front of Con's heart.

"Oh yeah, you wanna fuck with me now, golden boy!?" Matt was screaming.

"Don't do this, just walk -" Dulcie tried to talk him down.

"*Shut up*," Con snapped. She shut her mouth.

"This is fuckin' hilarious. Rich boy here likes fucking trailer trash, huh? Should've come and talked to me, man, I could've found you something way hotter than her."

"Thanks, but I'll stick with this particular piece of trailer trash."

"Nah nah, friend, you have to wait your turn. I was here first."

"You are very mistaken. You know how to use that toy, little boy?" Con asked. Matt's sickly gray skin flushed bright pink.

"Is that a fucking joke!? I was fucking running this town when you assholes were still in kindergarten!" Matt informed them.

"Running it, really. Running what? Maybe a meth den. Or a local chapter of incestuous bastards anonymous," Con kept needling him. Dulcie wanted to laugh, but Matt's trigger finger didn't exactly look steady. The guy was obviously high as fuck, not to mention royally pissed off. It wouldn't take much for him to pull the trigger, and as god-like as Con was, she was pretty sure even he couldn't survive a point-blank shot to the heart.

"Real funny, huh? Pretty boy thinks he's so funny. Should fucking come down to where I live, I'll fucking show you what a mouth like yours would be good for," Matt spit out.

"I've got a better plan," Con suggested. "Why don't *you* come down to where *I* live, and after I shove that gun up your ass and pull the trigger, I rip off your fucking arms and beat you to death with them."

Dulcie actually did laugh out loud at that one, and the sound startled Matt, drawing his attention to her. Distracting him. Con wasn't distracted at all and without any warning, he snapped his hand out and grabbed for the gun.

Remember, he's so quick.

A shot was fired and she screamed. Actually screamed, like a scared little girl. Before that moment, Dulcie hadn't really ever felt true fear, but when she heard the shot, it blossomed in her chest. Con had been shot, and he would die, and she would be as good as dead without him. Life wasn't worth living without the technicolor he provided.

Before her scream had even died off, though, she saw he hadn't been shot. He'd grabbed the front of the gun and yanked it away from them. By the time Matt pulled the trigger, the barrel was pointing up at the sky. Con punched him in the face, and as the other guy went down, he yanked the gun free. Then he turned it around in his hand and pointed it down at his fallen opponent.

"*No!*" Dulcie yelled, then leapt around him and shoved him in the arm. He fired a shot into the back panel of her car.

"What the fuck do you think you're doing!?" he demanded, staring at her like she was crazy. She kept a hand on his wrist and watched as Matt scrambled to his feet. He didn't waste any time, he immediately ran off into the woods that abutted the edge of the golf course.

"C'mon, gun shots this close to the club, people might come look," she realized she was almost gasping for air, and she shoved him towards her car.

He looked pissed off, but Con didn't argue and he slid into the passenger seat. She peeled out of the parking space and raced off the property, making a hasty escape. It wasn't until they were halfway to Fuller that she realized they'd left Con's car behind.

"Why the fuck didn't you let me shoot him?" he growled. She took a deep breath.

"Because it's too easy," she said in a simple voice.

"I don't care. He fucking touched you. How long has this been going on?" he demanded.

"Forever? I used to barricade my door when I lived at home. It comes and goes, now. It's like he'll forget about me for a while, then get a wild hair and harass me for a couple weeks. Last time was right before you came back to town. He followed me into my building, I caught his arm in the elevator's gate and broke his wrist," she broke it down for him.

"You should've told me."

Worse than him sounding angry, worse than him yelling. He sounded *disappointed*. If she hadn't known any better, she also would've said he sounded a little hurt. Upset that she'd kept something from him.

"You weren't here," was all she could think to say. "You were gone, remember? I've gotten so used to dealing with him, I didn't even think about it after you came back. He hadn't been around. Out of sight, out of mind."

Dulcie couldn't be sure if her explanation appeased Con or not. He stayed silent for the rest of the car ride home, but he wasn't always the most talkative person, anyway. When they got into Fuller proper, he still didn't say anything, so she automatically drove them to her apartment.

"Let me see."

He spoke as soon they got through her door, and she wasn't even given a chance to turn around. Her grabbed her arm and yanked her over to her kitchen area. He turned on a set of fluorescent lights, then cupped his hand under her chin, forcing her to look up at him. His thumb brushed across the top of her cheek and she winced.

"That broken wrist really came back to bite me in the ass," she tried to joke. He kept frowning.

"You're lucky he didn't break your eye socket."

"Thank god."

"We need to take care of him," he said. Made a statement. Dulcie took a deep breath.

"I know. But it's not that easy. And not yet, we have some unfinished business."

"Apparently. I got to your work around ten."

She was shocked.

"Were you spying on me!?" she demanded. He laughed and let go of her face.

"You sound so angry. If I want to spy on you, Dulcie, there's nothing you can fucking do to stop it, but *no*, I was not spying on you. I had dinner at the other spot, thought I'd stop in and say hi," he explained.

"Oh. Why didn't you?" she asked.

"Because you were busy saying hi to Jared Foster. You looked deep in conversation. Is that part of a shift-manager's job?" he checked.

"I'm allowed to sit and have conversations with old friends," she insisted. He shoved his hands into his pants pockets and leaned down so his face was level with her own.

"Sure you are – with *actual* friends. *Not* with people we've committed felonies against," he informed her. "I want to know every single fucking word he said to you."

"Don't trust me?" she snapped.

"I trust you. Stop changing the subject. Tell me what he said."

"Tell me what happened to your dad."

Con had been home for almost two months, but Jebediah Masters still hadn't put in an appearance. At first, Con had told everyone his dad was away on business in New York, but eventually that had just given way to "I don't know". No, he didn't know where his father was, and yes, he was concerned. Yes, their lawyers had been contacted and the police in New York had been called. Yes, that was why he was staying in Fuller – he wanted to be there in case his dad showed up. But no, he wasn't overly concerned. Jebediah Masters had a habit of taking off on his own; hunting, fishing, whoring around, whatever, and not telling anyone. He always turned up in his own time.

Dulcie knew he wouldn't be "turning up". She could feel it. Con had done something. Something very, very bad, and he was keeping it from her. *That's* what bothered her. They were supposed to be in this together. In her mind, it was ride-or-die. He knew all her dark little secrets, was allowed right into the center of her black little soul. She let him have carte blanche, yet he kept his own dark little deeds to himself. Why?

"Why do you want to know?" he asked, glaring down at her.

"Because I deserve to know. Because I've earned it. Because if this is a need-to-know-basis relationship, then I'm not interested," she laid it all out.

Constantine laughed. He had a big laugh, it almost didn't fit his persona. Well, the persona she got to see. His laugh was something made for the field. Made for jokes in the locker room, or laughing around a bar after a game. She could just picture him in college, using that laugh to pull people in, to make them want to laugh with him. Usually it settled around her, made her want to smile and revel in his happiness. But not in that moment.

I don't fucking feel like laughing.

"Do you really think it's that easy? That you can just walk away, little girl? Oh no. We're in too deep, now. You can't leave me anymore than I can leave you. So I hope you're ready to buckle up, cause it's gonna be a bumpy fucking ride."

NINETEEN

IT MADE CON ANGRY THAT DULCIE QUESTIONED HIM. HE QUESTIONED her about so little. For instance, her wanting to destroy the Foster home. She said it was for Frannie, so Con believed her. The fact that Jared Foster was Dulcie's ex-boyfriend didn't factor into it, she claimed, and Con believed that, too. Not that it was easy – Jared was the first boy she'd ever dated. First lots of things, he was sure. It wasn't fair. Con had only gotten to be first for one thing.

Though I'll definitely get to be the last.

So that she was questioning him and doubting things, it bothered him. Made him sad, as well. They did unspeakable things with each other and to each other. Barely even needed to speak and could still understand what the other was thinking. Was he the only one experiencing it?

When Con had grabbed the gun from Matt, the shot had burned the palm of his hand. While he cleaned the wound, Dulcie went about changing the sheets on her bed. She was a stickler for clean sheets, he'd noticed. She changed them out every afternoon, and every time they had sex.

She spent a lot of time doing laundry.

"Are you going to pout all night?" he asked, watching as she crawled under the top sheet and turned her back to him.

"I don't know. Are you going to tell me what I want to know?" she threw back at him. He rolled his eyes and moved onto the mattress.

"You're being childish," he informed her, sitting down. She snorted.

"I'm twenty-one. I'm allowed to be childish."

"That's debatable."

"If you have nothing to say, then you should stop talking."

Con took a deep breath and stretched out behind her. He stared at the back of her head for a moment, then reached out and touched his fingertips to her spine.

"The first time I saw you," he kept his voice soft. "I mean, *really* saw you, we were in eighth grade. They were having an award assembly for some basketball thing, I don't even remember. You were in the front row, and while everyone was clapping and cheering, you were drawing in a notebook. Then when it was my turn and they said my name, you looked up. First time in the whole assembly. You looked up and stared right at me."

"That long ago? You never talked to me," she pointed out. He nodded and continued moving his fingers over her vertebrae.

"I know. School ended, we went on vacation, all the usual stuff. Then I was a freshman, we were in different schools. I kind of forgot about you, but then my sophomore year, there you were again. We had an art class together, did you know that?"

That got her attention. She rolled around till she was facing him.

"*Liar.* I would've remembered."

"Okay, I wasn't *in* the class, I was a T.A., but still. The teacher kept me in his office, inputting grades, cleaning brushes, boring shit. One day, you left your sketchbook. Just got up and walked out without it," he told her.

"I remember – it was lunch time. I went back and the door was locked."

"Because I was inside looking through your book."

"Nosy."

"No shit. And it was like ... without even talking to you, I knew you knew me. It sounds fucking stupid, but that's how it felt. So before I even registered to you in your little Dulcie-world, I was having conversations with you in my head. You were just so shy back then, I was so worried I'd scare you. That I'd scare you and ruin us, and we'd never have a chance to be ... to be ..." he was at a loss for words.

"*Greatness.*"

See? You know me so well. Just trust that, and we'll get through this.

"Yeah. So you see? It feels like I've known you for so much longer than you've known me. I would go to all the art shows the school had, would sneak into the art room before football practice. I kept waiting for you to notice me, to *see me,* for you to get it. I almost began to think you never would. And then I saw the drawing you did of us, the shadow man and the little girl, and that was it. I didn't worry anymore. You weren't ready then, and you still weren't ready the following year, but I knew we'd be together," he let it all out.

"So you stalked me all through high school," she clarified.

"Kind of romantic, isn't it?"

"It's creepy as fuck."

"Yeah, exactly – *romantic.* Anyway, I'm telling you all this to help you understand me the way I understand you. You have catching up to do, and I -"

"Hey! I do not -"

"*You do.* I've long since accepted what we are. Crazy. Fucked up. *Murderers.* You haven't fully. Don't lie to me and say you have, because I know you haven't. And it's okay. I waited for you for years. I'll wait however long it takes," he assured her.

There was silence for a long moment and she stared up at him. He was kind of nervous. Admitting to stalking a girl and then basically stating he knew her better than she knew herself, there was a strong chance it wouldn't go over well. She could call the whole thing off. Could leave him alone in the darkness.

He wouldn't handle it well. He stared right back, memorizing the way she looked. Her eyes were huge amber pools, trying to drown him. She was naked, with the sheet pulled up to her collar bone, so only her smooth shoulders were exposed. She looked every bit her age, so young. So vulnerable. Just a stupid girl, trusting a very bad boy.

Please. Please trust me. Please understand me. Please let me love you in the only way I know how. Please don't let me destroy us.

"Tell me what happened to your father."

Her voice was soft, but like every other time, he just knew. Everything was okay. She wasn't scared of what he'd done. She wasn't afraid of him. She wasn't disgusted. She wanted to know, because they were together. Because they were partners. Because they were *lovers*.

"I killed him the night I came back," he stated. She didn't flinch. Barely even blinked.

"How did you do it?"

"I got home late at night, and he'd been drinking. He was mad because I was late. Started yelling. Cursing. And I was just so tired. So tired of pretending to be someone else. He kept shouting, and I was just staring at him. I remember, I was wondering if it would be weird if I called you. God, it was after midnight, it'd been three years since we'd last talked, and I was thinking of trying to call you. You've turned me into a puppy dog," he laughed.

"You did that all on your own, stud."

"He got mad that I wasn't scared. That always pissed him off. So he slapped me. I didn't do anything, so he did it again. Told me I was just like my mother, told me look what had happened to her, then he hit me again. It just set me off. She'd gone without a fight. I am *not* like her. So I pushed him and he fell down the stairs," he took a deep breath.

"The fall killed him?" Dulcie checked. He chuckled.

"No. Broke his arm, maybe a leg. He wouldn't shut the fuck up, he was sobbing when I got down there. I watched him for a while, he tried to crawl to the front door. Again, it's so stupid, but I thought of trying to find you. It's a small town, couldn't have been too hard. I didn't want to do that, not without you. But I was worried he'd get away, or get help, and then you and I wouldn't get a chance to get started. I did it for us," he explained why he'd done something so momentous without her.

"What did you do?"

"I put his head on the bottom stair and I stepped on his neck. *Snap*."

"Jesus."

"Quick and easy. Better than he deserved."

"Do you really think he killed your mother?"

"I don't care either way. I knew he would've become a problem for us at some point, would've stood in our way. I hated him. I never wanted to see him again, so I made damn sure I wouldn't."

There was a long silence. He'd just admitted to murdering his father. Not self-defense, not in a fair fight. He'd pushed a man down a set of stairs and he'd broken his neck. No going back now. Dulcie held his life in her hands. As he watched her, he realized how true that statement was; if she wanted to walk away, he wasn't sure how interested in life he'd be anymore.

Then she sighed and shifted forward. Her warm body pressed up against his, all her smooth skin flush with his rough clothing. Her head fit right underneath his jaw, and he could feel her nose in the hollow of his throat. He closed his eyes and wrapped his arms around her.

"I wish I'd been there," she whispered. He kissed the top of her head.

"You will be next time."

"Promise?"

"I promise. Now. I want to know everything you and Jared talk about."

TWENTY

DEEP BLUE EYES. THICK BROWN HAIR. LONG LEGS, BROAD SHOULDERS, and a *killer* smile.

They don't know the half of it.

Constantine knew his looks worked in his favor. Much the same way Ted Bundy's had worked in his; except Con had no interest in being a serial killer. He didn't even think of himself as *a* killer. He just didn't like obstructions, and human beings were little more than moving obstructions at the best of times.

A good looking man lured people into a false sense of security – particularly women. On top of his looks, he was also smart. Very smart. So he knew if he flashed the right kind of smiles, and said the right kind of words, he could get just about any damn thing he pleased. Dulcie was one of the few people who saw through his smile; she didn't buy any of his bullshit, she always demanded the truth. Everyone else, though, was fair game.

"*I was hoping to run into you.*"

Con smiled that perfect smile as Frannie McKey – no wait, *Foster*, he had to remember that – turned around. She obviously hadn't heard him come up behind her, and she looked absolutely shocked. As she should be; they were in a mall in a town about an hour outside of Fuller.

"Oh my gosh! Hi! What are you doing here?" she asked quickly.

"Just some shopping. Can't get anything decent at home," he commented. She laughed loudly.

"Oh god, I know. That stupid little town. I can't believe we bumped into each other like this! So good to see you again," she gushed, then leaned in and hugged him. Every inch of her body made contact with his and he held her tightly. High school really wasn't so far away, he could still remember her curves. Her skin, the little sounds she made when she was excited. Judging by the way she was shifting against him, she remembered, too.

"Yeah, it is. I kept thinking, that coffee we shared wasn't nearly enough. Wanna have dinner?" he asked, finally stepping back from her.

"*Of course!*" she responded before he'd fully finished talking. "I would love that, Con. When is good for you?"

"What are you doing tonight?"

He could've sworn she actually started panting.

"Nothing. Nothing at all. Are you staying here, or are you heading back home?" she asked.

"I was going to head home, but if I had something worthwhile to stay for, I could maybe stick around."

"Then I would *love* to have dinner with you tonight."

His smile got bigger.

She was staying at a Comfort Suites off the highway, closer to Fuller. He suggested they meet at an Applebee's. Not exactly candlelight and romance, but it was only a mile up the road from her hotel. Made life simpler, since neither of them wanted to be too far from her room.

When he got to the restaurant a little after eight, she was sitting at a high top table and was dressed to the nines. She was wearing a skin tight red dress – Dulcie had said Frannie was pregnant, but she wasn't showing at all. She looked *amazing*. She was all the things the universe required a cheerleader to be; tall, tan, and blonde. She had skinny hips and big tits, blue eyes and lips that were just made to be wrapped around a dick.

Tonight is going to be fun.

"I cannot get over how little you've changed," he laughed a while later, letting his eyes sweep up and down her form. She preened and smoothed her hands over her dress.

"Stop. I'm so fat now. I never should've had kids," she pouted. He chuckled.

"That's right. Kids. How is married life?" he asked, leaning back from the table as a waiter came to clear their empty plates. He'd had dinner while Frannie had picked at a salad. She'd talked *forever*, telling him all about her incredibly boring life – the people she hated, the job she hated, the customers she hated. Then she'd surprised him by ordering double desserts. So much for dinner being a quick in-and-out thing.

"So boring," she moaned. "I only did it cause Daddy said he'd cut me off if I had a baby outside of marriage."

"Well. Daddy's always right."

"I mean, Jared's nice and all, but he's just not ... y'know ..." her voice trailed off.

"Not enough?" he suggested. She let out a deep breath.

"*Yes.* I mean, how can anyone actually expect me to stay with him!? Look at me!" she insisted, gesturing to her body.

"I am. I have been all night," Con said, his eyes dipping down to her chest.

"We used to have a lot of fun in high school, right?" she asked, scooting her chair closer to him.

"God, yeah. Remember that time at Senior Sneak? In the woods?" he started laughing. She actually blushed.

"I used to hope you would come back and it could be like that again," she breathed, resting a hand on his thigh as she leaned close. "It *can* be like that again. You're staying, right?"

"C'mon, Frannie, you don't mean that," he told her.

"*I do.* I really, really do. What's to stop us?"

"Your husband, for one."

"Hasn't ever stopped me before."

"I don't know, it's such a small town. If anyone found out ..."

"No one will, and even if they did, *I'm* the one who's married – you're single, right? Nothing with that weird girl?"

"*Dulcie?*" he laughed loudly. "We're friends."

"Then there isn't a problem."

"You don't actually expect me to believe you'd cheat on your husband," he tried to call her bluff. Her hand moved up his thigh and cupped his crotch.

"I'd do anything you asked me to," she whispered.

"Then let's get out of here."

She'd barely managed to open the door to her hotel room before Con grabbed her from behind. He yanked her in a circle and pressed her against a wall. She seemed shocked, but he didn't give her a chance to process what was happening – he leaned close and kissed her hard, filling her mouth with his tongue.

"*God,* I missed this," she groaned when he moved to kiss her neck.

"When is your husband coming back?" he asked, his voice muffled as he buried his face in her cleavage.

"He's not ... he's not staying here. After the house got trashed, we stayed downtown for a while. But then he insisted on going home, so I came here," she explained, clawing at his jacket, yanking it down his arms

"Mmm, so we have the place to ourselves," Con's voice dropped into a growl and he grabbed the hem of her dress, his movements slow as he dragged the material up over her hips.

"All night. Every night. Any time you want. We could ... we could even go back to your place, sometime," she suggested. He chuckled and nipped at the edge of her shoulder. She wanted to worm her way into his house; worm her way into becoming the next Mrs. Masters.

"Could be fun. Remember after the homecoming game, when I brought you to my room for the first time?" he asked. She giggled.

"How could I forget? That was the first time a boy ever made me come."

"Let's see if we can reenact it tonight."

His hand was in her underwear, his middle finger finding its way inside her. She yelped and moaned, her fingers digging into his shoulders. He went back to kissing her neck, then sucked on her earlobe. Remembered all her old favorites.

"You're still so good," she groaned.

"You have no idea."

He pulled away then, but didn't stop kissing her as he walked backwards. She followed along till they got to the bed. Then he abruptly sat down. He kissed around the edge of her hip, then pulled her underwear down her legs. When she stepped free of them, he yanked her onto him so she was straddling his lap. His hand wound up back underneath her, and this time he wasn't being coy. Two fingers thrust in and out of her while his thumb rubbed in circles, sending her back to that long ago night in high school.

Frannie went nuts. She rode his fingers like it was the best sex of her life, which was really kind of sad. She had her hands in her hair, she was shrieking his name, and she was arching her back. It was picture perfect. He couldn't have made it look more erotic if he'd tried.

I swear, the universe always manages to unfold in my favor.

Dulcie glanced at her watch. Ten o'clock. Then she sat for another hour, drumming her fingers on the table top, before looking at her watch again.

10:05. Fuck me.

"Hey, sorry about that."

Jared smiled apologetically as he slid into the seat across from her. She smiled brightly at him.

"Oh, no worries. You had to call your babysitter, totally understandable."

They'd been at dinner for over two hours. Dulcie hadn't even want-ed to be there that long, but Jared seemed to be excited just to get out of his house. She was glad she could make him feel better, provide him with some escape, but her generosity had its limits. She was tired, she was bored, and she wanted to go home.

"You seem kind of distracted," his voice interrupted her thoughts. She shook her head.

"Me? No," she started, but the look on his face stopped her. "Just a lot on my mind, I'm sorry."

"Is it Constantine?" he asked.

"Why would you say that?" she was curious.

"I just remember things were kind of weird between you guys in school, and now he's back, and I've seen you two around town together. Is he your boyfriend?" Jared kept on with the questions. She frowned and began to nervously fiddle with her hair. She wasn't quite sure how best to answer the question.

"No, he's not my boyfriend. He's ... something else," she mumbled.

"Sounds ... complicated," he replied, and she snorted.

"You don't even know the half of it. Sometimes things are a little *intense,*" she stressed the last word.

"I'm not surprised. Everyone was always in love with him, but I always thought he was kind of weird."

"Really?"

"Yeah. Just the way he was in school, kind of closed off."

"Huh. I never noticed," her voice dropped into a whisper.

"Dulcie," Jared started, and his voice dropped low. "I know you said I can always talk to you, and I just want you to know, the feeling is mu-tual. If something is going on with him, if he's treating you bad, you can tell me. We have a spare bedroom, it's always open."

Dulcie almost burst out laughing. She managed to keep it at a gig-gle-level.

"Thank you, but it's fine, I promise. Besides, I don't think your sweet and generous wifey would particularly like me trespassing," she teased. Jared rolled his eyes.

"*Wifey* has been staying at the Comfort Suites. To be honest, I'm not sure when she's coming home," he sighed. Dulcie gasped.

"How awful! I'm so sorry! I always thought you two were so perfect together," she told him, then reached out and grabbed his hand.

"Really?"

"Yeah. I mean, like when I would see you in the store, or here at the club. You guys look so good together, and your baby is, like, the cutest thing ever. You're both always smiling. It seemed nice," she told him. He finally gave her a wistful smile.

"Yeah, Amy is adorable. Frannie and I may not always get along, but we sure make a damn good baby together," he chuckled. Dulcie nodded.

"You did. You *do* – you have another one on the way," she reminded him.

"Yeah, we do," his voice was softer still. Dulcie licked her lips and leaned in close.

"Look, Jared, I know you thought coming here yesterday, us having dinner, that it might be something. But it's not," she started, then held up her hand when he went to interject. "You're married. And you're a good guy. A good *man*. And a man doesn't just give up on his wife and children. I meant what I said, I'm here for you, *as a friend*, but you need to be there for her, *as her husband*."

When his eyes glassed over with tears, Dulcie almost gagged. Jesus, the man was a pussy. But he sniffled and nodded and managed to keep the crying at bay. He told her she was right about everything, and said he owed it to Frannie to keep trying. He owed it to their kids. He wasn't the type of guy to cheat on his wife, and he wasn't about to become one.

They hugged, then made their way out to the parking lot. He walked her to her car and gave her another hug. A long one; it felt like she was in his arms forever. Then he finally pulled away and thanked her again. But before he got into his own car, he called out to her one last time.

"Remember what I said, too. Constantine's not normal, don't fall for him the way everyone else does," he warned her. She smiled at him.

"I don't intend to."

Dulcie was pretty sure no one had ever fallen for anyone the way she'd fallen for Con.

By the time she pulled up to his big house, it was almost eleven o'clock at night. She let herself into the house and called out a greeting, but no one answered. She went upstairs, but it was empty as well.

She wandered around Con's room for a bit. He'd moved into the master suite, it was where he kept all his clothing, but his old bedroom still held his life from before; pennants and ribbons and awards on the wall. Pictures and books on shelves. His letterman jacket was still draped across the back of a chair.

She laid on his bed and wondered what it would've been like to lay there in high school. To have dated the star quarterback, to have been the envy of all the girls. Would she have done it? At that Halloween dance so long ago, would she have let him take her home, let him take her virginity in that same bed?

Well, you gave it to him in a dirty old truck, not exactly a whole lot better.

She sat up and swung her legs over the side of the bed. She figured nosiness didn't really apply to them and she yanked open the drawer on his nightstand. She almost laughed as the standard stash of porno mags came into view, but then something stopped her. She reached under the stack of magazines and pulled out a piece of paper. It was thick stock, not regular notebook paper, and the moment her fingertips touched it, she knew what it was.

It was a picture she'd drawn. When and where, she couldn't be sure. Probably at school. It was wrinkled and creased, a throw away. She'd balled it up at some point and tossed it into a trash can. It was detailed sketch of a schooner, nothing special, yet Con must have fished it out and kept it. She smiled and smoothed her fingers across the picture.

Also in the drawer was his senior yearbook. She turned to his color portrait and had a full on girly moment over how good he looked. Then she flipped through the pages, laughing at some of the notes and signatures people had written for him. But when she got to her own picture, she paused.

The small black and white photo had been circled in red, and not just once, but dozens of times. He'd gone round and round with a marker, over and over. Multiple times, and she was guessing not all at once. Enough times that there was an indentation in the paper, and for several pages behind it. In the center of the red circle, her unsmiling face peered out of the page, which wasn't abnormal in itself – Dulcie wasn't a big smiler. No, what was unusual was the fact that her eyes had been completely blacked out with a pen.

You weren't ready for me to see you, but you were too late – I knew what you were from the beginning.

She carried the yearbook and the drawing back into the master suite. She left them on the dresser, then went and took a hot shower. When she came back into the room, she called out again. Listened for an answer that she never got. She frowned and walked over to the closet. She put on the first shirt she grabbed, a pastel pink polo shirt that was frayed at the collar. She pulled it into place at the top of her thighs, then she sat at the foot of the bed.

And she waited.

Where the fuck is he!?

TWENTY-ONE

CON HEARD THE FOOTSTEPS BEFORE HE SAW ANYONE, AND HE breathed out a sigh of relief. He wasn't sure how much longer he could've gone on for – Frannie was perilously close to coming, and he couldn't have that, but he couldn't pull away, either. She'd expect him to start getting naked. So he kept teasing her as much as he could, and was beyond happy when he realized someone was standing in the open doorway.

"*What. The. Fuck.*"

Jared Foster actually didn't look too mad. If anything, he looked blank. Devoid of emotion. His wife was straddling another man's lap, grinding against that man's hand, and still. Jared just stared into the room.

Frannie shrieked and fell backwards off Con. He smiled and rubbed his hands down the front of his pants.

"Hey, man, how's it going?" he asked in a nonchalant voice. Jared turned to look at him, and finally there was a spark in his eyes. Some anger. Some fire.

"Can you leave? I need to have a private moment with *my wife*," he hissed. Frannie scrambled to her feet while shoving her dress into place.

"Honey, I know what this looks like ... Con and I, we're old friends,

172 pages172

we just -"

"Shut up, Frannie."

"You left me here, and it was only dinner, and it's not what you think -"

"Shut. Up."

"What did you think would happen!? You just left me out here, you don't understand what it's been like without -"

"*Shut the fuck up, Frannie!*"

Con had been in the middle of pulling on his jacket and he paused, his eyes bouncing between the couple. Jared's face was red, his eyes full of venom. Frannie couldn't seem to decide whether she wanted to look bitchy or pathetic. Con stood up and got between them.

"Hey, no need to yell, you're freaking her out," he said.

"Are you serious? Get the fuck out, Constantine!" Jared shouted, then pointed out the door.

"Fine. But take it easy on her, she's just a chick. Frannie," Con turned his attention to her as he walked backwards out the door. "If you need anything, don't hesitate to come see me."

Her face lit up like Christmas Day, and Con moved into the hallway as Jared started shouting again. The damage had been done, there was nothing more he could do, so he simply went downstairs and headed out to the parking lot.

When he finally pulled up in front of his house, it was almost midnight. The entire downstairs was dark, but when he got inside, he could see lights glowing upstairs. He stopped to use a bathroom, then hurried up the stairs, calling out as he headed towards the bedroom.

"*I thought you were going to be gone all night.*"

He paused in the doorway to take off his jacket, and he took in the sight. Dulcie was laying at the end of the bed, with her knees raised up and her feet on the edge of the mattress. She was wearing an old polo shirt of his and nothing else. She didn't bother to look up as he walked towards her.

"Took longer than I thought," was all he said, then he tossed his jacket into a nearby chair. She nodded, but still didn't look at him.

"Did you sleep with her?"

"Ooohhh, is that jealousy I detect?" he made fun of her, then pushed down on her knees. Her feet dropped to the floor and he crawled up so he was laying alongside her.

"Just answer the question, Con."

He propped himself up on his elbow and looked down at her. She kept her eyes on the ceiling. Her hair looked a little damp, and her face was devoid of make up, making her look even younger than normal. He put his finger on the side of her jaw and forced her to look at him.

"I did *exactly* what you told me to do," he informed her, then he leaned in and kissed the side of her neck.

"Tell me everything," she instructed him.

"I waited at her hotel and followed her to the mall," he started to explain, basically rehashing the plan they'd come up with the other night, after he'd confessed to killing his dad. "Convinced her to have dinner with me. The woman talked *forever*, took me a while to get her back on track."

"What time did you get to her hotel?"

"I don't know, like eleven."

"Jesus, Jared left the club at around ten-thirty. Cutting it a little close, Romeo."

"Hey, you're the one who told me to be subtle," he reminded her. "I even got her to invite me back, had her convinced it was her idea."

"So smooth," she teased, pursing her lips at him.

"I know, right? I impress myself."

"What next, lover boy."

"We got to her hotel room and I shoved my tongue down her throat. That's pretty much all it took, I could've done anything I wanted to the girl," he said. Dulcie went back to staring at the ceiling.

"Bummer for you."

"Hey, this was *your* plan, remember?"

"Did you fuck her?"

"No," he answered plainly, and she smiled.

"Good boy. So what all went down?" she asked.

"I sat on the bed and she straddled me. Jared walked in on us like that, she was fucking my fingers like it was her job. She just about had a panic attack when she realized she was caught," he answered. Dulcie's eyes fluttered shut and she let out a sigh.

"I wish I'd been there. I miss all the fun stuff," she breathed.

"Oh, yeah. Super fun," he joked, moving his hand over her body and pushing the shirt up her stomach.

"If you'd spent the night like I had, you'd be jealous, too," she assured him.

"Okay then, next time, you get to finger the girl in the relationship we're trying to break up," he told her.

"I'd prefer that – he almost started crying at one point. I can't handle that shit," she grumbled.

"Hey, I'm not arguing. You wanna be with another woman, I'm all for it," he whispered, placing his hand flat on her abdomen. Her skin jumped and started at his touch, then he made his way to the valley between her breasts.

"What else happened?" she asked, her voice little more than a sigh. He leaned in close and bit down on the side of her jaw before sucking on the pulse point in her neck.

"She tried to play it off, he yelled at her, standard stuff," he mumbled into her skin. He pressed himself up against her side and began sliding his hand back down her body. Before he could reach her legs, though, she grabbed his wrist and stopped him.

"Did you wash your hands?" she asked, her voice loud in the quiet room. He laughed.

"Excuse me?"

"It's bad enough you had to touch her -"

"*Your* idea."

"- but I'm certainly not letting you touch me if you're still stained with her," Dulcie finished. He kept laughing and kissed down the side of her arm.

"*Yes*, I washed my hands. Twice," he promised, then he moved so he was on top of her. He braced his hands on either side of her head and pushed himself up.

"Maybe you should shower," she suggested. He playfully glared at her.

"I have an idea. Do you trust me?" he asked.

"Hmmm, have to think on that one ..."

Con didn't wait for her to answer, he crawled off her and walked over to the closet. It took a bit of digging before he found something suitable, and when he moved back over to the bed, he was holding a handful of old computer cables and telephones wires.

Dulcie stared at him with wide eyes, but didn't say anything when he grabbed her arms. Didn't resist when he stretched them out above her head and tied her wrists together. He figured that was as good as an actual answer, so he ran a cable from the headboard to her bindings and knotted them all together. If she rolled from side to side, she would be able to fall off the bed and stand up, but she wouldn't be getting loose anytime soon.

"Are you scared now?" he whispered, leaning over her again. She took a shaky breath.

"I could never be scared of you," she whispered back.

He kissed her then. It felt like it had been a long time since his lips had touched hers. Probably because they'd spent the whole day apart, the first since they'd been together. Being with Frannie hadn't helped at all, it had just made it worse. No one kissed like Dulcie, no one tasted like her. When she wrapped her legs around his waist, he groaned and let himself fall flat on her, the bulge in his pants fitting squarely against her very naked crotch.

"I am going to spend hours feasting on you," he growled into her ear, and he could feel her shiver at his words.

"God, that sounds amazing. Yes, yes I want that."

He smiled.

"Good."

Then he shoved himself up and walked into the bathroom.

Con took a long, hot shower, scrubbing every inch of his body. She'd had made a good point, he did need to bathe after being with Frannie. She'd sullied him, and Dulcie deserved to touch something pristine.

When he finally walked back into the bedroom, it was to find Dulcie rolling from side to side. She was muttering under her breath and yanking on her restraints. When she noticed him, she glared.

"What the fuck, Con?" she snapped. He pulled on a pair of pants and moved to the side of the mattress.

"You don't like it?" he asked, running his fingers along the taught telephone wire that stretched from her wrists to other end of the bed.

"Not when you leave me like this for half an hour! If you're not going to fuck me, then let me go," she insisted. He crossed his arms over his chest.

"You didn't say please."

She spit on him.

As punishment, he held her thighs open as wide as they would go and went down on her like he was starving. When she was crying his name, begging him for an orgasm, he stood up again. He gave her a messy kiss, then even as she was leaning in for another one, he turned and walked out of the room.

Her curses followed him all the way downstairs, but he ignored her. She begged and pleaded, faked crying, called him every dirty name he'd ever heard, and eventually moved on to bribing. She threw out some very interesting suggestions, but he stayed strong and wouldn't respond. Besides, he also knew he could do anything to her any time he wanted, so sexual bribes weren't very effective.

The windows in the living room faced out over a long driveway, and during the day, he could see clear to the street. It was night time, and though he couldn't see anything in the pitch black, he pulled a dining room chair up to the windows and sat down. He stared out into the darkness and listened to Dulcie's voice as it began to grow hoarse.

She was an amazing woman, and her evil, malicious little plot to end Jared and Frannie's marriage had been pretty dastardly, but still. Con couldn't let her one up him. He still had a couple hands to play. So even though it got later, and his raging hard on was growing to an epic level of uncomfortable, he still didn't move. He shoved his hands down his pants, trying to readjust, giving his cock a few slow strokes while he listened to her voice. Then he stopped. He didn't want to ruin all the fun before it even got started.

By the time he saw lights out on the street, Dulcie had grown quiet. He stood up and stared outside for a moment longer, then he grabbed something out of the kitchen and headed back up the stairs. Wondered if his captive had fallen asleep.

She had moved up the bed, loosening the slack on the chord, but it still wasn't long enough to allow her to touch herself. Her head had gotten buried under the pillows and he watched for a second while she rubbed her legs together, obviously seeking some kind of friction to relieve the pressure he'd built up in her.

"Doing okay?" he practically yelled, startling her. She tried to lift her head, but the pillows didn't move.

"*Mo fock yarshelf.*"

He grabbed her by the ankle and yanked her down the bed. She cried out when her bindings pulled tight, jerking painfully against her wrists. He slowly crawled over her, and though she was glaring, her legs very willingly parted for him.

"Listening to you scream and beg, I almost did just that," he informed her. She strained her body towards his, trying to rub her breasts against his chest.

"What were you doing down there? I've been *dying*," she moaned.

"*Do you trust me?*"

He'd asked the question earlier and she hadn't answered. Now he stared down at her, into her wide amber eyes. It wasn't really fair to ask right then, she was so turned on, she almost looked drugged. But she focused on him and she took a deep breath.

"I … I do," she finally answered. He sighed.

"Such a good girl, Dulcie."

He'd dropped the item he'd brought with him onto the bed and he felt around for it. When he finally found it and lifted it into view, Dulcie's eyes got even wider as she took in the knife he held.

"Oh my, what big fangs you have," she whispered. He chuckled and pressed the dull side of the blade to her cheek.

"Still trust me?"

"*Always.*"

He reached over her and cut through the chords around her wrist. She didn't hesitate, she just immediately wrapped her arms around his neck. He dropped the knife and it bounced off the bed, making a clanging noise as it hit the hardwood floor.

She was biting down on his shoulder when he pulled away, causing her teeth to scrape painfully across his skin. It didn't slow him down though, and he grabbed her arm, yanking her up so she had to move onto her knees.

"This is an awful color," he commented as he roughly pulled the polo shirt off her.

"It's your shirt," she panted, pushing his pants down his legs. He stepped out of them, then knelt on the bed in front of her. She kept trying to wrap her arms around him, but he was shifting and moving, sliding against her and kissing his way around her shoulders.

"I just want you to remember that," he whispered, lifting her hair away from her back and lightly touching her neck.

"Your awful taste in clothing?" she joked.

"No, that you said you trust me."

"I do. What was that noise? Did you -"

He didn't give her a chance to finish. His hand went around her neck and he shoved her down flat on the mattress. Then he grabbed the side of her hip and held on, forcing her to keep her ass in the air. He shoved his dick into her without any ceremony, no attempt at foreplay, but it didn't matter. Her little time-out had worked wonders for turning her on and he felt zero resistance as he slid himself to a snug fit.

She tried to push herself up onto her hands, but he leaned forward and pressed down on her shoulders, forcing her to keep her head flat on the bed. Then he pummeled her ass, fucking her as hard as possible. She screamed at first as he bottomed out, then she just whimpered. Moaned his name. Began bucking her hips back against him.

Con was impressed by his unique ability to know what would and wouldn't work with her. They'd never played with bondage, but he'd just known it would get her riled up. Taking away her toys and leaving her all alone. She'd be coming in no time flat, and he was so worked up, he knew he'd be right behind her. As he watched a shadow fall across the hallway outside the open bedroom door, he smirked to himself and grabbed a fistful of her hair.

"Good girl Dulcie, does everything I say," he hissed as he jerked back, forcing her upright. She cried out and one of her hands reached out to a bed post, using it to keep her balance. He let go of her hair and ran his hand over her hip.

"Yes, yes, anything you say," she was gasping for air as she turned her face to look at him.

"Do you have any idea how perfect you are?" he sighed into her ear, slowing his thrusts, but increasing their intensity.

"Only when I'm with you," she managed to answer, then gave him a deep kiss.

"Perfect breasts," he whispered, his hand going to her chest and playing with her nipples. "Perfect body." Again his fingers splayed across her stomach. "And the most beautiful pussy I have *ever* fucked."

When he touched the aforementioned pussy, she let out a sob and a massive shudder shut down her body for a moment. It was at that same time she turned her head forward and noticed they had a visitor.

It could have gone poorly, but Con's instincts proved right once again – when Dulcie saw Frannie standing in the doorway, her body erupted in an orgasm of apocalyptic proportions. She moaned low in her throat and started shaking. She lost her grip on the bedpost and fell forward, into the same position she'd been in at the start – face down, ass up. Her body seized around his cock, halting his movements, and while he stared Frannie in the eye, he came inside of Dulcie.

"What the fuck is going on here!?" the blonde screeched. Con had his hands gripping Dulcie's waist, his head bent forward, and he was struggling to catch his breath.

"Love the likes of which you've never experienced," Dulcie finally whispered.

"But ... we were ... I thought you and I were ..." Frannie's voice trailed off, and Con finally lifted his head. She was staring at him, looking equal parts shocked and confused.

"You and I were never anything. I thought maybe if you witnessed something this perfect, you could fully understand that," Con managed to explain as he knelt upright once again. With his weight off her back, Dulcie finally slid away till she laying flat on her stomach, her legs on either side of him. Frannie's eyes skated over his naked form and he smiled at her.

"Then what was tonight all about?" she demanded, clutching her purse to her chest, as if the overpriced bag could somehow protect her from the horrifying scene she was witnessing.

"This. Just this," he sighed, running his fingers down Dulcie's calf. She twitched, then slowly rolled away from him and onto her back.

"I cannot believe I let you touch me, and you're choosing *that* over me," Frannie shrieked. "You're sick. You two are FREAKS, you did this on purpose. I think you're disgusting."

"Geez, *Fran*, keep talking sexy like that and you might turn me on," Dulcie said in a snide tone.

"I'm going to be sick. I can't ... I just can't. I *cannot*," Frannie actually started crying, and she turned and hurried away from the door. They listened as she pounded down the stairs, and both smiled when they heard the front door slam shut.

"You were outstanding," Con groaned, dropping down and planting a kiss between Dulcie's breasts.

"You know," she started as he stretched out at her side. "When you asked me if I trusted you, I thought it was about the knife. I thought you wanted to cut me."

"Oh no. No knife. Not this time. I wanted to do something that would cause permanent damage," he sighed, cupping her breast in his hand. He could feel her heartbeat, feel how fast it was racing.

"You could've told me, let me prepare," she pointed out. He chuckled and leaned close to kiss the side of her chest.

"And ruin the fun? It was my little treat for you. The last nail in the coffin," he explained, trailing his tongue across her nipple and then watching it tighten up.

"How sweet," she whispered, and he realized she was still staring at the ceiling. He scooted up and kissed underneath her ear.

"I knew you'd love it," he whispered back, and listened as she took a ragged breath.

"I did. I *do*. I love everything you do."

"And that's why you're such a good girl."

"But now everyone will know. About us."

"I *want* everyone to know. By the time we're done in this town, they'll never be able to forget us."

Her eyes fell shut again.

"*Promise?*"

"*I promise.*"

TWENTY-TWO

DULCIE COULD FEEL THE CHANGE THE MOMENT SHE WALKED INTO work. When she went out onto the floor, she could tell people were staring at her. Frannie had probably started making phone calls the moment she'd left Con's house, and then had all Monday to gossip about the incident. Fuller was a very small town, news spread fast. But Dulcie just narrowed her eyes and barked at people to get back to work, knowing that at least in the restaurant, no one would dare to question her about it.

Well, almost no one.

"Heard some crazy shit about you today," David said the moment she went behind the bar.

"Fascinating," was her only response as she dropped off a case of wine.

"You told me you weren't dating that Con dude," he pointed out. She nodded.

"I know."

"But I heard ..."

"Heard what?"

"Heard some *stuff.*"

She turned away from what she was doing and fully faced him.

"If you have the balls to bring it up, then at least have the balls to say it," she told him. "Heard *what*, David? That someone walked in on us having sex? That I was fucking him? Yeah, that all happened, but last I checked, sex didn't equal dating someone, and even if it did, I'm still not sure how it's any of your business."

David looked shocked. At her demeanor, at her tone of voice. He'd only ever seen at-work-Dulcie. He'd never seen the real Dulcie, and now that he was getting a glimpse, he didn't seem to like her too much.

"Jesus, what's gotten into you?" he asked in a soft voice. She rolled her eyes.

"Did you also hear that we were in a house, in a bedroom? It wasn't exactly on the side of the street – she came in, uninvited, and then went running all over town. What he and I do is private."

And I ain't just whistlin' Dixie …

"You've changed. Remember, I said it the other week? I bet it's this guy. Don't change for some guy, Dulcie," David urged her.

"I'm not changing for some guy, we're just -"

"*You are.* Look, I heard some other stuff, too. Stuff he was doing right before he was doing you. You deserve better than that," he stressed. She narrowed her eyes.

"You know," Dulcie slid her hip along the side of the counter, moving so she was right in front of him. "This is super cute. I get it. Big bad boy comes back to town, you save the girl, I start sleeping with you, right? *Wrong.* I wouldn't fuck you if you begged me to, and nothing will *ever* change that. So how about you keep your mouth shut, don't talk about shit you don't know anything about, and make the goddamn drinks."

Again, a look of shock covering his face. She stared at him for a moment longer, almost daring him to speak, but when it was obvious he wouldn't, she turned and walked away.

Everyone avoided her after that – all her orders were obeyed without a word, no one tried to chat her up or asked her any questions. The doors opened and things returned to normal for a bit. Most of their regulars were older people, fifties and above, who either didn't have time for gossip, or just didn't care. She was only a lowly waiter in their eyes.

Still. David's questioning had just been a precursor to a bigger moment that was coming, she knew. As the hours went by, she prayed that maybe it would wait till the end of the night, after closing. But no such luck.

A little after eight o'clock, Jared strode through the restaurant, and he *did not* look happy. Dulcie was just coming out of the office when she saw him, and she quickly hurried to intercept him.

"I am *at work,* Jared," she hissed, holding up her hands. "Can we *please* do this later?"

"Was it on purpose!?" he demanded.

"What!? What are you talking about? Stop, come in here," she said, then grabbed his hand and dragged him to the office. He stopped in the doorway, though, and refused to budge.

"You know what I'm talking about, Dulcie. What the fuck is going on!? Why would you do something like that to me?"

"To you!? Jared, she walked in on *us!* Do you have an idea how embarrassing it was?" Dulcie pointed out. That seemed to surprise him and he frowned for a moment.

"Still. You told me he wasn't your boyfriend, and -"

"I said it was complicated. Remember?"

"Yeah, looks real fucking complicated. I walk in on him fucking my wife, then find out an hour later, he was fucking you," Jared snarled. Now it was Dulcie's turn to pause. She hoped he didn't notice.

"You saw them having sex?" she checked.

"Close enough! What the fuck, Dulcie? After your little pep talk, I raced off to tell her she needed to come home, but instead I walked into the room to find him practically elbow deep inside her," he broke everything down. She let out a deep breath.

"Look, Con is entitled to do whatever he wants, and if that means having sex with me and messing around with other people, then he can do that," she told him.

"This is not 'other people'! This is *my wife!* He's not entitled to 'do' my wife!" Jared yelled, and she winced. The office was at one end of the bar and opened directly onto the floor. Their interaction would not go unnoticed.

"Sounds to me like that's something you should be explaining to your wife."

Jared's eyes got wide and he stared at her. It was like he was just realizing he had no clue who the person in front of him was; that he'd never actually met Dulcie.

"Do you even care?" he whispered, then cleared his throat. "My marriage is over, and he was a part of that. He told her if she needed him, to come find him. And what did she do? She went there an hour later and found him – *with you.*"

Dulcie should've felt bad. Jared had never really done anything wrong, he wasn't a bad guy. She couldn't muster up the proper feelings, though. She was annoyed and she was angry and she was so very tired.

"Yeah, Jared. *Your wife* went to the home of the man you had just caught her cheating with, *THAT'S* the important part of the story. Not what or who *he* was doing," she snapped.

"Believe me, I know that's important. What the fuck is his deal with me? What did I ever do to him?" he demanded. She threw up her hands.

"Are you serious? *He's irrelevant.* How can you not see that? What the fuck is wrong with you? She's a disgusting human being who's been fucking other men for years, but *now* you have an issue? Because it's Con? Because it's me? Your wife is a cum dumpster who left you for a guy who doesn't even care about her, yet you're here yelling at me? *That's* fucked up. I'm nothing to you, Jared," she was almost yelling by the end. He looked blown away.

"What is that supposed to mean!? You're not nothing to me," he insisted. She took another deep breath.

"Let me rephrase it – *you're* nothing to *me*. You don't exist to me. Why are you here? For a pity party? Well you came to the wrong place, because I don't care. I don't care what your wife did or how your marriage is ending or how bad Con made you feel. Your wife has treated me like shit for years, and you never said a word. Now that paradise is rocky and the magnificent Constantine is showing me attention again, suddenly I'm an option? Get fucked, Jared. Though you should probably get tested first, because safety doesn't seem like a high priority for your wife when she's *fucking anything that moves.*"

The entire restaurant was silent and Dulcie could hear as a fork fell onto a plate.

"This isn't you," Jared mumbled, taking a step back. "He's done something to you. He ruins things, and he's ruining you. He did this on purpose, I know it. He did it to end my marriage, and then he made sure Frannie saw you two together. You just can't see it."

*See it? I **orchestrated** it. Con is just the star of the show – I'm the producer.*

"If you need to tell yourself that to help you sleep better at night, Jared, then okay. Because you know what? Con sleeps perfectly fine, and I know that for *a fact*," she kept her tone snide.

That one cut deep. It was obvious that for the most part, Jared assumed she was an innocent bystander. Just a stupid girl, caught up in Constantine's sick little games. Blinded by his beauty, lost in love with him. But rubbing in the fact she was sleeping with him, it ruined the image a little bit. Made it harder to ignore the fact that maybe, just maybe, Con wasn't the only big bad wolf lurking around.

"This is wrong, and you know it. You don't mean any of this. What has he been saying to you? Just come with me, Dulcie. Come stay at my house, I can make sure -"

She burst out laughing. A loud, harsh sound. More like a cackle.

"Is that a fucking joke? *Come stay with you!?* Jesus, I'd rather just slit my wrists now and get it over with. You know what, fuck this. Fuck this place, fuck this town, and fuck you."

Part of the uniform at the Blue Rock was a small black apron that all but covered the short skirts they wore. She yanked it off as she talked, then threw it in his face. While he stood there, stunned, she shoved him out of the way and stomped out of the office.

"Dulcie, maybe you should -" David was talking under his breath as she moved past him, and he reached out to grab her arm. She yanked away and continued on her war path.

"What's the matter?" she yelled, turning in a circle as she walked and looking over the whole room, at the staring customers. "You all just love to whisper about shit, but when it's in your face, suddenly you've got nothing to say? Cat got your tongue? C'mon! Can't you say any-thing? *Why can't you say anything!?* Jesus, none of you are real! None of you are actually alive, and you're all just too stupid to even fucking realize it!"

She was shrieking by the end of her rant, but she couldn't help it. She'd spoken the truth, and the truth was not meek. It was bold and it was brash, it knocked down doors and bellowed through hallways. Raced down train tracks and burned down buildings. Screaming it was like ripping a hole into reality. She may have been a wallflower, but most of the time, she felt like she was the only real thing around her. A 3D image in a cardboard cutout town. People just slid past her in their fake existence, not seeing her because she wasn't in their dimension. She was on a higher plane.

As she ripped her hair out of its bun and stalked out of the build-ing, she did realize one thing. There was a very distinct possibility she was also completely insane.

So what'll it be? Exist on a higher plane from mere mortals and be crazy? Or retain some sanity and live amongst the flat people of the word?

TWENTY-THREE

"**D**ULCIE."

She burrowed further under her blanket.

"*Duuuuuulcie.*"

She squeezed her eyes shut tight.

"Why are you shutting me out?"

Con was on the other side of her apartment door. He could walk in at any moment, the thing was still busted. One solid hit and it would fall back off its hinges. Still, he stayed on his side and she listened as he scratched at the wood.

After her epic freak out, she'd gotten in her car and driven off. A half hour was a long time to sit with all the thoughts pinging around in her head. Constantine, her, the things they did together. The things they did apart. Was it growing into something great? Or was it all spiraling out of control? Con was playing a game, Jared had seen it from a mile away, and sure, Dulcie had arranged the game, had picked out the players. But Con had gone a step above and beyond her. Really dug salt into the wound. And he'd done it all without saying a word to her. Just like with his dad. Just like with leaving town. She'd never left Con in the dark, about anything, but he loved to let her wallow in it. Loved to leave her blind.

Oh, what big eyes you have …

After a couple more minutes of her ignoring him, he did push in the door. She listened as he shoved it to the side, then propped it back over the doorway. Then his footsteps, ominous in their slow approach to her bed. She had her back to him and she stayed under the sheet, curled into a ball.

"Little girl, what are we going to do with you?" he sighed, then she felt the mattress dip down as he laid behind her.

"What's wrong with me?" she whispered. His arm wrapped around her middle, then he slid her across the bed, pulling her into his chest.

"Ah, yes. I heard about your little explosion, a friend called me. His dad witnessed the whole thing."

"Awesome. I hope he recorded it."

"Don't be like this," Con urged, squeezing her tight. "Talk to me. We're in this together."

"No," she snapped. "No, we're not. Was anyone busting your balls about our little peep show last night? *Didn't think so.*"

"That's what you're upset about? You seemed pretty happy about it last night," he laughed at her.

"Still. I didn't know it was going to happen, I didn't get a say in it, and now I'm having to deal with it. He was yelling at me, did you hear that? In front of everyone. I don't like being part of a scene," she informed him.

"Really? Cause I think screaming at everyone and saying they're basically the walking dead is kinda creating a scene."

"I was angry, and frustrated, and *pissed off.* First thing when I got there, David – the bartender – was giving me shit, asking about us, and I don't know what to say, cause what the fuck are we?" she asked.

"That's what's bothering you?" Con sounded surprised.

"No. *Yes.* And I was alone, *again,* dealing with these questions about you, and not knowing what to say," she tried to explain it.

"Don't say anything. You don't owe anything to anyone, Dulcie. I told you to quit your job," he reminded her, and she listened as he moved to sit up, his back against the window behind them.

"Easy for you to say, *Daddy's boy*."

Her voice held a lot of venom, but Con just laughed at her again.

"I like that. Make sure you scream it out when we're having sex later tonight."

"Fuck off. And then Jared showed up halfway through the night and started freaking out in front of customers. I don't think he even really cared about Frannie cheating on him, he just cared because it was with you. That I was sleeping with you. You, you, you. I wanted to rip my hair out," she kept explaining.

"Ah. I see now. Little girl is jealous," he chuckled. She rolled over and from under the blanket, she punched him in the leg.

"I'm not jealous!" she shouted, continuing to hit him. "I'm angry because I have to deal with bullshit while you lead some life of luxury, doing god knows what during the day! That you make plans and do things and have thoughts without me! I'm upset because I … I …"

She ran out of words, but she still kept hitting. Con was laughing again, and he finally reached down and grabbed her. He wrestled around with her form and finally got his arms around her. She struggled as he lifted her, blankets and all, and deposited her on his lap.

"I know what your problem is," he said, pulling the blanket away from her head. Then his arms locked around her, cradling her to him and preventing her from getting away.

"*You're* my problem," she complained, refusing to look at him. It was the truth. Things at once seemed clearer yet murkier when she was around Con. Were they in the dark together? Or was he blinding her? Swallowing her whole?

"You don't care about your job, so quitting isn't a big deal," Con continued, his voice dropping low. "And the bartender is nobody to us, so obviously you can't be upset over him. You *enjoyed* what we did to Jared, so don't even try to tell me that's an issue."

"I don't know why I speak, when clearly you know me so much better than I know myself," she grumbled, pressing her cheek to his chest.

"I do," he agreed with her, and she felt his chin come to rest on top of her head.

"Then tell me, Mr. Masters. What is my problem? Why am I so upset? Why didn't I want to see you tonight?" she asked. He laughed again, and it reminded her of a snake rattling its tail.

"You're worried because you just cut a very big tie with your old world. You're upset because you think you might be in love with me and you don't know what that means. You're scared because you think I don't love you back."

Dulcie held her breath for a second.

"Ah. You do know me better than I know myself," she whispered. He nodded against her.

"I know. It's very frustrating."

"Why?"

"Because I keep hoping you'll get to know me."

"I'm trying. I'm just ..."

" ... *scared*."

"All I've ever wanted was to be myself, all the time," her voice was shaky. "And for you to love me."

"Just trust me. Trust *us*, and you'll get everything you want," he assured her.

"I hope so," she breathed.

"You know what, I know what you need," his voice got loud again.

"Of course you do."

"Stop being a brat. I hate self-pity. Let's go."

He didn't give her a choice. Con's arms went tight around her and he held her close as he stood up, lifting her as he went. She laughed when he started walking out the door, carrying her while she was only wearing the bed sheet and nothing else.

Resisting him had always been impossible, so Dulcie got dressed and followed him outside. His car was parked right in front her building, so they climbed in it and he drove them off into the night.

Of course, she knew where they were going, so she wasn't surprised when he parked his car near the abandoned train station. Possibly even in the same spot as that important night, so long ago.

They got out of the car, but Con didn't head down to the railroad crossing. He climbed the fence, then straddled the top of it and waited for her. Dulcie wasn't quite as nimble as him, she'd never been any kind of athlete, and when she got near the top, he simply grabbed her arm and pulled her the rest of the way. He was already on the ground before she'd even climbed down a couple feet on the opposite side, and he yelled at her to just jump.

"Super idea, Con," she grumbled through gritted teeth as she hopped around on one foot. He'd caught her for the most part, prevented her from falling, but her ankle had rolled under her weight.

"You're like Bambi on ice," he made fun of her, but before she could snap back at him, he pulled her around to his back and instructed her to climb on.

She laughed while he galloped down the track, then shrieked when he spun them in a tight circle. When she threatened to puke down his back, he reached behind him and pawed at her, making her giggle and shriek as he yanked her over his shoulder. He walked with her bent over him like that, spanking her until she thought she was going to pass out from laughing so hard.

Even maniacs can have a little fun.

He finally put her down when they got to their special spot. There had been a heavy rain the week before, and all the cardboard was officially gone. It was just a plain old ditch running alongside the tracks. There was no marker now, no sign to say "this is where we buried a body". But still, they could just tell. Dulcie would always know the spot.

"I'm sorry I'm difficult," she sighed. Con stood behind her and blocked her body as a strong breeze ripped across them.

"I like that you're difficult. I like that you're the perfect size, made to fit inside me," he replied, and his arms came around her. He was right, she could stand in front of him and his whole body was able to wrap around her. Envelope her. Consume her. "I like that I can tell you anything, and I don't have to worry about what you'll think – I can tell you I killed someone, or had my fingers in someone, or I short changed a clerk, and you'll still like me."

"You short changed someone!? That's it, this is over," she joked, struggling against his hold. He chuckled and held her tighter.

"I like that we did something like this together, before we even knew how far we could go," he whispered in her ear, and she shivered as she stared at the grave. "And I like knowing we'll go even farther. But we're not done here yet. I can't just leave, not with my dad missing, that all needs to settle down first. And I can't let you leave, because I don't want to be here alone. So please, *please*, trust me. We'll get through this."

"Fine," she sighed. "But if anyone else gives me any shit, I'm going to stab them in the eye."

"And I'll help you bury the body," he promised.

"Such a clever boy, Constantine Masters."

"Such a good girl, Dulcie Travers."

"You know what I like?" she asked, turning in his arms so she was facing him.

"Hmmm?" was all he said as he ran his hands up and down her arms.

"I like that we're out here all alone, and you can do anything you want to me," she whispered, hooking her fingers around the top of his pants. He smiled that Cheshire grin, and his hands moved all the way to her neck. His fingers felt cold as they wrapped around her throat.

"Anything I want," he echoed her, applying more and more pressure. She let her eyes fall shut and remembered their first time together. When he'd choked her to the point she'd almost passed out. His fingers got tighter and she felt him lean close, felt his tongue on the side of her face, and she sighed.

What a beautiful darkness we are.

They barely made it back to the car. As it was, he laid her out on the hood and shoved her dress up her body, pushed her panties to the side. One of his hands went back around her neck, preventing her from crying out too loudly. Not that it mattered, they were alone in the night. Alone in their dark place.

Or at least, she thought they were …

TWENTY-FOUR

DULCIE RECONCILED HERSELF TO THE FACT THEY WOULD MOST likely be spending another year in the town. Con had more than enough money to support both of them, he assured her, so at least she wouldn't need to get another job. He even told her she could move in with him any time she wanted. They spent all their free time with each other, anyway, and everyone knew they were together. The scandal of the football hero sleeping with the girl from the wrong side of the tracks would wear off as soon as people saw they were serious about each other.

So a week after she walked out of her job, Dulcie packed up her meager belongings and loaded them into the backseat of her car. She was on her last load, carrying a stack of books through the front door of her building, when someone rammed into her from the side. She let out a cry as she was forced against a wall.

"Thought I forgot about you, didn't you?" Matt was growling in her face. He looked worse than she'd ever seen him, with open sores on his face and deep bags under his eyes, and he appeared to be missing a bottom tooth.

"God, how could I? I think I smelled you coming," she gagged. He was absolutely filthy, but apparently didn't appreciate hearing it. He growled and got close to her face.

"Look here, you fucking bitch, I know what you did."

Matt had said a lot of things to her over the years, and she usually just ignored them. That, though, managed to catch her attention.

"What do you mean?" she gritted her teeth. He had all his weight on her, which wasn't very much, but he was bony and she could feel his hips digging into her.

"I saw you. The other night? Down at the old station. You and your boyfriend. Quite a show, Dulcie. Never knew you had it in you," his voice lowered to a grumble, and suddenly his bony hips weren't all she could feel. She gagged again.

"I don't care if you watched me have sex, pervert. Get off me," she demanded, trying to push at him.

"But I saw more than that. I've seen you guys there before, on the tracks. Always stopping at the same spot. I was there last night. After you let that guy fuck you, I went down there to see what the big deal was."

Okay, shit was serious now. They'd been so stupid, just assuming they were alone. The station had long been a hangout for the derelicts of the area, she'd always known it was only a matter of time before they'd come back to claim it. Just because there hadn't been tents outside, didn't mean people weren't lurking about inside.

"It's just some fucking train tracks," she cursed. "There's never anybody down there, we can do what we want."

"Oh, I see that now. *Whatever you want*. I found Larry. We all wondered what happened to him," he said. She completely froze.

"I don't know who Larry is."

"He used to blow me for meth," Matt explained, and again, Dulcie almost lost her lunch. "One day I went down there to drop off a delivery, make a deposit for him. He wasn't there. I thought he'd finally moved on to the next town. Never thought to look for a grave. Shit, I even slept in that cardboard box. Right above him, never even knew it."

"What the fuck do I have to do with some homeless meth head's body you found under -"

"Shut up, Dulcie. I know that's where you go all the time. I know that's what you two are always looking at, you fucking sickos. Look at a grave, then hump like bunnies."

"Look, Matt, you don't know what you're doing. If Con finds out you're saying all this, finds out you know any of this, *he will kill you.* Do you hear me? You need to shut the fuck up and disappear," she said quickly, her voice dropping to a whisper as her mind started racing.

"Oh no. I'm not going anywhere. You want me to shut up? Then you gotta give me what I want," he growled.

"What do you want? Money? I can -"

Her voice froze in her throat when his hand roughly grabbed at her crotch. His fingers clawed at the denim between her thighs, trying to dig into a place he certainly wasn't allowed to go.

"*You know what I want.*"

"Oh my god. Stop. Please, I can't do that."

"Unless you give me what I want, I'm going to the cops."

Dulcie's mind went from simply racing to warp speed.

"I can't," she whispered. "He'd kill me, too."

That seemed to surprise Matt, but before he could say anything, the sound of pounding footsteps interrupted them. Someone started yelling and it took a second for her brain to realize it was Jared. He was running towards them, calling out her name.

Matt beat it, letting her go before he bolted down the street. Jared chased after him, but he ducked down an alley. Dulcie stood up against the wall for a second, trying gain control of her breathing, slow her heart beat. When Jared came back around the corner, she lurched away from her spot and hurried around to her driver's side.

"Dulcie!" he yelled, but she ignored him and got in the car. He didn't even hesitate, he hopped into the passenger seat. "Dulcie, *stop.*"

Her hand was shaking so bad, she couldn't get the key in the ignition. Jared gently grabbed her forearm, forcing her to stop moving. She took a couple deep breaths, then held onto her steering wheel.

"I'm sorry I yelled at you," she managed to squeak out.

"Are you joking? I don't even care about that right now – are you okay?" he asked, then started rubbing her back.

"Yeah. Yeah, I'm fine. What are you doing here?" she wondered out loud, glancing over at him.

"I was coming to talk to you, I wanted to see how you were. What the fuck is going on?" he demanded. She swallowed thickly.

"That was Matt. He … has a thing for me. Likes to give me shit. He kinda took it a little far this time," was all she said.

"You think!? Dulcie, we need to call the cops," Jared insisted. She shook her head.

"No! No police. No cops."

"But -"

"*I said no.*"

There was a heavy silence and she started breathing fast. It was a warm day and easily had to be over ninety degrees in her car.

"Tell me what's wrong," Jared whispered. She took a deep breath, trying to collect her thoughts. They were scattered all around her, likes leaves in the wind. She had to get control of the situation.

You have to think of something.

"I can't," she whispered back as she turned to stare at him. "*Please.*"

She burst out crying and fell against him. His arms came around her, holding her tightly while rubbing at her arms.

"It's all so fucked up, Jared. I'm sorry," she breathed into his chest.

"What's fucked up? Is it Con? Does he know that guy is harassing you?" Jared asked.

"He knows about him, but not stuff like that," she answered.

"You need to tell him."

"You don't even like him."

"I know," Jared sighed. "But it's his job to protect you, not mine."

Dulcie leaned away then, but kept her hands pressed to his chest. His arms stayed loosely around her.

"Do you ever wonder? If we hadn't broken up that night? If I hadn't left the party?" she whispered.

"If Con hadn't followed you," he added, and she nodded.

"Yeah. What would've happened?" she asked. He managed to smile and brushed his thumb across her cheek, wiping away tears.

"I don't know, Dulcie. But I'm beginning to think I never would've been enough for you."

She didn't get a chance to respond. She'd barely opened her mouth when the door behind Jared was ripped open. Someone grabbed him by the shoulders and he was yanked out of the car. She gasped as Constantine threw him to the ground.

"Get it through your fucking head, she didn't choose you."

Dulcie was out of her seat and running around the car in time to see Jared get punched in the face. She tried to grab Con's arm, but he shook free of her.

"Stop it!" she ordered him.

"What the fuck is going on!? I come down here to help you get your shit, and what do I find? Him falling all over you, *again,*" Con sneered, cocking back his arm to hit him once more.

"He was helping me!" she shrieked, and that made him pause. *"He was helping me.* Matt showed up, and he grabbed me, and he touched me, and Jared scared him away. I was upset, we were just talking. *He was just helping!"*

She'd reached her breaking point. Things were spinning out of control, for both of them, and not in the fun way. Losing her shit at work had been the tip of the iceberg. There was a whole ocean of crazy threatening to spill out, and Matt had just opened the spillways. Something had to give, and it looked like her sanity was up for grabs.

She didn't wait for a response. She turned and ran back around her car. Con yelled her name, but she ignored him. Just got behind the wheel and burned rubber as she pulled out of the spot.

Not yet. Don't go crazy yet. You still have to find out if he really loves you.

By the time Con got home, Dulcie had calmed down. She'd had a lot of time to think about her options. Matt knew what they'd done, and no amount of lying could convince him otherwise. He'd always been like a tickle in her throat, a cough she couldn't quite get rid of. Now, he'd graduated to full blown tumor.

Also, the little lovers' paradise she'd been living in was officially over. Dulcie wondered if it even would've lasted the year. They were simply too dangerous together. Con had been right to stay away those three years. They had no self-control when they were together, they indulged each other. It was too much. At the rate they were going, they really would destroy each other, and she couldn't allow that too happen. He was too beautiful for prison, too exquisite for death, and she couldn't bear the thought of him suffering if either of those things were to happen. So if one of them had to make a sacrifice, it would be her.

That thought had her brushing away tears when he finally walked into the house.

"Did you beat him up?" she called out.

She watched as he looked around for a moment, trying to place where her voice had come from. She was sitting in his formal dining room, a spot in the house they'd never used. He finally located her and she watched his eyebrows shoot up in surprise. He slowly walked towards her, taking in the scene in front of him.

"No. We went and had a beer. What are you doing?" he asked, not moving past his end of the table.

Constantine had a twelve seat dining room table. Rumor had it back in high school, it had caught on fire during a drunken brawl between his parents. Dulcie knew he'd been the one to set it aflame. It had long since been sanded down and refinished – the fire hadn't caused any structural damage and it was an antique. Mrs. Masters had wanted to save it. So it sat in an empty room and was never used.

Until that night. Dulcie had set the entire table. Every seat had an immaculate setting – dinner plates, salad plates, solid silver cutlery, wine glasses, champagne glasses, water glasses, *the works*. It was fit for royalty to sit at, and she'd taken a seat at the head of the table. Con slowly sank into the chair at the foot.

"I wanted to see what it would look like if this was our home. If we were Mr. and Mrs. Masters, and this was our table," she explained. He narrowed his eyes.

"Apparently, Mrs. Masters would like to entertain," he guessed. She shrugged.

"Not really. What did you guys talk about?" she asked, putting her elbows on the table and resting her chin in her hands.

"We shot the shit, had some drinks. I had a Corona, he had a Bud."

"*Constantine.*"

"*Dulcie.*"

"You lost your shit out there," she called him out. He gave her a tight smile.

"He was *touching you*. You know how I feel about that," he reminded her. She shook her head.

"No, no, I was *allowing him* to touch me. There's a difference, Con."

"Not one that I can see."

"You touched Frannie, correct?"

"Yeah, but only as part of a greater scheme."

"*Exactly.*"

He looked surprised again.

"How was I supposed to know that's what was going on?" he demanded.

"Maybe by asking me? Instead of just running up and beating on any guy who's standing too close to me!" she snapped. "We're supposed to have trust, right? I didn't see any this afternoon."

"Don't talk to me about trust, Dulcie, when you can't even figure out how you really feel about me."

Ouch.

"I know how I feel about you," she whispered.

"You sure about that?" he challenged her. She took a deep breath.

"Matt knows," she barreled ahead with her plans.

"Knows what?"

"Everything."

"What, that we're fucking? Dulcie, the entire town knows. We're banned from the theatre because of that blowjob the other night. It's not a secret," he assured her. She shook her head.

"He knows *everything*."

That extra little emphasis on the word made all the difference, and she watched as clarity washed over his face.

"Ah. Does he. And how did he figure out our little secret?" Con's voice was so soft, it was hard to hear from how far away he was sitting.

"He saw us last week. He watched us while we were at the tracks, when we were on your car," she explained.

"He watched us have sex?" Con checked, and she burst out laughing.

"Well, yeah, but he also saw what we were looking at, then he went down there and found the body," she spelled it out for him.

"I don't care. That disgusting little twat watched me fuck you. I'm going to rip his head off," he informed her, and it wasn't just a passing threat made in anger. She watched him clench his fists, saw the muscles in his arms bunch and come together, his biceps straining against his t-shirt sleeves.

"You can't do that," she sighed.

"Why the fuck not!?"

"Because it'll just be one more problem. We were able to bury the last one, but not Matt. He has friends, people he'll have talked to about us. He can't just disappear, they'll know we had something to do with it," she pointed out. "On top of that, Jared is a problem."

"I told you, we hashed it out. I have him convinced I'm some love-struck puppy that's scared of losing you to him. He went home with an ego two sizes bigger than when we'd started drinking," Con chuckled.

"I doubt that," she grumbled.

"What?"

"He thinks you're this ... bad influence on me. He's been saying it since we had dinner, he yelled it at me when I had my breakdown. That's what he was saying in the car. He thinks you're some crazy possessive psycho boyfriend. Even if you got rid of Matt, and even if we managed to make it look like an accident, we *still* have a problem," she broke it down for him.

"I don't think I'd really classify Jared as a problem," he laughed. She let out a shout and banged her hand on the table.

"I'm fucking serious, Con! We're sitting here calmly discussing killing someone! Is that how it's always going to be? Just waiting for someone else to realize how fucked up we are, and then killing them, too!?" she yelled at him.

"You knew what you were getting into!" he yelled back at her. "You knew this is what I am, what *we* are! Don't fucking act naive! You delivered that final blow, little girl, not me. *You* wanted to destroy their house, and *you* wanted to end that marriage. So *do not* paint me out to be the monster in this story. Your claws are just as bloody as mine."

Dulcie jumped out of her chair, sending it flying over backwards. She went to stride out of the room, but Con was quicker. He stood up and moved in front of her, blocking her exit and penning her in by the wall.

"So I'm the bad guy!?" she screamed, slapping him in the chest. "Does that make you feel less like a psycho, Con? Fine. *FINE.* I'm the fucking bad guy! I did it all!"

"I didn't say that!" he was shouting in her face, trying to grab hold of her wrists.

"I'm just this awful fucking thing who kills people and just drags you along with me!" she kept yelling, tears streaming down her face.

"No one is saying that, Dulcie. Why are you doing this? I thought we were in this together," he reminded her.

"Well, we're not," she said boldly, wiping at her face.

"What the fuck did you just say to me!?"

"We're just two fucking crazy people, making each other crazier," she told him.

"You think I'm crazy. You think *we're* crazy, that what's going on between us is crazy," he double and triple checked, his voice getting loud again.

"I do, now get away from me."

"Don't talk to me like that."

"Get your fucking hands off me!" she shouted, trying to push him away.

"I touch you whenever I want," he growled as he put a hand on her chest, holding her in place.

"You don't own me!" she shrieked. Rage finally boiled over and Con lost it. He began beating his fist into the wall next to her head. She screamed and covered her face.

"Don't you ever fucking say that to me! Of course I fucking own you!"

She felt like she was going to have a heart attack. Was this fear? She didn't care for it one bit.

You need to do this, for both of you. Be strong.

Dulcie broke free and ran for the door, but of course she didn't make it. She had a hand on the knob when Con grabbed her from behind and spun her around.

"Stop! Let me go! *Let me go!*" she was yelling and hitting at him.

"That's what you want, isn't it? You're hurting, so you want me to hurt," his voice was loud in her ear.

"I want you to let me go," she snapped, and she slapped him across the face. She was shocked when right after, he emulated the move and slapped himself.

"Is this what you want!?" he shouted, hitting himself again. "You think I don't feel pain?" Another hit. "I told you I'd bleed for you." He kept hitting himself, over and over. "Why can't you trust me? If you want me to hurt, then fine. Fucking fine, Dulcie. I'll hurt for you. I'll bleed for you. *All you have to do is ask.*"

He went to hit himself again, and she couldn't take it. She broke. She grabbed his wrist and held on, preventing him from moving. Then she fell forward, gasping for air as she let her forehead rest against his chest.

"That's the problem," she whispered, watching her tears fall onto his shirt. "I don't want you to bleed."

He abruptly walked away from her and she almost fell over, so much of her weight had been resting against him. She watched as he staggered back into the dining room. He collapsed into his chair and put his head in his hands.

Now was her chance. He'd seen right through her – she *had* wanted him to hurt. She'd been cruel and she'd said things that weren't true, because she'd wanted him to be upset. Maybe if she hurt him bad enough, he'd leave her, and then he'd be safe from the crazy darkness that swirled between them. He'd gotten out once, for three whole years. He could do it again.

She couldn't go through with it, though. Couldn't stand to see him in any kind of pain. It caused *her* pain. They were connected. For better or for worse, now. By more than some unmarked grave in a ditch. By destiny, or fate. By some evil power. There would be no getting away from each other.

She moved into the dining room as well, sitting at a chair about halfway down the table. They sat in silence, both breathing heavy from their exertions. Finally, after about five minutes, Con sat upright.

"You're not the bad guy in this story," he whispered.

"I know. I know that's not what you were saying."

"And neither am I," he continued.

"I know."

"*We* are," he said, finally looking right at her. "Both of us. We're the bad ones. *Together.*"

She nodded.

"Together."

"And we'll figure this out, *together*. But Dulcie, you *have* to trust me," he urged her. She nodded again.

"I know. I do. I was just scared for you. I don't want anything to happen to you," she tried to explain.

"Nothing will happen to me, as long as we're together, okay? You made me promise to never leave. It works both ways, you know – don't you get it? *You own me, too.* I'm a part of you, you can't just push me away when you get scared."

Okay, now Dulcie was pretty sure she'd never stop crying. He looked heartbroken, and it killed her to know she'd caused him to feel that way.

"I'm sorry," she gasped for air. "I'm so sorry."

He slowly reached forward and grabbed the corner of the table cloth. It was pristine white, with a gold border all around it. Gorgeous. He pulled until it started to move, and then he kept going. Dragged the whole thing down the length of the table, sending all the expensive fine china crashing to the floor. She sat there till he was finished, till every-thing was in a pile on the ground.

"*Come here.*"

Dulcie stood up and moved onto the table. Then she crawled down the length of it until she was kneeling right in front of him. He stared at her for a second, his eyes so big and blue. So huge, she almost fell into them. She took a deep breath.

"I'm not scared of you," she assured him. He slowly stood up, then pressed his hands against either side of her face.

"*Liar,*" he whispered. She shook her head.

"No. I'm scared of myself," she breathed.

"Don't be scared," he said, then he leaned in and kissed a tear away. "Don't ever be scared. It kills me. From now on, tell me when-ever you're scared, and I'll take away your fears. Tell me when you're hurting, and I'll bleed for you."

He's so goddamn beautiful. Shines so bright, I can't even see him.

She gasped into his mouth as it covered hers. Raised up onto her knees so she could hold onto him. He wrapped an arm around her waist and swept her off the table. The moment her feet hit the ground, he reached under her dress and pulled her underwear down. She stepped out of them as he moved back and sat in his chair again. She followed suit, swinging a leg over his lap and lowering herself.

"We can't stay here anymore," she breathed into his ear.

"I know."

"It's not going to be easy. There's so many things we'll have to do ..." she let her voice trail off. She felt his hands moving between them, unbuckling his belt and shoving at his pants.

"*I know*. We'll get through it. We just have to trust each other," he reminded her, then pushed on her hips. She lifted herself up and could feel him under her, all burning heat and sinewy hard.

"I trust you," she moaned as she slid down his length. He undid the top buttons on her dress, enough so he could reach inside the material and kiss along her cleavage.

"Not yet, you don't," he informed her. She shook her head.

"No, I do, I -"

"It's okay," he whispered, lifting his head and kissing her on the lips. "Some day you will. Some day, you'll really love me, and if it's even half as much as I love you, we'll set the world on fire."

Dulcie had never realized beauty could hurt, and she sobbed as he began moving under her. Thrusting up inside her. She clung to his shoulders and cried into his neck, sitting still while he worked away. She couldn't give anything in return.

Just my heart.

He stood up, shocking her a little, but he didn't break their connection as he held her in his arms. He was gentle as he laid her on the table, careful as he moved them so they were stretched out together. God, who knew Constantine could be so gentle? He unbuttoned the rest of her dress, pulled apart the belt at the middle, and she was finally completely naked. How she always wanted to be when she was around him.

After he'd disposed of his own shirt, he laid down on top of her. She hooked her legs around his and followed his movements. His hips drew back, then pumped forward at an angle, striking places so deep, he was beyond moving her soul.

"I don't want this to ever end," she moaned, rubbing her hands down his back.

"It doesn't have to," he sighed, moving his hips faster. She worked hers back against him, building up a friction that was threatening to melt her from top to bottom.

"Together ... the two of us ... forever," she was gasping again. One of his hands slid down her body and pressed over her breast.

"You promised," he said, and she felt his teeth along the side of her neck. He bit down so hard, she shrieked.

"Con, please, I can't ... you ... I ... I'm ..."

"*Please,*" he groaned, and she felt his hand on the side of her face. "Please, look at me."

"*Yes.*"

Sex was such a ferocious act between them. Sweet and gentle weren't things that existed between wild beasts. But they did that night. She'd never been so aware of him, had never felt him so deeply. She stared into his eyes as the orgasm took over her body. Didn't stop looking even as she cried out and bit down into her bottom lip so hard she drew blood. Kept looking as his hips pumped faster and faster till they finally hitched in tight against hers, not moving again. Only when he dropped his head to her shoulder did she let her eyes close, and she concentrated on feeling him as he pulsed and throbbed inside her.

Don't say it. Not yet. Not till you know for sure.

"*I love you,*" he was fighting for breath. "I love you so goddamn much, I would tear apart this whole world for you."

Dulcie opened her eyes and stared at the ceiling.

"I know, Constantine. I know."

TWENTY-FIVE

"**S**OMETIMES, I FEEL LIKE COLORS ARE TOO BRIGHT. I CAN'T LOOK at them, they hurt my eyes. That's why I used to only draw, only paint, in black. It's the only safe color. When I was in high school, it was my favorite color. Something I could hide behind. Later it was red. Still is. Crimson, scarlet, burgundy, maroon, all of them. So beautiful on paper. So lovely on my fingertips.

"For years, I felt like I wanted to scream. That's it. Just stand and scream. And scream and scream and scream. If I could've just screamed all day, every day, maybe I could scream all the crazy out. I never cared, you know. About where I came from, about the trailer park, about my mom, about Matt. None of it ever bothered me because I could just hide in my blacks and reds and block it all out. No, what bothered me was the fucked up thoughts I would have.

"Crazy people have it easy – they don't know they're crazy. Being fully aware of how fucked up you are? That's the worst. Looking at your mom and wondering if you were strong enough to drag her dead body under the trailer, so you could leave her to rot, and *knowing* that's not normal, *that's the worst*. Knowing something is wrong with you, but not wanting to change even then. I spent hours wondering what was wrong with me. So many moments outside the counselor's office, trying to talk myself into going inside.

"But self-preservation is strong, and my brand of crazy has it in spades. I was holding out for something better, anyway. For *greatness*. If I just bided my time and drew my pictures and held my tongue, it would all pay off. I just had to believe, I had to have *faith*.

"And god delivered unto me a beautiful boy. With big blues eyes and pearly white teeth, and a body so fucking fantastic, I still can't believe I get to touch it. Talk about a reward for enduring a shitty childhood. How could this be for real? *The* Constantine Masters, the belle of the ball, the toast of the town, and he was made just for me! Oh yes, I fucking believe in the power of prayer, you don't even know the half of it.

"Before then, I thought you were bad. And not like 'oh, look at that *bad boy* over there, he's so *hot*', but like *bad*. Like more fucked up than two of me put together. Like maybe if god was really good, you'd be worse than me, and then my crazy would pale in comparison. It was easy to pretend for so long. Till now. Your shoulders are so big and broad, so tough and strong. You could carry that burden, I figured. You could be the bad one.

"I gotta hand it to you, though, you actually are as smart as everyone says you are. You saw right through me, even before I could see myself. You saw through the blacks and the reds and you saw this beautiful horror, these terrifying dreams, and you just loved them. You *knew* me. You pinned me down and you ripped me open and you showed me things inside me that I didn't even know were there. Whole new levels of sex and love and depravity, the likes of which the waking world isn't ready for. And you held them up in front of my face, yet I still refused to look. I've had my eyes closed for so long. Why did it take me so long to open them?"

The silence lasted long enough that Dulcie finally glanced over her shoulder. Con was sitting on the floor, looking up at her. He had a beer in one hand and he sipped at it. He was only wearing a pair of pants, no shirt, and his arms were filthy, coated in dirt clear up to his elbows.

He had his knees bent and his feet flat on the floor. They were covered in mud, too.

"That it?" he asked, then took another drink. She turned away from him again.

"I guess so."

"So many words, Dulcie," he sighed. "All because you can't say three little ones."

"Yeah, yeah. Keep ripping things out, keep showing them to me," she whispered, then she lifted her paint brush and pushed it in a broad stroke across the wall. Thick, black paint followed in its wake. Left over paint from when Mr. Masters had his shed painted. Dulcie had found it in the garage.

"Is it done?" Con asked, when she stepped back to look over her work.

"It'll never be done," she replied, tilting her head to the side. There was only one light in the room. She'd ripped the shade off it, but it hadn't helped much. Since they'd tossed all the room's furniture out back, she'd had to set the lamp on the floor. She could only clearly see her artwork from one angle.

"Is it done *for now?*" he corrected his question, and she listened as he climbed to his feet.

"For now," she sighed, dropping the paint brush. He moved behind her and she shivered. She was only wearing his t-shirt.

"Fucking fantastic body, huh?" he grunted, his breath hot on her ear.

"Glad you paid attention to the pertinent parts of my confession," she laughed.

"I paid attention to the whole thing. Don't worry, I love you, too," he assured her. She leaned back then, trusting him to take her weight. When she made contact with his chest, she let out a sigh.

"That's why it can't ever be done."

She couldn't say the words because she didn't trust him enough yet; didn't trust *herself.* But she could give him this – a moment in time they'd always remember. A beating heart that would only ever belong to him. It was all in black, and her memory of anatomy was shaky at best, but one entire wall was covered in a heart. A *real* heart, with arteries and ventricles and blood. So much blood.

"I love it. It's perfect," he whispered as he kissed her temple.

"It is, isn't it?" she agreed. His arm wrapped around her waist.

"It really is. Pity it won't be here for long. C'mon, we have a lot of work to do."

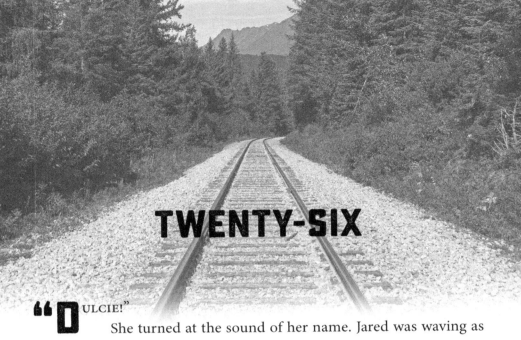

TWENTY-SIX

"**D**ULCIE!"

She turned at the sound of her name. Jared was waving as he jogged towards her. She smiled and stood up.

"Hey, thanks for meeting me on such short notice," she said, then leaned in to hug him when he got close enough.

"No problem, I was glad you called."

She winced when she took in his bruised cheek. Con hadn't held back.

"I just wanted to say thank you, for helping me yesterday," she got right down to it as she took her seat again. They were in the middle of the park and he sat down next to her.

"God, don't thank me. I would hope anyone would do that if they'd seen what I saw," he told her.

"Yeah, I know. But still, it was nice. And I also wanted to say sorry, for Con," she continued. He nodded.

"It's okay. We talked for a while. That guy really has a thing for you."

"He's got something, that's for sure."

"Y'know," Jared spoke slowly. "He told me a lot of stuff, about Matt … your brother."

"*Half*-brother," she was quick to correct him.

"He said stuff like that's been going on for a while," he kept talking.

"Yeah. Yeah, it has. It's gotten worse since I moved into the big house. It's driving Con crazy," she explained.

"I can imagine."

"No," she shook her head. "Like *really* crazy. We got into this huge fight last night, he was hitting himself, he broke a bunch of dishes. He's … he's going to do something."

She stared at Jared with wide eyes. She knew she didn't look very good; she hadn't put on a stitch of makeup before leaving the house, and she'd been up all night. No sleep had left her with bags under her eyes and less than glowing skin.

"What's he going to do?" Jared asked. She sighed and shoved her messy hair behind her ears.

"Something bad. I don't know. I shouldn't have said anything," she mumbled, tapping her fingers against her lips. He reached out and grabbed her wrist.

"No, you should. You have to talk to someone. If he's acting this way, Dulcie, you need to get away from him," he insisted, holding her hand close to his chest. She shook her head.

"No. It's not like that, he wouldn't hurt me," she said, but her voice was shaking.

"It doesn't matter. You're scared, and that's bad enough. Please, Dulcie. I know … I know things got weird between us. But we're friends, at the end of the day. At least, I think of you as a friend. *Let me help you,*" he insisted.

"After everything I said to you," her voice lowered to a whisper. "You'd still help me?"

"In a heartbeat."

Dulcie frowned and looked away from him, but didn't pull her hand free. He was squeezing her fingers, almost massaging them. She realized he was trying to warm them up; she was ice cold.

Silly man, that's room temperature for me. Careful, you might get frostbite.

"I shouldn't have come here," she stood up abruptly. He held fast to her hand.

"*You should've.* I'm glad you did. You're seriously freaking me out."

"I have to go. If Con finds out I talked to you about this, he'll ..."

"He'll what? I'm not scared of him," Jared sneered. She finally looked down at him.

"You should be."

Then she yanked free of his grasp and jogged to her car. By the time he was even halfway to her, she was already driving away. She let out a deep breath and glanced in her rear view mirror. Barely recognized the eyes looking back at her. The amber was being swallowed by black. She shook her head and looked forward.

One down. One more to go. Just keep moving.

Dulcie rarely saw her mother anymore. Since she'd moved out, she'd never once been back to the trailer. Never had a reason to, as far as she was concerned. It was just a box on wheels. A holding pen for the not-quite-dead.

She didn't bother knocking when she went inside. Her step-dad was passed out on the couch, snoring loudly while the TV hissed, full of static and snow. There was some muffled noises from the back of the trailer, a distinct squeaking sound. Like mattress springs.

"*Momma!*" Dulcie shouted, then she pounded on a wall. The snoring on the couch continued, but the mattress springs stopped squeaking. A couple minutes later, her mother came out from a back bedroom, pulling a tank top into place.

"That you, baby girl? Lord, it's been ages!" she called out, enveloping Dulcie in a hug when she reached her.

"It has. I just wanted to stop by, see how you were doing," she replied, cringing and trying not to breathe through her nose.

"How sweet! Want some tea?"

Dulcie said yes, and they sat down at a tiny table in the front of the trailer. While her mother searched for some clean cups, a man came out of the back, loudly clearing his throat while he did up his pants. When he finally dislodged whatever it was that was bothering him, he spit it onto the floor, then nodded at the women in the kitchen.

"Ladies," he said, then winked at Dulcie before heading out the front door.

If I pulled the stove out of the wall, it would rip open the propane hose. One spark, and this place wouldn't exist anymore. Did I bring any matches?

Her mom poured them both glasses of sweet tea. Then they chit chatted about brainless stuff. Her mother prattled on and on about a new Walmart that had just opened, how she was thinking of getting a job, how she hoped Matt would get a job.

Dulcie talked less and less, letting her mother fill in the gaps. She stared at the older woman, wondering what had happened in their lives to turn them into the people they were in that moment. Tessa Bottle was a shell of a human being, only half-alive at best. She sucked dick for crack, fucked strangers for meth, and she didn't even hardly do the drugs herself – almost all of it went to her husband.

Why was she such a shadow of a person? Dulcie didn't have one single memory of her mother being decent. Being full. Maybe she'd given it all to her children, maybe they'd sucked the life from her. Sometimes, Dulcie felt like she was overflowing with life. Like she was so full of energy and ether and dark matter, she might explode at any moment.

"... proud of you, being with a boy like him," her mom's voice cut into her thoughts.

"I'm sorry, what?" Dulcie shook her head, dragging herself into the present.

"I heard you were seeing the Masters boy. *My* daughter, with the mayor's son! I can't believe it. I always told you that you were pretty, didn't I? Just need to do somethin' with your hair once and a while, but other than that, so pretty," her mother sighed, then reached out to fiddle with the end of Dulcie's braid. She slapped her hand away.

"Thank you, I'll be sure to remember that next time we go out on a date," she joked.

"Does he … does he have a lot of money?"

Ah, there it was. Dulcie had wondered how long it would take. The conversation had been way too normal up until that point. She looked around, then leaned close and smiled conspiratorially.

"He does. I moved into that big house of theirs. Momma, it's *gorgeous*. So many bedrooms, we don't even know what to do with them all. He buys me presents and takes me places, it's … it's like a dream," she sighed.

Or a nightmare. Hard to tell.

"That's wonderful, darling. You know, things have been awful rough around here. Your step-daddy hurt his back, y'know, and hasn't been able to work at the factory, and Matt, well, he's just so sick, baby. We could really use your help," she told her. Dulcie frowned and nodded.

"Of course, Momma. All you had to do was say something, I feel awful."

She dug into her messenger bag and pulled out her wallet. Con had given her five hundred dollars that morning. She was supposed to be saving it in case of an emergency, but she knew it would serve a better purpose right in that moment. She took out the bundle of twenties and slid it across the table. Her mother's eye almost bugged out of her head.

"Oh my lord, baby, thank you! Thank you so much! Tell that man thank you," she gushed as she grabbed at the money. There was a creak from behind them and when Dulcie looked over her shoulder, it was to see her step-father on his feet, watching the whole transaction.

"Yer boyfriend is awful generous," he said, his voice full of suspicion.

"He is," Dulcie agreed, then she stood up. "I have to go now."

Her mother made a big production of saying goodbye, all without looking up from the money. Dulcie finally just walked out, mid-sentence. When she stepped outside, it was to find Matt standing next to her car. He was smoking a cigarette and dropping the ashes onto her hood. She sighed and walked towards him. She'd hoped to run into him, but would've preferred it to be inside. She could only hope he'd ask her mother what the visit had been about; hope he'd investigate a little.

"Visiting Mommy and Daddy?" he asked. She came to a stop in front of him.

"Look," she started. "I left them a lot of money. There's more to come, if you leave me alone."

"Nah, that wasn't part of the deal, remember? I never said anything about giving Mom money," he chuckled, then blew a stream of smoke in her face.

"Matt, you don't understand. I can't ... I can't do what you want," she hissed.

"You'll do whatever I say, or I'm gonna run right to the fucking cops," he threatened.

"I can't! Matt ... he'll ... *he'll kill you,*" she whispered.

He suddenly grabbed her by the throat and swung her around, pinning her against the vehicle. She held her breath as he leaned in close.

"Who, *rich boy!?* He ain't got the balls," he growled. She shook her head.

"He does. He told me so. He found out what happened, he has it all planned out," she choked out the words.

"What fucking plans?"

"Please, Matt, just believe me. Just take the money, and no one will get hurt."

He slammed her back again, then raised the lit cigarette to her face. She stared as it got closer and closer, her eyelashes almost brushing the ash that was threatening to spill onto her cheek.

"You fucking tell me what rich boy has planned, or someone will get hurt *right now,*" he assured her. She gasped for air.

"He said he's gonna find you and make you pay. Gonna bulldoze this whole place to the ground, with you in it. Then he's going to bury you out by the train tracks," she wheezed.

He backed away and she bent in half, loudly sucking in air.

"Fucker thinks he can kill me? Thinks a fucking rich boy could kill me!? That motherfucker. Thinks he can fucking buy me off with his money, thinks he can threaten my home," Matt was growling as he paced back and forth. Dulcie finally stood upright, rubbing at her throat.

"I'm serious, Matt. He's dangerous. He'll hurt you, he'll hurt *them*," she insisted as she nodded her head at the trailer.

"Fuck that. You go tell that asshole I'm gonna come to *his* house and fuck *him up*. How would he like that? Maybe I'll fuck his little princess girlfriend, right in front of him," he suggested, moving close to her again. She slid down the side of the car.

"Just take the money. I left five hundred dollars inside," she told him.

"Five hundred!?"

"Yeah, he gave it to me this morning, I -"

"That motherfucker just *gave you* five hundred dollars?"

"Well, yeah. His parents, they're well off. I thought ... I thought maybe if you had it, you would calm down," she suggested. A wicked smile spread across his face.

"Oh, I'm calm. I'm real fuckin' calm."

"*Please,* Matt. He's crazy. I'm really *scared*," her voice dropped into whisper. He finally looked her in the eye.

"Good. You should be. Now go tell that asshole that *he* should be scared."

TWENTY-SEVEN

THE SMELL HIT DULCIE THE MOMENT SHE WALKED INTO CON'S house. She started to gag and she turned in a circle, looking around for him.

"Sorry," he called out, and she looked up to find him jogging down the stairs. "Sorry about the smell. I'm not sure which is worse."

"Is that *alcohol*? It smells like a vodka factory!" she snapped, holding her sleeve over her nose. His voice was loud as he laughed.

"I wish."

"And what is that … that … *god*, what is that!?" she wasn't able to articulate what the other smell was – just that it was the most vile odor she'd ever encountered.

"Oh, yeah. You didn't smell it last night cause I left him in the shed. I put him at the table – seemed fitting," Con said by way of an explanation. Dulcie turned to look in the dining room and instantly started retching.

The table cloth and dishes were still in a mess on the floor. Several chairs were overturned, including Con's, but not Dulcie's. Her chair had been placed upright again, and now held an occupant.

Jebediah Masters once again sat at the head of his dining room table. Though of course, he probably looked much worse than he had

221

the last time he'd been there. He'd been dead and buried for two months – the night before, while Dulcie had painted their heart, Con had dug him up. She'd known what he'd been doing, but she hadn't realized he was going to seat his dad at the table.

"I can't," she gagged again. "I'm gonna … throw up."

"Squeamish? I'm shocked," Con made fun of her, then moved past her into the dining room. He grabbed the tablecloth off the floor and draped it over the body.

"No, not squeamish. Just … the smell … good god," she tried to explain. It was too much, she really was going to vomit. She pressed both hands over her mouth and ran up the stairs. She made a beeline to the room with the heart and then she took great gasping breaths of air, smelling only the paint fumes.

"Better?" Con's voice was behind her.

"A little," she nodded her head.

"Good. How did it go?"

She turned around to face him.

"I went to my mom's place, I gave her all the money you gave me," she started.

"All of it!?"

"Yeah."

"Jesus, Dulcie. Awfully fucking generous."

"Matt wasn't there, I didn't know what to do. I wanted to offer him the money, try to bribe him, but he wasn't there. So I gave it to my mom, knowing she'd tell him about it. Then when I left, he was waiting outside," she told him.

"Did he try anything?" he asked. She nodded.

"Threatened to burn my eye out with a lit cigarette. Told me *you* should be afraid of *him*. Told me he was going to make you watch while he raped me," she laid it all out. Con clenched his teeth together for a second and took several deep breaths through his nose.

"I don't think you have any idea how much I'm going to enjoy this," he finally responded, his voice so low she had trouble hearing it. She swallowed thickly.

"I think I have an inkling. What if something goes wrong? What if -" she started talking fast. He reached out and pinched her lips together.

"Stop it. Be brave. *Be who you were* **meant** *to be*," he whispered, then he leaned in and kissed her.

Nothing on earth was like kissing Constantine. It was like for that moment, she was inside him. She was *fused* to him, one with him. He never held back, he poured every emotion he had into all his kisses. It blew her mind that he'd ever had casual sex, or that she had, for that matter, because there was *nothing* casual about what went on between them. It was as serious as ...

... as a heart attack.

He moaned into her mouth and speared his hands into her hair, holding her at the angle he liked. He pushed her into place, and she let him, because what other choice did she have? Her back hit the wall and she could feel her clothing sticking to the still tacky paint. Could feel it matting her hair. She sighed and dragged her nails down his forearms before hooking her fingers around his biceps.

"I never got to tell you," she whispered when he finally pulled away.

"What?" he asked, clenching his hands into fists while he kissed along the side of her jaw.

"I think you're beautiful. That's why I could never draw your face. I could never do you justice. You're the most beautiful thing I've ever seen. I just wanted you to know that," she blurted out.

He stopped kissing her and stood back a little so he could stare into her eyes. His beautiful blue eyes, surrounded by such dark lashes. He'd gotten a buttery tan over the summer, though he was nowhere near as brown as her – he was naturally fair skinned, and it suited him. His brown hair was messy and wavy, probably in need of a cut, but she liked it. It was a little wild, a look he wore well. Her eyes filled with tears and she moved her hands to his chest, pressing them over his heart.

"Little girl," he sighed. "You have *got* to start trusting me."

"*I do,*" she snapped, and a tear finally spilled over onto her cheek.

He was quick to wipe it up with his thumb.

"Then trust me when I say we'll get out of this just fine. Just trust me, and do everything I said, and *don't be scared*, and we'll be *just fine*," he assured her.

"If you say so," she mumbled. He chuckled.

"*I do*. And you will get to experience all this magnificent beauty for as long as you want," he teased, pressing his forehead to hers. "And I'll get to experience yours. Just get through tonight. That's all you have to do, and then we can be together in whatever way we want."

At the end of his statement, a thought flashed across Dulcie's mind.

And what way is that? Without this town, without this kindling for our fire, what do we have?

She wasn't given a chance to explore her thoughts. Con's hands moved to her ribs and he squeezed, gently lifting her off the ground. He was so much stronger than her. So much bigger. He could almost lift her small frame over his head. He didn't, though, and she wrapped her legs around him. She was pressed back up against the wall, then his pelvis was pressed to hers, and suddenly there was a much more important issue at hand. They might not survive the night – did she really want to spend their last moments together talking about the future?

Con apparently felt the same way, and in a matter of minutes she was stripped of her shorts and thrown to the floor. They knocked over a can of paint, and as they pushed and pulled against each others bodies, screamed and cried out as they tore into each others souls, everything was coated in black.

TWENTY-EIGHT

IN HINDSIGHT, TAKING A SHOWER WAS STUPID. BUT THE PAINT WAS drying and itchy, and the bits of her that weren't covered in paint were soaked in sweat, so they didn't even think about it. They went into the big bathroom at the end of the hall and both stood under the spray, wiping away the layers of paint.

She wanted to wash her hair, so after giving her a big kiss and stealing her breath away, Con stepped out of the shower. She watched through the glass shower door as he pulled on a pair of old jeans, then he walked out of the room.

It was maybe ten minutes later when the power went out.

Thank god I rinsed out the shampoo.

In an instant, she had the water turned off. She stood in the stall for a second, holding as still as possible while she strained her ears. All she could hear was water dripping off her body, so she pushed open the door and stepped out onto the bath mat.

The room was pitch black, no windows at all. She dropped to a crouch and shuffled across the floor, her arm stretched out in front of her. When her hand finally collided with the wicker hamper, she breathed a sigh of relief. The master bedroom's en suite was nice enough, but the bathroom at the back of the house was much bigger, with a jacuzzi tub and a separate shower that was easily big enough for eight people. She and Con preferred to use it when they showered together, and so a lot of their clothing was shed in that bathroom.

She pulled items out of the hamper till she felt a small piece of denim. Shorts. She wiggled into them, still staying low to the floor, then went back to digging. When she grabbed what felt like a t-shirt, she pulled it on, then quickly realized it was one of Con's. At least she wasn't naked, she figured, so she stood up and shuffled back towards the door.

She pressed her ear to the wood and listened. She could hear something, but it was faint. It almost sounded like laughing. People, hooting and hollering, rummaging around in the rooms. She couldn't tell how many, though. There was a faint light coming in under the door, so she laid flat on her stomach and tried to look out.

BANG.

Something hitting the door. So quick, so abruptly, she actually shrieked. She jumped to her feet and took a couple steps back. There was some more banging, then the knob slowly began to turn. She hadn't bothered to lock it. The door swung open, and she was blind for a moment as a lantern was held in her face.

"Well, well, well! What do we have here? And she's already wet, my favorite," a voice hissed.

Dulcie had no clue who the man in front of her was; he was tall, with dark hair and spotty skin. He was holding a camping lantern and was swinging it gently. Back and forth, to and fro. She held up her hand to block the light and frowned.

"What are you doing in my house?" she demanded.

"Don't play that game with me, girlie. Matty told us all about yer rich boyfriend. Told us all about what you done to poor ol' Larry. I think we're gonna be movin' in with y'all. So why don't you come over here and give us a good welcome home," he suggested, then reached out to grab her arm. She slapped at his hand.

"Don't you fucking touch me!" she shouted.

"Quiet now! Wouldn't want the cops showin' up, would ya? I might

226

have to have a conversation with 'em about some of your extra-curricular activities," he warned her, then managed to get a grip on her wrist. He braced his shoulder against the door frame and began pulling her to him.

"Stop it! *Stop!*" she shrieked.

There was a loud thunking noise and something wet splashed across her neck. She was struggling to pull his fingers off her wrist when it happened, and she froze for a second. His hand fell away and she looked up, then promptly screamed.

His left eyeball was bulging out of his head. It was frighteningly unnatural looking, with his eyelid almost completely closed behind the orb. He didn't look too bothered, though. His mouth was slack and he seemed to be mumbling something, though she couldn't make sense of it. As she covered her mouth with her hand, she watched as his good eye rolled back in his head and he dropped to his knees. When he pitched forward, she scrambled to get out of the way.

"You okay?"

She looked out the doorway to find Con standing there. The lantern had fallen to the floor in the hall, casting the light up harshly from under him, making him look slightly ghoulish. He still wasn't wearing a shirt, and he had red splatter marks across his chest. She realized it was blood, and she looked down at herself. There was blood on the white t-shirt she was wearing, and when she touched her throat, she saw that's what had splashed against her.

"Fine," she breathed, her eyes moving to the bat he had in his hand. The same bat she'd used to destroy Jared's house. "Are you?"

The end of the bat had blood on it, so she turned to look down at their fallen guest. Where the back of his skull should have been, there was just mush. Blood and hair and bone. Probably brain matter, she didn't look too close. Con must have come up right next to him, and then just swung away, trying to hit it out of the park.

I would never expect anything less than a home run from Constantine.

"Peachy keen. Let's move," he answered her, then he pulled her out of the bathroom and shut the door, hiding the body.

Dulcie scooped up the lantern and hurried behind him. He was stalking down the hallway, completely fearless of who might be in the house, or how many of them there were. He stood at the top of the stairs and looked down into the darkness, so she moved to stand next to him and held up the light.

"What now?" she whispered, glancing up at him. He kept staring at the dark.

"We finish what we started."

He roughly grabbed her by the arm and started dragging her back down the hall. The lantern fell to the floor and bumped up against a wall. It must have knocked a battery loose, because the light began to flicker erratically, acting like a strobe in the dark house. Con shoved her into their room. Not the master suite, but the room with the heart on the wall.

"What are you doing?" she was stunned as he all but threw her across the doorway. She stumbled and fell against the giant heart.

"You'll be safe in here," he informed her, then he slammed the door shut.

She pushed off the wall and ran after him, but when she jerked on the knob, she found it was locked. It was an old house, the doors had ancient looking key holes, and a master key worked on all of them. Con had locked her in the room.

"*Stop it!*" she yelled, pounding on the door. "Stop it, don't do this!"

There were footsteps then, but she couldn't tell if it was him running away, or someone else moving around. She could hear movement on the stairs, the hollow thumping sound of someone rushing up them. She lost her shit and began screaming, jerking and yanking on the knob.

What if he gets hurt? What if something happens? I need to be there. If he dies, I have to be a part of it. How could he do this to us?

Something heavy rammed into the door and she jumped back.

Then there was complete silence. The only light in the room was coming from the moon outside, making everything around her look silver. Except for the heart on the wall. That was still as black as ever.

Dulcie took a deep breath and dropped to her knees. She leaned in close, trying to look out the key hole. The lantern was still flickering away on the floor. There was a noise in the distance, something or someone shuffling around. She pressed her ear flat to the door for a second, trying to figure out what it was, then she moved to look out the hole again.

"*Dulcie.*"

She was startled, but she didn't move when she saw an eyeball looking back at her. It was blue, but not the deep blue of Con's eye. This blue was dull and pale, surrounded by skin that looked grayer than normal in the strobing light.

"Matt," she gasped his name. "What are you doing!?"

"You invited me to a party," he laughed.

"*I did not.*"

"Sure you did. Tell me this guy has lots of money, tell me he's gonna mess me up. Sounds like an invitation to me. So I brought some of my friends to party, hope you're ready," he told her, then she listened as he jiggled the knob.

"You can't get in here," she warned him.

"We'll see about that."

Before he could make good on his threat, though, there was a crashing noise, followed by a shout. More like a roar. An animalistic sound that made Dulcie's heart beat faster and harder. Matt jumped up and disappeared from her view.

"No! Don't you run away! You fucking come back here!" she started screaming again, beating on the door.

Another figure ran past the key hole, but it was just blackness moving in the bright light. A shadow passing her by. She couldn't tell who it was – where was Con? Was he okay? She couldn't handle this, she was going to go crazy.

Well, *crazier.*

She jumped to her feet and hurried to the other side of the room, careful to skirt where the paint had spilled earlier. The rollers and paintbrushes she'd used the night before were still laid out, but none of them would help her. Then she found Con's shovel, the one he'd used to dig up his father. He'd carried it upstairs with him when he'd joined her in the room.

Dulcie grabbed it and charged back to the front of the room. With a yell, she thrust the blade into the side of the door. She wiggled it back and forth, pulled it out, then shoved it in again. Really worked it in between the door and the frame. One more hit, and when she threw her weight against the handle, the door bowed and the bolt ripped through the frame.

She ran into the hall in time to see Con and Matt struggling at the top of the stairs. She watched as Con was able to hook an arm around the smaller man's torso, allowing him to trip the other guy and send him crashing down the stairs. She listened as the body rolled down the steps. There was yelling, a sickening crunching sound, and then silence for a moment. Then, soft weeping.

"Why?" she whispered, moving to stand next to Con. He was breathing heavy.

"It was him or us, Dulcie, you know I had -"

She smacked him in the back with the shovel, hard enough to make him wince.

"*Why'd you lock me in that fucking room!?*" she shrieked.

"Because you were right, you've done all the heavy hitting up until now. It was my turn."

Before she could hit him again for making such a selfish statement, he jogged down the steps. It was darker downstairs, all the drapes were drawn, though the front door was standing wide open and letting in moonlight. It fell across Matt's crumpled form, showing a pair of badly broken legs. Something else didn't look right, but Dulcie couldn't put her finger on it.

"Wait," she called out, following after Con at a more sedate pace. He reached the crying figure and moved to stand over him.

"Oh, I've waited too long for this," Con sighed, then he bent over and grabbed the other man's head. Dulcie gasped, and at the same time, movement in the doorway caught her eye.

"No, wait! Don't -"

He was beyond listening, though. Con jerked his arms back with such a force, Dulcie could hear the spine break from where she was standing on the stairs. She grimaced as he rested the head backwards at an impossible angle, so it was laying against the body's shoulder blades.

"God, that felt good," Con groaned, standing upright.

"It wasn't him," Dulcie whispered, looking past him and out the door.

"What?" he asked, finally turning to see what she was looking at.

"*Holy shit.*"

Matt was standing in the doorway, staring wide eyed at the act of murder he'd just witnessed. Sure, Matt was a bad guy, and probably had no qualms about committing some nasty crimes. He'd been ready to rape his own sister, he was no goody-two-shoes. But murder was another thing entirely, and watching someone do it in cold blood wasn't easy for the average person to witness. Especially when the person being killed was a friend.

"I told you to come see where I live," Con breathed, and Dulcie watched as his trademark grin spread across his face.

"*You're fucking crazy!*" Matt screamed, stumbling away from the porch.

Con took off after him, laughing loudly and shouting threats.

Dulcie let out a deep breath and went to the foot of the stairs. Stared down at the dead body. It was some guy she'd never met. More like a boy – she couldn't place his age, but he looked young. Probably close to her own age. Matt must have seemed cool to him, probably gave him drugs and promised him a good time. "*Hey, come to a party on the hill, we'll scare some people, steal some shit, have a laugh*", and now the kid was dead.

She dropped the shovel on him and walked out the door. Con was standing in the driveway, staring into the woods that surrounded the property. She stood next to him for a second, then reached out and grabbed his hand. Linked their fingers together.

"He got away?" she asked.

"Yeah."

"He watched you do that."

"I know."

"He's probably out there, watching us."

"I hope so."

Con turned to face the house and Dulcie was forced to follow. They looked up at the big white building, took in the dark green shutters and impressive columns. She remembered looking at it when she was little, thinking it was a magical place. She almost laughed at how right that thought had turned out to be.

Con let go of her hand and walked over to where the Cutlass was parked. He opened the trunk and rooted around inside it. When he came back, he held a small box in his hand. He grabbed her arm and pulled her back a couple steps, staring hard at her feet.

"No going back," she whispered. He shook his head.

"We're long past that, anyway. Forward only, from here on out. Say goodbye, Dulcie."

"*Goodbye, Dulcie.*"

He struck a wooden match against the box, then tossed it to the ground in front of them. To where a divot had been dug into the gravel. There was a puddle of liquid in it, and the moment the match came close, it burst into flames. The fire followed the path of liquid up over the porch and through the door. Once inside, it caught onto the soaking wet carpet of the living room and the windows burst with the swell of heat that rolled through the house.

While Dulcie had been running all over town during the day, Con had gone and bought a couple industrial sized bottles of isopropyl alcohol. He'd left jugs of gasoline in a couple of the bedrooms and the basement, and had poured out a bunch around the back of the house, but the smell was too much to just toss it around the home. Matt and his friends would've smelled it the moment they'd stepped foot in the house. Alcohol, though, wasn't a smell that usually scared people, and isopropyl alcohol burned exceptionally well.

A little fact Con had retained from school.

As they stood together and watched the house go up in flames, she was surprised to find she felt a little sad. She was watching a childhood fantasy burn. Watching some of her memories turn to ash. She wished she'd taken a picture of their heart.

A breeze blew across her back and she shivered, then glanced up at Con. He had his arms folded across his bare chest and his stare was intense as he watched the fire burn. He had blood on his hands and smeared down one cheek. His bare feet were dirty, as well. He looked like a wild thing, like something that had crawled out of a nightmare. *Like a monster.* And as if he could read her thoughts, he slowly turned towards her and leaned down close. She realized he was grinning. Grinning so big, she could see all his fangs.

"This is the part where you run away, little girl."

TWENTY-NINE

BRANCHES AND TWIGS SMACKED HER IN THE FACE, SLICED INTO HER bare feet, as Dulcie barreled through the forest. She was breathing heavy, pumping her legs as hard as she could. She felt like she'd been running forever, but she knew she wasn't far enough away. Not yet.

She was caught off guard when she reached the edge of the treeline and she shrieked as she stumbled and fell down the side of a hill. More like a large embankment. She tumbled through bushes and grass till she smacked into something hard. She groaned and rubbed at her ribs as she climbed to her knees. Looked down to see what she'd hit.

A rail. She'd ran clear to the train tracks. Con's house was only about two miles from the abandoned station, and when she lifted her head, the large building loomed up ahead of her. She wiped at her face, then got to her feet and began running again. Sprinting down the middle of the tracks.

She hoisted herself up onto the platform and dashed across it. The first set of doors she came across were locked – someone had wrapped a chain through the handles and padlocked it together. She cursed out loud and hurried to the next set, only to find them chained as well. She hadn't been expecting this; if all the doors were locked, she wasn't sure what she would do.

When she got to the last set, though, they burst open before she could try the handles. She screamed as an arm reached out and grabbed the front of her t-shirt. She was yanked into the building.

"What the fuck are you doing here," a voice hissed in her ear as an arm wrapped around her throat. She'd been shocked at first, but once she recognized the owner of the voice, she heaved a sigh of relief.

"Matt. Thank god," she breathed, gripping onto his wrist. He dragged her backwards, farther into the station.

"Come to kill me, too!?" he yelled. She shook her head.

"I told you. I warned you he's crazy," she said quickly. "He burned down the house, to get rid of the evidence. I ran away."

"That fucker killed my friends," his voice was suddenly a little shaky. Matt was scared. She let her eyes close for a second.

"I know. He's going to kill me, too," she whispered.

"Fuck that. Fuck all this," he groaned, and he abruptly let her go. She stumbled a little, then turned to watch him head for the stairs. She went to follow, then cried out when something sliced into her foot.

There was glass all over the floor – Matt must have broken a window to get into the building. She gingerly tiptoed around the other shards, then left droplets of blood in her wake as she went up the stairs.

"What are you doing?" she asked, straining her eyes to see him. There were flood lights from the highway that shown into the building, but it was still dim.

"I need this," he grunted, and when she came around to his side, she saw that he was holding a small glass pipe. It had a wide bowl at the end, and he flicked on a lighter underneath it.

Jesus, he watched his friend get murdered, and he comes here to get high. I wonder if he heard that noise outside?

"What are we going to do!?" she suddenly yelled, dropping into a crouch at his side. Her voice carried through the old building, echoed down the stairs.

"Fuck, I don't know! He's your fucking crazy boyfriend!" he hissed. She nodded and began chewing on her fingernails.

"I didn't know. I didn't know it would end like this," she mumbled, glancing around the space. Looking for a weapon. But there was nothing. Matt was kneeling on a filthy looking mattress, with only a sheet crumpled up on it. There were some old comic books and some empty food containers, but that was it. Nothing useful.

"He won't touch us," Matt took another hit of meth. "He can't fucking touch me. Not when I'm here. I told him not to come to my house."

Dulcie heard another noise and she whipped her head around, looking behind her. They were crouched below the railing that overlooked the station floor. It also blocked her view of the stairs. Staying low, she began moving backwards, to the far wall.

"You don't get it," she whispered, slowly moving farther away from Matt.

"Oh, I fucking get it," he coughed out, then sucked on the pipe some more.

"This *is* his house."

A window downstairs burst, startling a shriek out of Dulcie. She pressed herself against the wall and curled into a ball. Matt, though, had new found strength from the massive amount of stimulant now flowing through his body. He jumped to his feet and leaned over the banister.

"You wanna fuck with me now!? Not hiding in some dark room anymore, rich boy!" he shouted. There was a banging sound from below them, something metal hitting the marble floor in rapid succession.

"You're the one who cut the power," Con's voice floated up to them. "I would've been fine killing your friends with the lights on."

"You motherfucker, I'm gonna cut you open," Matt threatened, and Dulcie was a little surprised when he produced a large blade from the inside of his pants. She looked twice and her surprise turned to shock – it was Con's knife, from his kitchen. It was recognizable because it was a very distinct knife. Wolfgang Puck brand, razor sharp, and the entire thing – blade and handle – was bright red. It was the same knife Con had used to cut her free when he'd tied her to the bed. Matt must have stolen it when he'd been prowling around the house.

"Is she up there?"

"Who!?"

"Little Red Riding Hood," Con laughed. Matt glanced down at her, and she wrapped her arms around her knees.

"Yeah. Yeah, your fucking girlfriend ran to me. How does that feel, you psycho?"

"Feels like I need to reclaim my property."

"Just try it, motherfucker. Just you fucking try it!"

Dulcie had moved so she was almost across from the steps, so she could see when Con started walking up them. His tousled brown hair came into view, then his face, though it was too dark to see his features. When she caught sight of his chest, she almost laughed – he'd gotten fully dressed before coming to the station, and he'd put on his letterman jacket, the one from high school. He looked *exactly* like the picture she'd drawn of him, so many years ago.

A shadow man, come to do very bad things in the night. She wasn't wearing a hood, but her shirt was marked in red. Splattered with blood.

Close enough.

"Did he touch you?" Con asked once he got to the top of the stairs.

"No," she whispered.

He turned towards Matt and she finally saw what had been making the banging noise. He'd brought the shovel from the house, the one she'd used to break out of the room. The one he'd use to dig up his dead father. He let the blade drag across the floor as he walked past her.

"You think that scares me!?" Matt was shouting with such violence, spit flew from his lips. "C'mon, asshole! *C'mon!*"

Con swung the shovel, knocking the knife out of the other man's hand. It flew onto the mattress in the corner, but it didn't seem to faze Matt. He swung his other hand and caught Con in the side of the head with his fist. The shovel dropped to the ground and Matt hit him again, causing him to stumble backwards. The garden tool was kicked, sliding across the floor till it hit her in the toes. She squeezed her eyes shut tight for a moment.

It's okay. It's all going to be okay. Okay. OK. Two little letters in exchange for three little words. It has to be okay.

When Dulcie opened her eyes, the two boys were locked in battle. Con was obviously the bigger one, the stronger of the two, but Matt was so pumped full of drugs, he was beyond feeling any pain. So when Con slammed a fist across his face, it didn't even make the drug addict pause. He shouted and charged forward, ramming into him and forcing them back.

They teetered at the edge of the stairs and Dulcie screamed when it looked like they were going to go down. But then Matt grabbed the sides of Con's jacket and swung him around, slamming him up against the banister. He immediately began pummeling the bigger guy, landing his fists everywhere.

"Who's scared now, huh? Who's fucking getting killed now!?" Matt was shouting. He hooked his fist into Con's jaw, and Dulcie watched as blood sprayed through the air.

She slowly climbed to her feet, and from over Matt's shoulders, she could see that the big bad wolf could, in fact, bleed. It was streaming out of his mouth, running down the side of his cheek. But still, he smiled that amazing smile. Showed those fangs that she knew could eat her up oh so quickly.

"Hard for me to kill you … when you're already dead," Con sighed. Matt let out a yell and punched him in the side, causing him to spit out more blood.

"*Fucking psycho! I'm not scared of you!*" Matt screamed.

A shrill noise filled the small space. That same scraping sound. Dulcie took a couple steps forward, till she was right behind Matt, and she looked down at Con. His big blue eyes finally locked onto her own and he stared at her.

"Good, because *I'm not the one you should be scared of,*" he whispered.

Matt had barely looked over his shoulder when Dulcie let out a shriek and swung the shovel. The flat side caught him in the face, hard enough to send him flying backwards. He'd just bumped into the wall when she swung at him again, this time hitting him in the chest. He cried out in pain, but she was beyond hearing anything. The shovel came down on his head, sending him to his knees.

"Couldn't just leave me alone!" she shouted, moving in a slow circle around him.

"Why … what are you ..." Matt was gurgling. Now he was the one spitting out blood.

"I told you. I warned you not to fucking touch me. I told you something bad would happen. God, you're disgusting, wanting to fuck your sister," she spit out. "And you just had to bring your fucking friends! You wanted a party, right? You certainly fucking got one! Having a good time, Matty? Your friends had a *blast*."

"Please … please," he whispered. She laughed at him.

"Are you fucking joking?"

An underhanded swing brought the shovel up under his chin. She'd used both her arms, really put a lot of torque on it, and he actually lifted off the ground. When he landed on his back, more blood flew through the air. From behind her, she heard Con clapping.

"Beautiful form, little girl."

Dulcie stood over Matt for a second, her legs on either side of his torso, then she lowered herself so she was actually sitting on his chest. She cocked her head to the side and let her eyes wander over his face. He might have been crying, she couldn't tell. There was too much blood. He was definitely missing more teeth, though, that was for sure.

"Why couldn't you leave me alone?" she sighed, wiping a fingertip through the mess on his face. A clean path for his tears.

"I'm sorry," he coughed out.

"Ooohhh, too late for that, Matt. Much too late for that, isn't it?" she whispered back, then got to her feet again.

"You're … you're a fucking crazy bitch. *Fucking crazy*," he finally said with some gusto.

Dulcie held very still for a moment and stared down at him. Looked into his eyes and tried to see how she felt. How she *truly* felt. She'd lured him to Con's house, she'd let Con kill his friends, and then she'd convinced him she was scared and needed his protection. Those were such bad things. So very, very bad.

… you're a fucking crazy bitch …

"You better fucking believe it," she breathed.

Then she gripped the shovel between her hands and lifted her arms up high before driving the blade straight down through his head.

"Took you long enough."

Dulcie let go of the handle and stumbled backwards. The shovel stayed standing upright. She was pretty sure she'd gone straight through his skull and had embedded the tool in the actual floor.

"What do you mean?" she asked, wiping her hands down the front of her shirt. She looked over her shoulder, but Con wasn't by the railing anymore. He was over by Matt's makeshift bed and moving towards her. She hadn't even realized he'd moved, she'd been so lost in the moment.

"Fucker broke my tooth," Con commented, and she watched as he spit out half of a molar. "I began to think you were enjoying letting him kick my ass."

"You said you wanted your DNA spread around," she reminded him as she raked her hands through her hair.

"I wanted it to look like there was a struggle, like you put up a fight. I didn't want permanent damage," he explained, his fingers feeling around the side of his cheek. They slid around and he flattened his hand, wiping away the excess blood from his face.

"What can I say? I like to see you bleed," she sighed, looking at all the blood he'd spit everywhere.

"You were amazing," he told her, moving so he was touching her.

"You locked me in a room," she growled, remembering that little fact. She glared up at him.

"I didn't trust you," he chuckled, trailing his fingers through her hair. "I had to be the one to kill them, not you, but I knew given half the chance, you'd fly off half cocked and kill someone yourself."

"Fair point."

The plan had been to lure Matt to the house and either kill him there, or convince him Dulcie was just some poor girl in an abusive relationship with a psycho – at Con's insistence. That way if he managed to escape early on and get the police involved, she would be free from any guilt. One of them had to remain free, that was crucial, and of the two of them, Dulcie was the best at pulling off innocent and unassuming.

Matt being at the station was fortuitous, Dulcie had honestly thought she wouldn't get the chance to kill him. When he'd run away from Con's house, they'd figured he'd gone straight to the cops. Not too much of a problem – they're plan had already been accomplished, Con looked like the bad guy. Hopefully, they'd be long gone before anyone would even know they were missing. It would, though, perfectly set up an alibi for what had happened.

Con had gone crazy, killed his father, killed Matt's friends, burned down his house, and then taken Dulcie to the station, to their *special spot*, which Matt knew *alllll about*. Who knew what happened after that? Con was crazy, after all. Clearly, he'd done something with Dulcie. Absconded with her. Kidnapped her. *Killed her.*

"You're so beautiful right now," he whispered, his hand cupping the side of her face, tilting her up so she had to look at him. He fell on her mouth, kissing her in a way fit for the end of a fairy tale.

One of those stories that came out of the Black Forest, and ended with children being eaten and big bad wolves going home satisfied.

"So close to done. I can't believe we're gonna pull this off," she gasped. His fingers slid further into her hair, and she could feel the bloody hand print he left behind on her cheek.

"I can. We're unstoppable. We're goddamn amazing," he growled, then pushed his tongue into her mouth. She kissed him back, wanting more from him. Wanting everything.

If I could just die like this … what a beautiful moment … what a beautiful man ...

"*Dulcie,*" he whispered when he pulled away. She had her eyes closed and one of her hands on the back of his neck, holding him close.

"What?"

"You're bleeding."

She opened her eyes and saw that he was looking down, so she followed his gaze. There was blood underneath her heel, and she remembered she'd slashed open her foot when she'd been downstairs.

"Oh, from the glass on the floor, I cut myself. It's not very deep."

"*Too bad.*"

There was a flash of red and Dulcie gasped. Squeezed her eyes shut tight and dug her fingernails into his neck. She took a couple deep breaths, then looked down at herself again.

The knife from Con's kitchen, the one Matt had stolen, was now buried in her. Con's free hand was still wrapped around the handle. She struggled to keep calm and watched as blood began to stain her white shirt.

"I didn't ... I wasn't ..." she panted. She felt his lips against her forehead.

"Baby, I wish you could feel this the way I do. *Fucking amazing.*"

He twisted the knife and she finally cried out. She jerked away from him and almost threw up as she felt the blade slide free from her body. Her hands instantly went to cover the wound, though it didn't help any. Warm blood flowed over and around her fingers.

Dulcie fell to her knees and started laughing. She lifted her right hand and turned it over in front of her face. Let her eyes wander over the crimson red. Such a beautiful color. Her laughter turned to sobbing and she let her head fall forward.

"I wasn't ready," she cried. He moved to squat in front of her and she felt the tip of the blade under her chin, then he pushed up, forcing her to look at him again.

"Doesn't matter. It had to be done," he assured her. She stared at him through her tears. Stared at those blue, blue eyes.

"But I wanted to tell you I love you," she whispered.

Finally. Now it can't poison me anymore.

"Ah," he breathed, and his Cheshire grin was back in place. "Now, Dulcie. Now we can *finally* be together." She smiled back at him and nodded.

Then he stabbed her again.

THIRTY

THE SMALL TOWN OF FULLER, WEST VIRGINIA WAS ROCKED BY A series of events that took place late one Tuesday evening.

A 9-1-1 call brought fire trucks to the Masters household, which was engulfed in flames by the time they got there. They were nowhere close to having it under control when a second phone call came in – the old train station was on fire, as well. A second fire truck was sent to deal with it. Luckily, that fire was much easier to take care of, and by morning, investigators were able to start crawling all over the smoke damaged interior.

It was late the next day before they got into the Masters house, and what they found wasn't pretty. Three bodies in the wreckage, all badly burned. Mr. Jebediah Masters was easily identified by dental records, but there was something strange. Investigators later determined Mr. Masters had died long before the fire. It was also readily obvious that the fire had not been an accident – the ground around the back part of the house was soaked in gasoline, and burned out metal gas cans were found in some of the rooms.

The heights of the other two bodies completely ruled out the possibility of Constantine Masters being either of them, but no one had seen the young man since the day of the fire. He was an immediate suspect, much to the shock of the town.

Well, to most of the town.

Jared Foster came forward and was adamant Constantine was responsible for the fires, and more so, that he'd done something to Dulcie Travers, the girl Con had reportedly been dating. Jared stated that Dulcie had come to him, had admitted to being afraid of Con, and that he'd personally witnessed Con acting strangely towards the girl.

The body of Dulcie's half-brother, Matthew Reid, was found in the train station. He'd been violently murdered. A lot of blood was found at the scene, but not all of it could be attributed to Matthew's injuries. Tests showed that blood on the banister and blood on Matt's fists had come from one Constantine Masters. A partial tooth belonging to Con was also found, indicating some sort of fight had taken place.

It was also quickly revealed that a large amount of the blood belonged to Dulcie Travers. There was a pool of it on the second story, then a bloody trail lead down the stairs and out the door and all the way to the railroad crossing. From there, it disappeared into the woods.

Many measures were taken to find out what had happened. Dulcie's mother admitted that her daughter had come to her on the day of the fires and had been acting strangely. That her son had said some strange things about the couple, as well. The state police were brought in, but to no avail. While it was determined that both the Masters fire and the train station fire were intentional, there were no other clues as to what had happened to the young couple.

Of course, there were whispers. That it was all a drug deal gone bad. That Con had gone crazy and killed Dulcie, then killed himself, leaving their bodies for the bears. Or that he'd buried her in the woods and then ran; both his and his father's bank accounts had been cleaned out. It seemed like the most likely scenario.

The town was shaken up for a long time, but as summer turned into fall without any answers, and fall turned into winter, it faded away. The Masters' home was torn down, and by the next summer, the train station had gained a reputation of being haunted. People were coming from all over the state to see if they could catch sight of a young woman's ghost. A restless spirit, doomed to wander the station after her lover had murdered her.

Right after the fires, Jared Foster quietly got divorced. He gained custody of his daughter and moved them into a small apartment. Later, he took custody of his newborn son. Then he saved his money, and by the following summer, he had enough to move. He was getting out of Fuller. What he should've done right after graduation. What Dulcie should have done.

And as he drove past that old train station, he let his eyes wander over it. Let his foot ease off the gas pedal. There was a window on the second floor, and for just a moment, he thought he saw someone standing there. Someone with dark blonde hair and light amber eyes. Someone who'd always existed on another plane from him.

I'm sorry I couldn't help you, Dulcie, but for what it's worth ... thank you for helping me.

EPILOGUE

"STOP IT."

"You stop."

"I'm not doing anything. *Stop it!*"

"I can't help it that you're ticklish."

"I swear to god, if you don't -"

"*There you are!*" a shrill voice shouted. A brunette in a flowing maxi dress was hurrying towards them, waving her hand. A man followed in her wake.

"*Uh oh, we're busted.*"

"Mr. Ford, this lovely woman is Shannon Cork," the brunette, Carmen Enger, introduced them. "And this is her husband, Michael Cork."

The woman who'd been introduced as Shannon gave a big smile, shaking hands with Mr. Ford. The man claiming the title of husband smiled as well, but didn't offer his hand. Instead, he wrapped his arm around his wife's waist.

"Such a pleasure! I'm so happy to meet you, Mrs. Cork. I have to tell you, I just adore -" the man started going on, but her husband held up his hand.

"I'm sorry, so sorry, but could you excuse us for just a second? I forgot something I needed to tell my wife," he apologized, pulling at her

247

as he tried to step backwards. She held her ground.

"But babe, Carmen just brought him over here, we can't -"

"Please, *Shannon*."

She stared at him for a second, her lips pursed together tightly, then she sighed and turned back to their guests. Made apologies and assured them they'd be back. Then she followed him out of the room. He held onto her arm and dragged her around the building, hauling her outside and onto the beach.

"What was that?" she hissed, slapping at his hand when they were well out of sight of other people.

"When I tell you I want to talk to you, it means I want to talk to you *right now*," he explained. She rolled her eyes.

"I'm not talking about that."

"Then what?"

"I *hate it* when you call me Shannon."

Constantine burst out laughing. That loud laugh that she loved so much.

"What do you want me to do? I can't exactly call you by your real name."

Dulcie sighed and walked away from him, moving to where a palm tree had fallen at the edge of the beach. She sat down in the sand and leaned against its trunk.

"God, why did I ever agree to Shannon. It sounds so ... *girly*," she complained. He laughed again and sat down next to her.

"Hey, I like Shannon. We were in a hurry. Next time we have to evade the law, we'll plan it out better and you can pick whatever name you want."

It was only about a twelve hour drive from Fuller to Miami. They'd had to stop in Roanoke, Virginia to get her some much needed stitches. He'd kept the stab close to the side of her torso, nowhere near any organs, but it had still bled like a bitch.

Con had bought their new identities in Miami. She'd been stoned out of her mind on pain pills at the time, and it wasn't till they were landing on the French island of Martinique that she even knew she had a new name.

Though really, living a whole new life in the Caribbean, with the man she loved, where no one knew the old Dulcie, where she could be *whoever the fuck she wanted to be,* was a pretty fair trade for having a name she didn't care for.

"So what's the emergency? Why'd you drag me out here? That guy was gonna buy something," she said, gesturing with her head to the building they'd walked away from. Lights and conversation poured out into the night air. It was an art show, being hosted by one of the top galleries in Martinique. Dulcie was the featured artist.

"So? We don't need the money," Con reminded her, then he scooted lower down in the sand so he was stretched out next to her.

"It's not about the money, Con. It's also nice knowing my art is hanging in someone's home," she tried to explain. He snorted and pulled at her gauzy dress, dragging it up her body and revealing the white bikini she was wearing underneath.

"You mean *Shannon Cork's* art is hanging in someone's home," he corrected her. She smacked him in the back of the head.

"Don't make me hurt you."

"Oh, keep talking like that and we'll never make it back to the party."

He planted kisses along the edge of her hip, working his way to the nasty scar on her side. It had been a year, but it was still sensitive. It stood out starkly against the dark tan she now permanently wore. The tan that went so well with the new brunette dye job she always sported. He kissed the scar, too.

"You had to make it so big," she sighed, combing her fingers through his hair.

"Thank god Matt brought that knife – the puny little pocket knife I was gonna use wouldn't have left nearly so beautiful a mark."

"Beautiful? Con, it's *huge*, and I didn't think it would ever stop bleeding."

"That was the whole point – they had to believe you were dead, that I killed you," he explained for the hundredth time.

"Last I saw online, they still consider the case open," she told him. He snorted.

"Yeah, and last I saw, your ghost is roaming the halls of West Virginia's newest haunted attraction. Mission fucking accomplished, Dulcie."

She laughed and moved so she was even with him on the ground.

"Pretty amazing. We are *pretty amazing*," she sighed, smoothing her hand over the mark on her skin.

"We shine like stars, little girl," he agreed, his fingers moving alongside hers.

"And you know, I actually like the scar," she admitted.

"Good. It took that stab to get you to admit you love me," he reminded her.

"It needed to be said in blood," she whispered.

"Well, you certainly gave a lot that night."

"That's how much I love you."

He kissed her then. Even after a year. Even after fires and murders and dwelling in darkness, *loving* in darkness, kissing him still felt exactly the same as it had when she was seventeen years old. Like all her favorites things, rolled into one. Like every dream, *every nightmare,* she'd ever had.

Still feels like that fairy tale.

"I did actually want to ask you something," he whispered, shifting around so he was on top of her.

"Hmmm, and what was that?" she asked, tilting her head back so he could kiss her exposed neck.

"I want to know," he breathed, his tongue moving between her breasts. "When do we get to be bad again?"

She smiled big.

"Baby, I thought you'd *never ask*."

ACKNOWLEDGEMENTS

This wasn't one of those books I had in the back of my mind, or on the back burner, or anything like that – it was really as simple as I saw a house.

Okay, maybe not that simple.

Many months ago (a year, maybe?) Jennifer L. encouraged me to sign up for the Rebels & Readers Author Event in West Virginia. So I did it. I love going to places I've never been before, so I thought of it as like an adventure.

I absolutely fell IN LOVE with West Virginia. It was November, but for this Alaskan chick, the weather was still warm, just perfect for me. The town was quaint and lovely, and the countryside absolutely stunning. I brought a friend with me and we decided to drive around for an entire day, going out to see our first ever Piggly Wiggly's, some covered bridges, and the super spooky Trans-Allegheny Lunatic Asylum.

While on the highway, I spotted this large house in a town somewhat below us. It stood out simply because it was the largest dwelling, but also because it was all white, with dark shutters and roofing. Very nice, with columns in the front. Then maybe a mile or two down the way, on the opposite side of the highway, there was a small trailer park. My friend and I started joking about the mayor lived in the "fancy house", and how his son was probably the star quarterback, and how he had a crush on one of the "weird chicks" from the trailer park. It was really that simple. Standard N.A.

So I don't know where Dulcie and Con came from, but I'm very glad for them, and even more glad that Jennifer thought of me for that signing event.

This book was truly like one long, 80,000 word primal scream therapy. Frustrations with the writing world, with the industry, with my personal life, all of it kind of came out in this book. I told my critique partner that I didn't think I had enough for a "full novel", but I didn't care. I'm just going to write whatever comes out of me, then if it's 50,000 words, so be it, I have a novella. If it's 230,000, whatever, I wrote War and Peace, I don't care.

And so Constantine Masters was born.

So many people to thank. Of course, Ratula, for my eight million messages about Tiny Dog and random thoughts and how best to deal with crazy husbands and the random projectile vomit. Sunny, for always making me laugh and loving Con quite possibly more than I do. Jo and Beatriz and Rebeka, for our group chats and silliness.

Christine at Shh Mom's Reading, for handling ALL my tours, over a year and a half later! I adore you and the way you handle your business. Thanks for always making it easy for me, because I know it's not easy for you, and it really means a lot.

Najla Qamber, who has made every single book cover, every single Facebook banner, and every single professional teaser. Two years running – I'm not going away any time soon! Thanks for your amazing attention to detail and the stunning covers you turn out.

To all the blogs that share and promote and read and do all that you do – to the events, to Teaser Tuesdays, to reviews, to … everything. You are everything. Thank you for helping me do what I love.

To the readers – your kind words and thoughts mean everything. It's been an interesting journey! Thanks for keeping life adventurous. I hope I keep bringing you stories that you enjoy.

To my friends – it's been an interesting year. Thanks for sticking with me and letting me do my thing. I'm not the easiest person at the best of times. At challenging times? Well …. just …. thank you. So much.

And to Mr. F. Seventeen years we've known each other. Here's to seventeen more. Thanks for being you, and for letting me be me. Two of the most important things in my world. Words aren't enough to express how important you've been in my journey.

The Kane Trilogy

degradation

Available Now

If you haven't met Jameson Kane yet, read below for a sneak peek …

~excerpt~

TATUM PLUCKED AT HER SHIRT in a nervous manner. She had tucked it into a tight pencil skirt and even put on a pair of sling back stilettos. If someone had personally requested her, she wanted to make an effort to look nice. She had blown out her hair and put curls in the ends, and toned down her make up. Even she had to admit it, she looked presentable.

For once.

Men in expensive business suits began to file into the conference room and she stood still, giving a polite smile to everyone who entered. A team of lawyers was meeting with their client. Six chairs were lined up on one side of a long table, with just a single chair on the other side.

Tate had been positioned at the back of the room, next to a sideboard filled with goodies and coffee and water. She fussed about, straightening napkins and setting up the glasses. When all six chairs were filled on the one side, she stared at their backs, wondering who the big shot was that got to stare them all down. The person who would be facing her. A door at the back of the room swung open and her breath caught in her threat.

Holy. Shit.

Jameson Kane strode into the room, only offering a curt smile to his lawyers. His eyes flashed to her for just a second, then he looked back. His smile became genuine and he tipped his head towards her, almost like a bow.

She gaped back at him, positive that her mouth was hanging open. What was he doing there!? Had he known she would be there? Had he been the one to request her? Impossible, he didn't know what temp agency she worked for – but what would be the chances? She hadn't seen him in seven years, and now twice in two days.

Tate felt like swallowing her tongue.

"Gentlemen," Jameson began, seating himself across from the lawyers. "Thanks for meeting with me today. Would anyone care for any coffee? Water? The lovely Ms. O'Shea will be helping us today." He gestured towards Tate, but no one turned around. Several people asked for coffee. Jameson asked for water, his smile still in place. It was almost a smirk. Like he knew something she didn't.

She began to grind her teeth.

She delivered everyone's drinks, then carried around a tray of snacks. No one took anything. She moved to the back of the room, refilled the water pitcher. Tidied up. Felt Jameson staring at her.

This is ridiculous. You're Tatum O'Shea. You eat boys for breakfast.

But thinking that made her remember when he had said something very similar to her, and she felt a blush creep up her cheeks.

She was pretty much ignored the whole time. They all argued back and forth about what business decisions Jameson should, or shouldn't, make. He was very keen on dismantling struggling companies and selling them off. They tried to curb his desires. His tax lawyer explained how his tax shelter in Hong Kong was doing. Another lawyer gave him a run down on property law in Switzerland. Tate tried to hide her yawns.

They took a five minute break after an hour had passed. Tate had her back to the room, rearranging some muffins on a tray, when she felt the hair on the back of her neck start to stand up. She turned around in slow motion, taking in Jameson as he walked up to her.

"Surprised?" he asked, smiling down at her.

"Very. Did you ask for me?" she questioned. He nodded.

"Yes. You ran away so quickly the other night. I wanted to get reacquainted," he explained. She laughed.

"Maybe I didn't," she responded. He shrugged.

"That doesn't really matter to me. What are you doing tonight?" he asked. She was a little caught off guard.

"Are you asking me out, Kane?" she blurted out. He threw back his head and laughed.

"Oh god, still a little girl. *No*. I don't ask people out. I was asking what you were doing tonight," Jameson replied.

She willed away the blush she felt coming on. He still had the ability to make her feel so stupid. She had been through so much since him, come so far with her esteem and her life. It wasn't fair that he could still make her feel so small. She wanted to return the favor. She cleared her throat.

"I'm working."

"Where?"

"At a bar."

"What bar?"

"A bar you don't know."

"And tomorrow night?"

"Busy."

"And the night after that?"

"*Every* night after that," Tate informed him, crossing her arms. He narrowed his eyes, but continued smiling.

"Surely you can find some time to meet up with an old friend," he said. She shook her head.

"We were never friends, Kane," she pointed out. He laughed.

"Then what is it? Are you scared of me? Scared I'll eat you alive?" he asked. She stepped closer to him, refusing to be intimidated.

"I think *you're* the one who should be scared. You don't know me, Kane. You never did. *And you never will*," she whispered. Jameson leaned down so his lips were almost against her ear.

"I know what you feel like from the inside. That's good enough for me," he whispered back. Tate stepped away. She felt like she couldn't breathe. He did something to her insides.

"You, and a lot of other people. You're not as big a deal as you think," she taunted. It was a complete lie, but she had to get the upper hand back. He smirked at her.

"That sounds like a challenge to me. I have to defend my honor," he warned her. She snorted.

"Whatever. Point to the challenger then, *me*. Defend away," she responded, rolling her eyes.

He didn't respond, just continued smirking down at her. The lawyers began filing back into the room and Jameson took his position on the other side of the table. She wasn't really sure what their little spar had been about, or what had come out of it. She was just going to try to get through the rest of the conference, and then she would scurry away before he could talk to her again. She didn't want anything to do with Jameson Kane, or his —,

"Ms. O'Shea," his sharp voice interrupted her thoughts. Tate lifted her head.

"Yes, sir?" she asked, making sure to keep her voice soft and polite.

"Could you bring me some water, and something to eat," he asked, not even bothering to look at her as he flipped through a contract.

She loaded up a tray with his requests and made her way around the table. No one even looked at her, they just threw legal jargon around at each other – a language she didn't know. She stood next to Jameson and leaned forward, setting his water down and then going about arranging cheese and crackers on a plate for him. She was about halfway done when she felt it.

Are those ... his fingers!?

Tate froze for a second. His touch was light as he ran his fingers up and down between her legs. She glanced down at her knees and then glanced over at him. He was still looking down, but she could see him smirking. She tried to ignore him, tried to go back to setting up his food, but his hand went higher. Daring to brush up past her knees, well underneath her skirt. He couldn't get any farther, not unless he pushed up her skirt, or sunk down in his chair. She dumped the rest of the cheese on his plate and started to scoot away. She had just gotten back to her station when she heard a thunking noise, followed by groans.

"No worries. Ms. O'Shea! So sorry, could you get this?" Jameson's voice was bored sounding.

She turned around and saw that he had knocked over his water glass. He was blotting at the liquid as it spread across the table. The lawyers were all holding their papers aloft, grumbling back and forth.

Tate groaned and grabbed a towel before striding back to the table. She glared at him the whole way, but he still refused to look at her. She started as far away from him as she could get, mopping everything up, but eventually she had to almost lean across him to reach the mess. She stood on her toes, stretching across the table top.

As she had assumed it would, his hand found its way back to her legs. Only this time he wasn't shy, and her position allowed for a lot of access. His hand shot straight up the back of her skirt, his fingertips brushing against the lace of her panties.

She swallowed a squeak and glanced around. If any of the other gentlemen lifted their heads, they would have been able to see their client with half of his arm up his assistant's skirt, plain as day. He managed to run his finger under the hem of her underwear, down the left side of her butt cheek, before she pulled away. She stomped back to the food station, throwing the towel down with such violence, she knocked over a stack of sugar cubes.

When she turned around, Jameson was finally looking at her. She plunked her fists on her hips, staring straight back. His smirk was in place – as she had expected it would be – and he held up a finger, pointing it straight up. *One.* Then he pointed at himself. One point. *Tied.* He thought they were playing a game. She hadn't wanted to play games with him, but she hated to lose at *anything*, and she never wanted to lose to a man like Jameson Kane.

An idea flitted across her mind. Tate wanted to make him as uncomfortable as he had just made her feel. She coolly raised an eyebrow and then took her time looking around the room. The lawyers all still had their backs to her – not one of them had turned around the entire time she'd been there. Blinds had been drawn over every window, no one could see in the office, but she knew the door wasn't locked. Anyone could walk into the room. She took a deep breath. It didn't matter anyway, what was the worst that could happen? She would get fired? It was a temp job, that Jameson had requested her for – he didn't even work there. Did she really care what happened?

She dragged her stare back to meet his and then ran her hands down the sides of her skirt. He raised an eyebrow as well, his eyes following her hands. When she got to the hem of the skirt, she pressed her palms flat and began to slowly, *achingly*, slide the material up her legs. Now both his eyebrows were raised. He flicked his gaze to her face, then went right back to her skirt. Higher, up past her knees. To the middle of her thighs. Higher still. If anyone turned around, they would be very surprised at what they saw. One more inch, and her skirt would be moot. Jameson's stare was practically burning holes through her.

Taking short, quick, breaths through her nose, Tate slid her hands around to her butt. She wiggled the material up higher back there, careful to keep the front low enough to hide her whole business, and was able to hook her fingers into her underwear. She didn't even think about what she was doing, couldn't take her eyes off of Jameson, as she slid her underwear over her butt and down her hips. As the lace slid to her ankles, she pushed her skirt back into place. Then she stepped out of the panties and bent over, picking them up. When she stood upright, she let the lace dangle from her hand while she held up one finger. Point.

Winning.

Jameson nodded his head at her, obviously conceding to her victory, then returned his attention to the papers in front of him. Tate let out a breath that she hadn't even realized she was holding, and turned around, bracing her hands against the table. She leaned forward and took deep breaths. She had just started to gain some ground on slowing her heart rate, when a throat cleared.

"What is that, Ms. O'Shea?" Jameson called out from behind her. She spun around, balling up her underwear in her fist.

"Excuse me, sir?" she asked.

"That," he continued, gesturing with his pen at her. "In your hands. You have something for me. Bring it here."

Now everyone turned towards her. Tate held herself as still as possible, her hands clasped together in front of her legs, hiding the underwear between her fingers. All eyes were on her. Jameson smirked at her and leaned back in his chair. She took a shaky breath.

"I don't know what —,"

"Bring it here, Ms. O'Shea, *now*," he ordered, tapping the table top with his pen. She glared at him.

Fuck this.

She turned around and pulled one of the silver trays in front of her. She laid her panties out neatly on top, making sure the material was smooth and flat. She was very thankful that she had gone all out and worn her good, expensive, "*I'm-successful-and-career-oriented!*", underwear. She balanced the tray on top of her fingertips and spun around, striding towards their table, a big smile on her face.

"For you, Mr. Kane," she said in a breathy voice, then dropped the tray in front of him. It clattered loudly and spun around a little before coming to a rest, the panties sliding off to one side.

As she walked away, she could hear some gasps. A couple laughs. A very familiar chuckle. When she got to the door, she pulled it open before turning back to the room. A couple of the lawyers were gawking at her, and the rest were laughing, gesturing to the display she had just put on; Jameson was looking straight at her, his smirk in place. She blew him a kiss and then stomped out the door.

ABOUT THE AUTHOR

Crazy woman living in an undisclosed location in Alaska (where the need for a creative mind is a necessity!), I have been writing since …, forever? Yeah, that sounds about right. I have been told that I remind people of Lucille Ball - I also see shades of Jennifer Saunders, and Denis Leary. So basically, I laugh a lot, I'm clumsy a lot, and I say the F-word A LOT.

I like dogs more than I like most people, and I don't trust anyone who doesn't drink. No, I do not live in an igloo, and no, the sun does not set for six months out of the year, there's your Alaska lesson for the day. I have mermaid hair - both a curse and a blessing - and most of the time I talk so fast, even I can't understand me.

Yeah. I think that about sums me up.

Made in the USA
Monee, IL
16 May 2020